HER
Guardian

CASSIA LEO

HER GUARDIAN
by Cassia Leo

First Edition
Copyright © 2017 by Cassia Leo

All rights reserved.

Cover art by Cassia Leo.
Editing by Jessica Anderegg of Red Adept Publishing.
Copy editing by Marianne Tatom.

ISBN-13: 978-1721766611
ISBN-10: 1721766618

This book, or parts thereof, may not be reproduced in any form without expressed written permission from the author; exceptions are made for brief excerpts used in published reviews.

All characters and events appearing in this work are fictitious. Any resemblance to real events or persons, living or dead, is purely coincidental.

HER
Guardian

For my mom.
You may not recognize me anymore, but your wit and strength will always be the common thread woven through all my stories. Keep dancing and smiling.

PART I: *Kristin*

1. Taken Care Of

THE DIMLY LIT STAIRWELLS in our five-floor walk-up in the Bronx smelled even more like cat piss than usual.

The August humidity had a lovely way of extracting the aromas that were usually trapped inside the dingy walls of our building. I tried to breathe through my mouth as I climbed the final steps to the fifth floor. But when I stepped into the corridor, a bright yellow notice taped to the front door of apartment 502 made me gasp, and the sharp smell got sucked into my nose again.

I gagged, then marched toward my apartment. "What the actual *fuck*?"

My curse came out much louder than I'd

anticipated.

Dropping my canvas bag of groceries on the floor, I quickly snatched the paper off the door, but not quickly enough. Mr. Williams walked out of his apartment as I bent over to stuff the notice into my grocery bag.

"Good morning, Mr. Williams," I said, breathing far too heavily for a casual walk to the bodega. "How's your day so far?"

He tilted his head a bit as his dark eyes remained focused on my bag. "Is that an eviction notice?"

I unzipped my purse and dug frantically through the receipts and half-used drugstore makeup, which had probably been there since I dropped out of college two years ago. "It's just a mix-up," I replied with a chuckle when I found my house key. "Same thing happened a couple weeks ago. At least this time it happened on a Monday morning instead of a Friday night. I'm heading straight to the property manager's office as soon as I get these groceries in the fridge."

"Is everything okay with you and your ma?" he asked through narrowed eyes.

"We're fine," I said, forcing a smile. "Thank you so much for asking, but we're just fine. This is just a huge mix-up."

Mr. Williams scratched his scraggly white beard,

which sparsely covered his chestnut-brown skin. "Okay," he said, slowly nodding. "Well, if you need anything, don't you hesitate to holler at this old fool."

My smile widened, and this time it was genuine. "Thank you, Mr. Williams. I promise I'll do that."

He stuck his chin out and beamed with pride. "That's a good girl. You take care now," he said, then ambled back into the apartment across the hall.

When I was five, I often wondered if I was invisible—not metaphorically speaking, but actually invisible. I would watch in complete silence as my mom came home from a fourteen-hour shift, cleaning up other people's messes. She'd collapse onto the sofa, turn on the evening news, and eat her dinner with a tired smile. Then I'd retreat to my bedroom and dream of a world where I existed.

It wasn't until a fateful evening in September two years ago, my fingernails peeling off as I desperately clawed my way up a highway embankment, that I finally realized how tangible I was, how heavily I was anchored to this merciless world.

Now, as I rushed inside the humid apartment I shared with my mother in the South Bronx, I wished I could be invisible again.

Closing the door softly behind me—so as not to attract the attention of any more neighbors—I power-walked into the kitchen and tossed my canvas grocery bag onto the counter. Yanking out the bright yellow eviction notice, I contemplated the ten-digit phone number scrawled on it in black marker.

No. I wasn't going to give those incompetent pricks at the property management office the courtesy of calling before I showed up. No way would I give them time to come up with some trumped-up violation that my mother or I had supposedly committed.

Despite the fact that our building was more than a hundred years old and in serious disrepair, the bylaws consisted of a list of rules—I kid you not—at least sixty pages long. The list was mailed to us every year with an offer to renew the lease—with another rent increase, of course. And every year, the list got longer.

One rule actually stipulated we were not allowed to walk around in high heels after ten p.m. I supposed it was a good thing I had no social life. I was in no danger of violating that rule.

Of course, whatever bone the management was picking with us now was probably not due to anything I did or didn't do. The eviction notice was almost certainly a response to what I had *threatened* to do. Three weeks ago, I threatened to file an ADA—Americans with Disabilities Act—complaint if they didn't fix the loose handrails in the stairwells.

When my mom and I moved into this apartment more than ten years ago, my mom was in excellent physical shape. Despite the fact that she had spent most of her life working as a housekeeper, she had managed to take good care of her body. Until she fell off a ladder at home and shattered her kneecap. Three surgeries later, she was desperate to return to work so I could return to NYU, but no one would hire her back.

If the eviction notice was left on our door, that meant my mom wasn't home when the notice was served, which meant our neighbor Leslie had come by to take her shopping.

I put the groceries away and stuffed the eviction notice into my purse before I left the apartment. I thought of leaving a message with Leslie's family, but decided against it. I didn't want to worry her or my mom.

Leslie was a stay-at-home mother with two kids in high school and a husband who drove a bus for the MTA. She helped my mom up and down the stairs once a week to go shopping. Having amazing neighbors like Leslie and Mr. Williams was one of the many reasons I was hesitant to move to another apartment building with an elevator.

One subway ride and nine blocks of walking in the glaring summer sun later, I arrived, sweaty and determined, at the front doors of Golde Property Management. I entered through the glass double doors, which squeaked on their hinges as I pushed my way inside. The black and gold confetti design on the linoleum looked like something straight out of a '70s discotheque. The faux oak furniture in the waiting room, with the wood-grain laminate peeling off the corners, confirmed that I had stepped into an office stuck in another century.

In the decade since we moved into our apartment, and ever since I began paying the rent a couple of years ago, I'd never had to visit Golde Property Management. I always paid the rent on time, and I always agreed to the new lease terms. If I had known that they were living in the '70s, I wouldn't have bothered asking them to bring our apartment up to modern building standards.

Nonetheless, I needed to clear up this eviction nonsense. The last thing I needed was for my mother and me to be thrown out on our asses over a clerical error.

The receptionist sat at a desk behind a sliding-glass window at the back of the waiting room. She watched me approach without even attempting to smile.

I slid the yellow eviction notice across the counter onto her side of the glass. "I want to know what this is about."

She spun in her chair to face the computer on her left, positioning her fingers over the keyboard. "What's the property address?"

"Twenty-four eighty-three Hughes," I replied sharply.

She typed in the address, then her eyes scanned down to the lower-right part of the computer screen and stopped. "It says here that the eviction notice was posted today at 10:02 a.m. by the Bronx County Sheriff's Department due to violation of the rental agreement. The violation listed here is nonpayment of rental dues in the amount of $7,050."

I couldn't help but laugh. "Are you kidding me? Our monthly rent is $1,175. That means $7,050 is what, like, six months' rent? We're not even late one month, let alone six. I want to speak to a manager."

She rolled her eyes as she picked up the beige phone handset and dialed an extension. "Is Jerry in his office?" she asked the person on the other end. "I've got a tenant here who says she's paid up, but she just got served." She sighed as she balanced the handset between her ear and shoulder. "Well, tell him when he's done with his meeting that I got someone waiting for him up here. Okay? Okay." She hung up the phone and looked up at me with a bored expression. "He's in a meeting with an investor. You'll have to wait a few minutes."

I wanted to protest for the simple fact that if I caused a scene it might ruin their chances with this investor, but I decided not to press my luck. "I'll be waiting right over there," I said, nodding toward the tweed sofa in the waiting area.

Taking a seat on the sofa that smelled like desperation, I picked up a copy of the *NY Post* from the coffee table. The paper was dated thirteen months ago. This place needed an investor more than my mom needed a disability-accessible apartment building with an elevator.

Of course, my mom would never admit that she needed anything.

The eldest of four sisters, my mom left her small hometown in South Dakota to make her way in New York City when she was just nineteen. After a brief brush with homelessness, she started cleaning houses and saving up money to start her own cleaning business. Not long after that, I was born, and her dreams of being her own boss were tossed out the window.

I had just finished reading a story about a feud between the hosts of two popular YouTube channels when a door leading into the back office opened. The first man who stepped into the waiting area—whom I assumed was Jerry—looked to be about sixty years old, and wore brown slacks and a short-sleeved blue button-up shirt, the fabric thin enough to show the dinginess of the tank top he wore underneath.

The second man who walked through the door looked more like a mirage than a man.

He was no more than twenty-eight years old, wearing a sharp navy-blue suit and a swagger in his step that said he didn't just own the place, he owned *the world*. His dark hair was short, but not so short you couldn't help but notice it held the perfect amount of wave. Every inch of him, from his prominent brow to his broad shoulders and beyond, looked sturdy. This man was built to last a thousand lifetimes.

But it was his face that made me wonder if I was actually staring at a desert mirage.

His strong jaw and brilliant green eyes looked as if they'd been chiseled by Michelangelo. As a former student of sculpture at NYU, I could make that type of comparison in the more literal sense.

If this investor bought out Golde Property Management, I'd probably sign a *hundred*-year lease.

I shrugged off this ridiculous thought. It wasn't as if this wealthy godlike man was going to send my next lease renewal along with a handwritten marriage proposal.

Will you be my wife? Check yes or no. Please send reply in the enclosed envelope with full rent payment by the first of the month.

"Are you Kristin?"

I snapped out of my absurd fantasy to find the man I suspected to be Jerry staring at me as he held the door to the back office open. "Excuse me?"

"Are you Kristin Owens?" he replied. "Here about the eviction notice?"

His question set my blood on fire with anger. "Yes. I want to know what this is all about," I said, getting to my feet as I held the yellow paper in front of me. "We've paid our rent on time every single month for the past ten years. If this is about me threatening to—"

Jerry held up his hand to interrupt me. "Okay, okay. Let's go into my office," he said, his expression a mixture of shame and anger, probably because I just made a scene in front of his potential investor. He looked up at the man. "I look forward to hearing from you again, Mr. Meyers. Jennie over there can validate your parking."

Mr. Meyers cocked an eyebrow as he looked me over. "Maybe I should sit in on this."

Jerry waved off the suggestion. "Oh, no, this is just routine admin stuff. It will be over in two minutes.

Don't want to waste your time."

I stared at Jerry, making no attempt to avoid looking directly at the huge hairy mole protruding from his temple. "So now I'm a waste of time?" I asked. "If you think you can get away with—"

"Excuse me," Meyers interrupted, taking a step forward. "Earlier, you said you've paid your rent on time every single month for the past ten years. So, forgive me if I'm wrong, but that allows you to continue living in the unit until any further disputes are settled in court. Am I right?"

Jerry shook his head. "But she hasn't paid her rent," he insisted. "I thought it was strange when the computer spat out the notice, but they only come up when a tenant is coming up on six months past due. Computers don't lie. *People* lie."

"Are you fucking kidding me?" I shouted. "Are you calling me a liar? You piece of trash. I swear to God, I will bury you in so many legal—"

"Whoa-whoa-whoa…" Meyers interrupted again. "Let's not get ahead of ourselves," he said, casting a calm, confident look in my direction, holding my gaze for a moment before he turned back to Jerry. "You said computers don't lie, but they do sometimes glitch. You even said you thought it was strange the computer spat out her name."

"Yeah, but it doesn't randomly spit out names all day long," Jerry objected.

Meyers nodded and pressed his lips together in an expression that said he understood where Jerry was coming from. This guy was good. He was refereeing this dispute like a seasoned mediator.

"But it's possible the computer got it wrong," Meyers continued as he looked back and forth between Jerry and me, smiling when I crossed my arms over my chest. "How about this? I'll pay the past-due amount until you can figure out the glitch in the system. Does that sound fair?"

I narrowed my eyes at him. "Who the hell are you?"

His veneer of confidence cracked for just a fraction of a second before he regained his composure. "I'm sorry, I didn't mean to offend you," he replied. "You're right. It's very presumptuous of me to think I could settle this with the swipe of a pen. Forgive me." He turned to Jerry and gave him a curt nod. "I have some…thinking to do. I'm not sure your organization is a good fit for us. We'll be in touch."

"Wait!" Jerry shrieked. "I think she was just taken by surprise with your offer. Right, Christina?"

"Kristin," I corrected him. "And I don't need him to pay my rent. I already paid it. I need you to fix this!"

I crumpled the yellow eviction notice and dropped it at his feet.

"I can't," Jerry replied as Meyers quietly made his way to the receptionist's desk. "My lawyer handles the evictions. He won't close the file until the rent's paid in full. I can't pay him if I don't have your money."

"You have my money!" I yelled so loudly I could almost hear my vocal cords snap.

I cursed myself as tears stung the corners of my eyes. Blinking them away, I glanced over my shoulder, expecting to find Meyers staring aghast at my lack of control. He probably wasn't accustomed to that sort of thing in his perfect world of privilege. But he wasn't there. He was gone. I didn't know if I felt more relieved that he hadn't witnessed my outburst, or disappointed that the only sure way out of this eviction mess—at least, temporarily—had just walked out of my life.

God, why didn't I just let him help me? It wasn't as if I knew the guy. I didn't need to maintain some foolish sense of pride in front of him.

I was becoming more and more like my mother every day.

"It's taken care of."

I looked up at the sound of the receptionist's bored voice.

She waved a piece of paper in the air, which looked suspiciously like a check. "He took care of your rent," she said, looking annoyed.

I turned to Jerry, but all he did was shrug.

What the fuck just happened?

2. Karma

IT TOOK ME A MINUTE to regain my bearings, then I raced outside to find Mr. Meyers. I charged through the double glass doors. Momentarily blinded by the bright sunlight, I blinked furiously to adjust my vision. The August heat pressed in on me as I frantically scanned the street for any sign of a man in a suit. But we were less than four blocks from the stock exchange in the heart of the financial district. There were suits everywhere.

Panic rose inside me as I realized I was now indebted to a complete stranger. Not exactly the resolution I was hoping for when I strode into Golde Property Management full of self-righteous anger. How could I let this happen?

My mind flashed back to that night. Every time I screwed up, my mind automatically conjured the memory of the night I fucked up worse than I ever would again. Almost as if my brain was trying to reassure me that whatever I'd done this time wasn't as bad as it seemed.

The only problem was that this time, my memories of that night couldn't distract me from how royally fucked I was.

I slid my phone out of my pocket, opened up my favorite contacts, and touched my mom's name. Two rings passed before someone tapped me on my shoulder. I gritted my teeth, prepared to turn around and face whatever transient was going to ask me for spare change and tell them that I could really use some spare change myself. But as I turned around, I found a face that I knew was going to cause me nightmares, and maybe a few naughty daydreams.

"Looking for someone?" Meyers quipped with a knowing smile.

"Uh…I…uh…" I was suddenly having trouble forming words. "I…I can't accept your money," I finally spat out, ending the call as I realized our answering machine was playing.

He cocked an eyebrow and I couldn't help but notice how his smooth, tanned skin seemed to glisten in the sunlight. "I don't understand. I didn't give you any money."

My jaw dropped. "What? Are you trying to pretend like you didn't just give that receptionist in there seven grand to pay my past-due rent, which, by the way, is not actually past due. It's just—"

"I know. It's a glitch," he said before I could finish. "Which, *by the way*, is why I wrote the check. And it wasn't a gift," he continued, his eyes flickering with satisfaction at the objection in my eyes. "I mean it wasn't a gift from *me*. It was a company check. It's really just an incentive for Jerry to fix your account."

"What kind of incentive is that? If you pay my debt—*that I don't even owe!*—what incentive does he have to fix my account if he just got paid double the rent?"

He looked down at me with a smile that made my heart stutter. "Because now it's my business. If he doesn't fix your account and return my money, I won't buy him out. Not many investors looking to buy these old property management firms anymore."

The way he said the word "property" caught me off guard. He pronounced it "prop-uh-tee." For a moment, he sounded like someone from *my* neighborhood.

"What did you say your name was?" I asked.

He looked confused for a split second before he replied. "I didn't. But my name is Daniel. Nice to formally make your acquaintance, Kristin."

Now *I* was the one scratching my head. I must have been hearing things. Or maybe he really was from the Bronx, and he used the magical world of finance to pick himself up by his bootstraps. You could take the sexy man out of the Bronx, but you couldn't take the sexy Bronx out of the man.

I smiled to myself as I thought of how much Petra would like that joke. Then, I shook my head to free myself of thoughts of my former best friend.

"You really think Jerry's going to fix this mess?" I asked, unable to hide the note of worry in my voice. "I really can't deal with getting thrown out on the street right now."

Daniel pursed his full lips. "Would next week work better?"

I narrowed my eyes at him. "Not funny."

He shook his head. "You have nothing to worry about," he said, looking cool as a cucumber. "Jerry's in so much debt right now. He won't do anything to jeopardize the deal we discussed. And if he does, well, let's just say…I know people who can help him change his mind." He laughed when my eyes widened, a deep, hearty laugh that was sexy as hell. "I'm kidding," he assured me. "I've always wanted to say that."

"Thanks for clarifying," I said sarcastically. "I really don't need to add co-conspirator in a murder plot to my resumé."

His gaze traveled down the length of my body and returned to my face. "Don't worry. I'll be your alibi."

Suddenly, I was aware of how hot my face felt, and I cursed my body for turning me into a blushing cliché. "It's really hot out here. I have to go," I said, fanning my face as I turned on my heel and headed for the subway.

"Wait a minute," Daniel said, catching up to me. "Shouldn't we at least exchange numbers so I can keep you abreast of any new developments in the hunt for your missing rent payments?"

I stopped in the middle of the sidewalk and a woman on her cell phone bumped into my back, then cursed at me as she passed. "Yeah, get over it!" I shouted at her as she sped away, her four-inch heels clicking on the pavement as she flipped me the bird.

Daniel smiled and shook his head. "You are something else. You really are," he said, pulling his cell phone out of his pocket. "What's your number?"

"Why do you need my number? I thought it was your company that paid my rent, not you. Shouldn't I be exchanging numbers with your accountant, or something?"

"Sweetheart, you do *not* want to give my accountant your phone number. Trust me."

The way he said *sweetheart*, with a smooth lilt, made me want to give him a lot more than just my phone number.

I sighed, as if he was really asking too much of me, then I gave him my phone number. Within a couple of seconds, my phone chimed with a new text message. I flashed him an amused grin as I slid my phone out of my pocket and read the text.

The receptionist gave me your address. I'll pick you up at 8 p.m.

When I looked up from my phone, I was not at all surprised to find him gone. What an arrogant, presumptuous, absolutely fuckable human being. Too bad I'd be working at eight.

I deleted his text and made my way home.

My mom should be back from shopping with Leslie by now. I didn't want to worry her, but I had to tell her what had happened. When I started working and paying all the bills, my mom made me promise to tell her if we were ever in danger of not making the rent.

We were in no danger of lapsing on the rent, not since I'd decided to take a double shift on Tuesdays and Fridays. But it seemed that even—or *especially*—when things were going well, karma was always waiting just around the corner with a baseball bat to deliver a death blow to my confidence.

Today, it was an eviction notice. Tomorrow, it could be a shitty customer who would complain to my boss because I didn't let him grab my ass. Whatever I did, the karma police were always hot on my trail.

Truthfully, I didn't know if I even believed in karma.

The saying "what goes around, comes around" was one I used to laugh at when I heard it repeated. But nowadays, I found myself hoping it was true, because if karma was real, then maybe I could turn my negative karmic value into a positive with enough good deeds. For instance, forgoing college to take care of my mom instead of pawning her off on one of her sisters in South Dakota, whom I'd never met.

Entering our apartment on the fifth floor, a cool air-conditioned breeze doused the flame of summer heat throbbing in my skin. My first instinct was to panic that I had left the window AC unit on full blast while no one was here, and I would surely pay for that mistake when our next electric bill arrived. But as soon as I saw my mother lying in her hospital bed in front of the TV, sound asleep, I knew it was she who had turned it on, probably so she could get some rest after what was probably an exhausting trip to Target.

Despite the fact that I was an only child, my mom never babied me. She taught me to cook dinner when I was six. I began making trips to the local bodega by myself when I was nine. Though, I did that mostly so I could pet the cats that wandered the aisles. Sometimes, though, I wished my mom would baby herself.

Closing the front door softly behind me, so as not to wake my mom from her nap, I quietly lifted the two un-emptied Target bags sitting at the foot of her bed and tiptoed to the bathroom. When I reached into the first bag, I smiled as I pulled out a bottle of coconut shampoo I mentioned in passing to my mom a few weeks ago.

I had been complaining about how difficult it was brushing the tangles out of my long brown hair. I told my mom how envious I was of Helen's—one of my coworkers—silky, coconut-scented locks. How I'd never have hair like Helen's because I couldn't afford fancy hair products.

I shook my head as I imagined my mom sitting in the electric shopping cart, asking Leslie to help her find a nice coconut-scented shampoo.

It's the little things people do for you that show how much they truly care.

My shift didn't start for more than two hours, so I took my time in the shower, washing and conditioning my hair twice with the new products my mom had bought. Then, I took my time blow-drying my hair and using the cheap flatiron I bought at a flea market to create a luxurious beach waves hairstyle I saw on Pinterest. It wasn't until I was finishing up my "no-makeup makeup" look that I realized I wasn't getting ready for work. I was getting ready for Daniel.

How stupid of me.

It wasn't as if I was going to skip work to go on a date with a guy I'd known all of ten minutes. The new Kristin didn't do things like that. She wasn't impulsive or flighty. She wouldn't hurt someone she loved—her mom—to satisfy a primal urge.

I hadn't taken a single sip of alcohol in almost two years, and I would not allow myself to become addicted to anything or any*one*.

The memories of that night returned and, before I could stop myself, tears spilled from my eyes, carving trails through my fresh makeup. I allowed myself to cry as I washed my face in the sink. If my mom walked in, she wouldn't be able to see the tears through the soapy water. But as soon as I patted my face dry, I drew in a deep breath and pushed aside all those feelings that had become a part of my daily life since the night I lost my best friend.

The loneliness, the sadness, the *fear* that the loneliness and sadness would never go away. I stuffed it all down, locking it away to be dealt with another day.

For now, I had to go to work and do my job, while trying to forget that I could be out there somewhere in this glittering city, probably enjoying a lavish dinner at a fancy restaurant with one of the hottest guys I'd ever laid eyes on.

3. Blood Sisters

Ten years earlier

BLOOD. EVERYWHERE.

I wanted to cry.

No, I didn't want to cry. If I cried, everyone would hear me.

I couldn't help it. I cried.

"Are you okay in there?" a voice called to me from the other side of the door of the restroom stall I occupied.

"I'm fine," I called back from inside the stall, unable to hide the desperation in my voice. "Just a headache. I'm fine."

It was just my luck. Less than two weeks had passed since I transferred to this new school. I hadn't made a single friend yet. I'd been eating lunch alone in the computer lab while surfing the six websites allowed through the "kid-safe" internet filter. I had actually just fallen into a *Webster's Dictionary* rabbit hole of words related to the word "pathetic," when I felt a strange, warm sensation in my crotch.

I had gotten my first period about a month ago, over the summer, so I had no idea I was supposed to wear *preemptive* feminine protection at school. Shit, between all the stuff we had to do to get me registered at this new school, and my abysmal first two weeks, I'd completely forgotten the disturbing appearance of my first period last month.

Now, I was sitting in the bathroom, and the bell was about to ring for everyone to get to their fifth-period class following lunch. The crotch of my panties, and the back of my blue skinny jeans, were soaked through with a ghastly splotch of blood the size of my fist. There was no way I'd make it to the nurse's office without at least one person seeing me. I was doomed.

Rumors of my bloody mishap would spread fast. I'd never have any friends at this new school, or whatever high school I went to next year. I'd be branded the "gross girl." I'd be a loner for the rest of my days. I'd probably be better off just waiting in this restroom stall until school let out in about two hours. No, that wouldn't work. I'd have to wait until all the sports teams and after-school clubs had let out. That wouldn't be for another four or five hours.

"Did you bleed through your pants?" the same voice asked.

My stomach ached as I realized this person probably saw me walk into the stall. She was probably going to go run and tell her friends how the new girl was in a restroom stall, crying over her gross panties.

"Here," she said.

I flinched as a large black T-shirt flew over the door of the bathroom stall and landed in my lap. I quickly scooped it up so it wouldn't accidentally come in contact with my bloody pants.

"That should cover your ass enough for you to make it to the nurse's office. And take this, too," she said, holding her chubby, freckled hand under the door.

I grabbed the pad she was holding, then quickly attempted to place the T-shirt back in her outstretched hand. "Thank you, but I can't take your shirt."

She drew her hand back swiftly, and I tightened my grip on the shirt to keep it from dropping on the grimy floor. "Don't feel too grateful. The only reason I had that shirt on me is because I was taking it home to wash. It's the undershirt I use for Phys Ed."

I tentatively brought the shirt to my face and

inhaled. My nose crinkled at the smell of grass and sweat. Laying the shirt over my shoulder, I cleaned myself up and stuck the pad over the bloody stain on my panties. Then, I pulled the plain black shirt over my pink Paramore T-shirt. I had never felt so cool in my life, wearing a complete stranger's plain shirt.

I never had trouble making friends. I had trouble keeping them. I finally found a group of friends I could settle in with last year, then we had to move out of our Brooklyn apartment to a shitty five-floor walk-up in the Bronx because my mom couldn't afford the "criminally sky-high Brooklyn rent," as she called it.

I peeked around the edge of the door, making sure we were alone, before I stepped out of the restroom stall. The red-haired girl standing by the sinks was at least six inches taller and forty pounds heavier than I was. She wore white canvas sneakers, blue skinny jeans, and a striped gray and black T-shirt, which was too long, even on her, as the hemline stopped mid-thigh. Glancing down at the shirt I'd just put on, I realized the hemline skimmed the tops of my knees.

"You're in my Algebra class," the girl said, turning back to the mirror and leaning over the sink to get a closer look as she plucked her thin ginger eyebrows.

I made my way to the sink and began washing my hands. "Am I?" I replied, knowing full well she sat two rows away from me in Mr. Caldwell's sixth-period Algebra class.

She chuckled. "Uh...yes. You're the one who laughed the loudest when Caldwell put that shitty word problem on the board about the bakery that used math to figure out why they ended the day with too many leftover apple pies, and I blurted out it was because I didn't work there."

I laughed again at the joke, recalling how funny I thought it was that a girl our age would make fun of her weight in front of a classroom. Then, how mortified I was when I accidentally let out a loud witch-like cackle and everyone turned toward me, and suddenly *I* became the brunt of the joke.

"Oh, yeah," I replied, regaining my composure. "Thanks again for the shirt. I'll wash it and bring it back to you tomorrow."

She looked at my reflection in the mirror and raised her eyebrows. "Tomorrow's Saturday."

"Oh, shit. I meant Monday. I'll bring it back on Monday."

She laughed and refocused her attention on her eyebrows. "Where do you live? I can pick it up this weekend."

I thought of the rundown apartment we'd moved into a month ago and how there were still unpacked boxes stacked up in the hallway. We had to turn sideways to pass them.

"I...I can take it to your house. Where do you live?" I asked, trying to sound as nonchalant as possible as I yanked a few paper towels out of the dispenser to dry my hands.

She bent over and tucked her tweezers into the red and black backpack on the floor. "Yeah, I don't live in a house. I live in a janky shithole on Belmont."

I chuckled. "Me, too. Well, not on Belmont. We're one street over on Hughes. We just moved in last month."

"Even better," she replied, hoisting her backpack onto her shoulder and sliding a silver flip phone out of her jeans pocket. "What's your number?"

I averted my gaze as I tried to think of a lie for why I didn't have a cell phone, but for some reason, I didn't want to lie to this girl. "I...don't have a cell phone. My mom can't afford it."

She didn't hesitate at all at this response as she then asked for my home phone number, which I gave willingly. "So...what name should I put on your contact? Blood Sister?"

I smiled at the mention of the word "sister." "Kristin is cool."

"Sweet," she replied, tucking the phone back into

her pocket. "I'm Petra, in case you didn't catch that in Caldwell's class. I'll call you tonight. Stay dry out there!" she said with a wink before she disappeared into the corridor.

Turning back to the mirror, I realized I was grinning like an idiot. I tempered my reaction as another girl walked into the restroom. She looked me up and down and let out a derisive chuckle as she sneered at the black T-shirt I was swimming in. I didn't care. This shirt was given to me by someone who didn't take herself seriously. Someone who extended her kindness to a complete stranger, turning that stranger into a friend.

I let out a tremendous sigh of relief.

I had a friend.

4. Hero

It wasn't until I started working at Cantina Joe's in Hell's Kitchen last year that I realized how, as long as I worked there, I would probably never feel invisible again. The catcalls I could deal with; it was the constant groping and hungry, lecherous looks that made me start carrying a pocketknife to work. I wasn't *afraid* of the customers. I just didn't trust them. Truthfully, I didn't trust anyone anymore, least of all myself.

No more than two seconds had passed since I'd clocked in after my last break of the night before Joe was shouting at me from behind the bar.

"Hey, Kris! Table eight needs a pitcher of sandía!"

The bar was small enough that Joe's resonant voice

reached even the farthest corner of the back kitchen. Jesus, our line cook, flashed me a look of pity as I tied my half-apron around my waist and sighed. Jesus felt sorry for me because he knew what I knew. An order for a pitcher of sandía coming from table eight at this time of night could only mean one thing: *He* was back.

Roger always sat at table eight and ordered a pitcher of sandía, a cocktail made with pureed watermelon, lime juice, simple syrup, and a generous pour of cheap white tequila. It was Cantina Joe's signature drink, and one of the only things that kept customers coming back for our uninspired small-plate menu. Roger was no exception. In fact, there was nothing he enjoyed more than reminding me how much the food sucked, and how the sandía and my sweet, round *melons* were the only things that kept him coming back.

Roger was very near the top of my List of Reasons I Wished I Could Go Back to Being Invisible.

I emerged from the back kitchen with confidence, determined not to let Roger get the best of me tonight. The savory smell of fried garlic and peppers transformed into the refreshingly sweet scent of tequila and watermelon. First, I slinked behind the bar with Joe, an imposingly large man with a leathery, red face that looked every bit of fifty-two. My boss cocked a gray eyebrow at me as I swiped my employee keycard on the touchscreen register and punched a few buttons to sign back into the computer system. I called up the order for table eight and changed the server from Joe to Kristin.

Joe nodded toward the counter, where a frosty pitcher of pink cocktail awaited me. Despite tending bar and chatting up drunks for nearly thirty years, Joe was a man of few words when it came to his managerial style. There were times I appreciated this approach, and times like tonight when I wished he'd use that deep bearlike growl of his to eighty-six Roger permanently.

Loading up a tray with the pitcher of sandía, a couple of glasses, a small bowl of lime wedges, and some napkins, I made my way through the maze of bar-height tables to the booth in the corner. Roger sat on the side of the booth facing the bar, so he could watch me as I came and went. His receding hairline and pinched features gave him a mousy appearance, but his faded Mets T-shirt and beer gut made him fit right in with all the other drunks who loved spending their evenings harassing cocktail waitresses.

Another guy at a table on my right held up a finger as I passed. "Can I get another Dos Equis?"

My breath caught in my chest as I recognized the

smooth voice, dark hair, and *enormous* shoulders, which appeared ready to burst through the seams of his expensive suit.

I smiled at Daniel as I tried not to drop my tray. "Sure. I'll be right back."

He smiled warmly, the kind of smile people reserved for babies and puppies, and it caught me off guard. My mind's eye was so focused on replaying the man's smile, I didn't see the barstool at the next table until I tripped over it, spilling the entire contents of my tray all over Roger's pant leg and sneaker.

"Jesus Christ! You *idiot*!" Roger bellowed, springing out of his booth to shake the pink liquid off his shoe.

"Oh, my God. I'm so sorry. I'll clean it up," I said, my eyes pleading with him not to make a scene.

A flicker of arousal lit up his taut features as I knelt down to pick up the tray. "Why don't you suck my dick while you're down there and I'll forget this ever happened?"

"What?" I replied, pretending I hadn't heard him as I placed the empty pitcher and shards of broken glasses on the tray.

The sudden pain in my scalp burned like someone had taken a blowtorch to it. Roger yanked me up by my dark-brown ponytail until I was looking up at him.

His eyes were wild with lust as he whispered just

loud enough for me to hear him over the pop music playing on the restaurant's sound system. "You heard what I said, bitch. I said suck my—"

Before he could finish, the fire in my scalp was extinguished and Roger was facedown on the floor. Daniel was on top of him, smashing his red face into the sticky, wet terra-cotta tiles.

"Listen to me, you sick fuck," he seethed through gritted teeth. "I'm gonna give you two fucking seconds to apologize to her, or I will fucking ice you. You got it, motherfucker?"

A deep panic arose inside me. If Joe saw one of our regulars facedown in the spill I'd made, I was going to get fired for this. I couldn't get fired.

"It's okay," I pleaded with Daniel, who seemed to be taking great pleasure smashing Roger's face into the sticky floor. "He's fine. I'm sure he didn't mean what he said. I'll clean this up and everything will be okay. I swear, everything's fine."

"You heard her, man. Everything's cool." Roger pushed the words out through the side of his mouth.

Joe arrived as the rest of the bar's patrons looked on in horror, clutching their glasses of beer and sandía closely. "What's going on here?"

Daniel growled as Roger tried to get up. "This piece of trash just attacked your waitress. I'm holding him here until she decides how to deal with him."

Joe turned to me, wide-eyed. "Is that true?" Something in his eyes begged me to tell him it wasn't true, that one of his regulars wasn't lying facedown on the floor, in a puddle of cocktails, and about to be eighty-sixed.

I closed my eyes and drew in a deep, sour breath as I nodded.

"It's a lie!" Roger shouted. "That bitch tossed the pitcher on *me*—on *purpose*!"

Joe wanted to believe me and Daniel. I could see it in the disappointed wrinkles around his gray eyes. But he hated the cops as much as any of the drug dealers that lived on my street.

"What do you want to do, Kristin?" he asked, his voice weary. This was serious if he was calling me Kristin instead of Kris.

"I don't think it's a big deal," I replied, my shaky words propelled forth by the fear of losing my job. "He can stay, but I'll ask Dina to take care of him."

Daniel looked up at me, unable to disguise his disappointment. "You're gonna let this fucker get away with that?"

I glared at him. "I need this job, okay?"

I felt as if I were being split in two. One part of me watched powerlessly as this handsome man pleaded with me to stand up for myself, wanting desperately for me to be the kind of plucky waitress he probably imagined I'd be. Another part of me thought of the terrible things I'd gotten away with. Putting up with Roger was just another part of my penance. It was God or the universe balancing the scales.

Daniel didn't know me. He didn't know what I was capable of. He didn't know that I didn't deserve his pity or his help.

Unfortunately, for some crazy reason, today felt different. Today, I wanted to be the person Daniel wanted me to be.

As I watched Joe helping Roger up off the floor, I slowly straightened my back so I could project my voice over the sound of the pop music. "Get rid of him or I quit."

Turning on my heel, I left the mess of sticky liquid on the floor, making a beeline for the swinging doors that led to the back kitchen. Passing the line cooks, I burst through the door into the employee restroom and locked it behind me before I dissolved into tears. Sitting on the toilet, tearing off squares of toilet tissue to wipe my face, ten minutes passed before I heard a knock on the door.

"Someone's in here!" I shouted.

"Kris, it's me," a deep voice echoed through the

crack in the door. "I eighty-sixed Roger."

My chest swelled with pride, in myself *and* Joe, for standing up to that bully.

"For a month," Joe continued, and my heart sank. "He'll have cooled off by then. If not, I'll eighty-six him again. Permanently. I promise." When I didn't reply, he knocked again. "Kris, that's the best I could do… Sorry."

Standing up from the toilet, I tossed the wad of used tissues into the waste bin and washed up before removing my apron and emerging from the restroom. Joe was still standing there, genuine worry etched all over his wrinkled face.

I flashed him a weak smile. "Thanks for looking out for me, Joe," I said, grabbing my purse off the hook on the wall. "I have to take the rest of the day off. I'm just…not feeling well."

"Yeah, of course. You take a couple of days if you need to."

I nodded as I slung the purse across my body and slunk out the back door. My heart leapt out of my chest as I found Daniel waiting in the alley behind the bar.

"Fuck. You scared the shit out of me," I complained.

"More than that creep in there?" he asked,

sounding slightly annoyed.

I set off down the short service alley toward 47th. "You nearly got me fired in there."

"He *assaulted* you."

I rolled my eyes as I dug my hand into my jeans pocket until my fingertips hit the warm steel of my pocketknife. "Roger isn't a rapist. He's just an asshole who thinks women owe him more than the time of day. He'll get what's coming to him, eventually. We all do."

Daniel kept up with me as we transitioned briskly and effortlessly onto the crowded city sidewalk. "Is that how you thank the guy who gave him what was coming to him?"

I sighed, trying to drown out the voice in my head that was in complete agreement with Daniel's actions, even if it did put my job in jeopardy. "Thank you, but you really didn't have to do that."

He chuckled. "Of course, because, just like earlier today, you were handling the situation so well on your own."

My jaw dropped and I stopped in the middle of the sidewalk to glare at him. "Listen here, you sexist little shit," I said, ignoring how his smile widened. "I am not a damsel in distress. I do not need to be *saved*. If you want to be a hero, there's an animal shelter six blocks away."

His smile disappeared. "Listen here, little lamb. I know you're not lost. But you sure as hell were about to be devoured by the Big Bad Wolf in there. Now, you don't have to thank me," he said, taking a step closer so our noses were just inches apart. "But please don't patronize me. I am *not*, nor have I ever been, a sexist little shit." He held my gaze for a moment, then he straightened his back and nodded toward the street. "Shall we?"

We walked side by side in silence until we reached the corner of 48th and 10th, when he said, "You're right, by the way… That guy had it coming. And I'm glad I was there to give it to him."

I scrunched my eyebrows as I looked up at him. "Why are you following me?"

"Following you?" he replied, looking just as confused as I felt. "I'm just making sure the Big Bad Wolf doesn't come back for another nip."

"So, are you gonna follow me around for the rest of my life to protect me from Big Bad Roger?"

He shrugged. "Are you looking to hire a bodyguard?"

I shook my head as I pulled my pocketknife out of my pocket. "This is the only bodyguard I need, thanks."

"Whoa, whoa. Put that thing away," he said, clasping his large hand softly over mine as his eyes scanned the intersection. "You never want to advertise you're carrying a weapon. It's like challenging thieves and rapists to a duel. And trust me, they're probably carrying something with a lot more punch than that puny thing."

"Are you calling Laser puny?"

The light turned green and he laughed as we stepped into the intersection to cross. "You call your knife Laser?"

"He may be small, but he'll cut you with precision," I replied, tucking Laser back into the warmth of my pocket, then sliding my bus pass out.

"You're headed for the bus stop?" he asked as we approached 49th.

"Yeah, how'd you know?"

He shrugged. "Wild guess," he said, pointing at the MetroCard in my hand. "You don't trust men, do you?"

My eyebrows shot into the stratosphere. "Uh…a bit of a loaded question for strangers, don't you think?"

He flashed me that warm, almost paternal smile again. "Not exactly strangers anymore. Are we, Kristin?"

"Do you always answer a question with a question?"

"Do *you*?"

I nodded as I took a seat on the bench. "Should have seen that coming."

He flicked an intense look at the homeless guy standing a few feet away, then he took a seat next to me. "Let me give you a ride home."

I held up my MetroCard. "I've got that covered, thanks."

Before Daniel could reply, the transient snatched the card out of my hand and took off down 10th faster than Usain Bolt on steroids.

I grabbed Daniel's arm before he could run after the guy and tackle him the way he did Roger. "It's fine. He won't get far with what's left on it."

Daniel took a couple of deep breaths. "You need a bodyguard," he replied, glancing at my hand gripped tightly around his solid forearm.

I quickly let go. "Nope, but I guess I do need a ride now," I said with a sheepish grin.

He shook his head. "Just you, or Laser too?"

"We're a package deal."

He sighed as he stood from the bench. "Well, then, it would be my pleasure," he said with a slight bow. Then he bent his arm, holding out his elbow for me to slip my arm inside his. "Shall we?"

I hesitated for a long moment, staring at the crook of his elbow as if it were the edge of a cliff and I was about to plunge off headfirst. I hadn't been with anyone—not even a random Tinder date—since that night. It was hard to meet guys when you had no more friends. I got plenty of invitations from men at the cantina, but I had a rule that I didn't date customers. Daniel certainly didn't look like our usual clientele. I was certain he went to Cantina Joe's tonight looking for me.

I felt as if I'd been staring at his elbow for ages, when I finally stood up and hesitantly slid my arm through his.

He flashed me a reassuring smile. "You surprised yourself."

I rolled my eyes, trying to downplay the truth in his words. But I couldn't bring myself to spit out a sarcastic retort. At the moment, I was focusing so hard on just trying to breathe, I didn't think I could remember my name if I were asked.

Soon, the nervous energy melted away and we walked in comfortable silence as we headed back toward the bar, as if we had done this a million times before. Just another night out on the town for Daniel and Kristin. I didn't know if it was a good thing that being near him made me feel safe. What if I was being lulled into a false sense of security?

Suddenly, I became painfully aware of how we must look together.

Daniel was so polished in his expensive suit, chiseled features, and perfect hair. My perfect hairstyle that I'd spent almost an hour on had become so frizzy that I'd had to put my hair up in a messy ponytail halfway through my shift. I didn't imagine my drugstore makeup was holding up very well against the onslaught of the summer humidity. I was wearing my Cantina Joe's uniform: frayed jean shorts and a red T-shirt featuring the restaurant's logo. I may have felt, for a brief moment, as if walking down the street arm-in-arm with Daniel was something we'd done a million times, but to everyone else we probably looked like a rich businessman and a prostitute.

I quickly yanked my arm out of his. "Sorry, I…I think my phone is vibrating," I lied as I dug through my purse for my phone, letting out a phony chuckle as I pulled it out and the screen was pitch black. "Guess not."

Luckily, we were less than a block away from the cantina, so the awkward silence that followed my fake phone call didn't last long. Daniel's gleaming black Range Rover with heavily tinted windows was parked on 47th.

"Now I see why you were so reluctant to take the bus," I remarked, eyeballing the flashy SUV.

He opened the passenger door for me. "It's a company car," he replied, looking flustered for the first time since we'd met.

"Company car…for a company you own, right?" I said, but he didn't respond as I slid onto the supple perforated leather seat. "What do you do for a living?"

He tilted his head as he looked down at me, as if the answer to this question was plainly obvious. "I'm in finance."

"Finance?" I replied, cocking my eyebrow. "Is that code for something?"

He smiled. "What? I don't look like your average Warren Buffett wannabe?"

I nodded. "Answering another question with a question. I think I'm beginning to see a pattern. Either you're stalling for time to come up with a lie, or you're one of those people who are obsessed with privacy. Should I be worried?"

"Only if you're one of those people who like to tell everyone your life story within the first ten minutes of meeting them. Are you one of those people?"

"Absolutely not," I replied.

He shrugged his massive shoulders. "Then we'll get

along just fine."

He closed the car door and the sounds of the city faded away into a silent and dark realization. If I wasn't working, I should go home. I should go home and thank my mom for the shampoo. It was such a thoughtful gesture, and I was repaying her by taking a night off.

Daniel slid into the driver's seat. "Where to, princess?"

"I thought you got my address from the receptionist."

"The night is young," he replied in that smooth voice as he tapped his steering wheel. "And this thing doesn't turn back into a pumpkin for a few more hours."

I searched his gorgeous face for any indication he meant me harm, but all I saw was a genuine guy who seemed to want nothing more than to give me a choice: go home or go for a ride.

I looked him in the eye. "What's the best place to go in Manhattan if you want to disappear?"

His smile dimmed a bit as he seemed to recognize my reluctance to go home might have less to do with wanting to spend time with him and more to do with a need to escape whatever was waiting for me at home. "That's easy, the Botanical Gardens."

I drew in a long, deep breath, then let it out slowly. "Let's disappear."

5. Smooth Jazz

"YOU LOOK HUNGRY," Daniel remarked, pulling his Range Rover into the sluggish traffic on 47th.

"I ate before my shift, thanks." I didn't bother telling him my shift started almost seven hours ago.

He chuckled at my response. "I wasn't offering to get you something to eat. You look hungry for something, but whatever it is, it's definitely not food."

I shifted uncomfortably in the leather seat, my gaze focused on the logo on the side of the work van parked against the curb beside us. "I don't know what the fuck that means."

After a brief silence, I turned to Daniel and found him wearing a curious smile, as if he were considering whether he should let me in on a secret. Ultimately, he turned away to focus on the road, then he turned right into even worse traffic on West Side Highway.

"You could have used some of this feisty attitude in the restaurant," he said, with what I interpreted as a note of disappointment in his voice. "Why didn't you speak up when your boss asked what that Ted Bundy wannabe did to you?"

I was not mistaken. For some reason, this privileged asshole who barely knew me was *disappointed* in me.

I shrugged. "Can we talk about something other than Roger?"

"Sure. Why don't we talk about why you want to disappear?"

I sighed. "You know, being good looking doesn't give you the right to be a nosy little prick."

His eyes widened, as did mine, as we both realized my slip. "So you find me good looking?"

I crossed my arms over my chest and stared out the window again. "All I meant is that you don't have a right to pry into my personal life just because you think you saved me from Roger and Jerry."

"I *think* I saved you?"

"I don't want to talk about this, okay?"

He focused his attention on the highway. "I won't ask any more questions about your job…except for one."

I narrowed my eyes at him. "What?"

"Why do you work there? I mean, shouldn't you be in college or graduate school?"

I snatched my purse off the floor and clutched it to my belly, suddenly feeling as if I needed something to hide behind. "It's not a huge mystery or anything. I dropped out because I couldn't afford it."

"Isn't that what scholarships are for? You're a…girl. There's scholarships for women in just about every field these days."

I shot him a scathing look. "Can we drop the inquisition, please? I wanted to disappear, not put myself on trial for being a loser."

Though I immediately regretted speaking these words aloud, I was grateful it managed to get Daniel to stop his interrogation. However, traffic slowed as we passed Pier 1 on our left, and the silence seemed too much for him to handle. He pressed a few things on his flashy touchscreen and crisp musical notes flowed out of his sound system. He leaned back with a satisfied grin spreading across his beautiful face.

I chuckled as the sound of elevator Muzak filled the air. "Very funny."

"What? You don't like jazz?" he replied without a hint of a smile.

I waited for him to burst into laughter, to say he was kidding, but he just stared at me as the car inched forward in traffic.

"Hey, keep your eyes on the road," I demanded.

"We're going, like, two miles per hour," he replied, his gaze locked on my face.

"My dad died in a car accident. I take driver safety very seriously," I replied, inwardly cringing at the words my mother had repeated to me so many times, which I was almost certain were a lie. But I didn't mind using this probable lie about my father's death if it got Daniel and his gorgeous green eyes to stop staring into my soul.

The Range Rover stopped dead as the other cars around us continued inching forward. "Your...your dad...died? What...I thought..."

I cocked an eyebrow at this odd response. "Hey, it's no big deal. It's not like I knew him. He died when I was a baby. But now I...I don't know, I guess I have a kind of phobia of car accidents. That's why I don't drive anymore."

I swallowed hard, trying to clear away the emotions that welled up as I thought of that night, and the *real* reason why I might never find the courage to get behind the wheel again. Suddenly, I could smell my own fear as the city lights burned streaks into my retinas while the car flipped over, spiraling into hell.

We both let out deep, audible sighs at the same time, which confused the fuck out of me.

"Are you okay?" I asked, unable to hide the note of torment in my voice, the result of allowing myself to remember that night.

He nodded vigorously as the Rover moved forward again. "Yeah, yeah. I'm great. I just...I guess what you said about your dad caught me a little off guard. I...I never really had a dad around. My dad...He's been in and out of prison since I was six."

I stared at him for a moment, searching for any indication that he was pulling my chain, trying to relate to me on some deeper level by constructing a fake sob story, but he appeared extremely uncomfortable, like someone who had just shared a shameful piece of their past with a complete stranger.

"I'm sorry to hear that," I replied, setting my purse back on the floor. "How about your mom?" I shook my head as the words came out of my mouth. Now *I* was the one being nosy.

"She's gone," he said, the solemn look on his face betrayed by the ridiculous soaring bellow of the saxophone coming from the speakers. "Breast cancer. She died a few years ago."

"I'm sorry," I whispered.

A sickening weed of guilt grew inside my belly as I thought of my mom, at home alone. I could have gone home to be with her instead of going to the Botanical Gardens with a complete stranger, but I needed a break. I needed to forget, just for a few minutes, that I was the only thing standing between my mother and me being homeless.

Daniel was saying something, but I couldn't hear him over the thundering roar of guilt drowning out every thought in my head.

"Can you just take me home?" I interrupted him. "I'm not far from the Botanical Gardens."

His gaze skimmed over my face, possibly searching for signs I had tired of his company. "Of course."

He seemed distant now, and I found myself wishing I had paid attention to whatever it was he was just saying. This happened often, tuning out in the middle of a conversation. I'd be speaking with a customer or coworker, then suddenly I'd find I hadn't been paying attention for an unknown period of time. Always lost in thoughts of all the things I needed to do for my mother, or all the things I'd never get to do for myself.

Or the terrible things I'd done in the past.

We were four blocks from Hughes Avenue when my phone began to ring. Looking at the screen, I saw

Leslie's name and face. Leslie knew who to call if she ever saw my mom trying to leave the apartment without me.

I understood my mom got bored up there with no one and nothing but the TV for company, but I couldn't afford to hire a caretaker to watch her while I worked. I wished we had family in New York who could help. With my mom's entire family in South Dakota, and my father supposedly dead, I was alone. Totally alone.

"Leslie, what's wrong?" I said, pressing the phone to my ear to hear her voice over the shrill bleat of the saxophone.

"Oh, honey, you should get down here as soon as you can," she said, her gravelly voice sounding as tired and weary as ever. "We're at the Bronx-Lebanon ER. Your mom took a spill."

6. A Keeper

PASSING THE PARKED ambulances on the way into the emergency entrance made me sick to my stomach. Despite Leslie's assurances that my mother was not in grave condition, the guilt from not being there when she needed me only amplified my concern. However, the moment we stepped through the sliding doors, a tiny bit of my anxiety was relieved.

Most people hated the smell of hospitals, but I actually found it soothing. Having spent so much time wandering these sterile corridors over the past few years, I'd come to associate the smell of hospital disinfectant with the feeling that my mother was in good hands, and I could rest. It was difficult to feel at ease when I was at work and she was home alone.

"You really don't have to stay here with me," I insisted as Daniel and I approached the nurses' station. "I can find my way home from here, thank you."

He ignored me as he sidled up next to me at the counter, and I couldn't decide if I found his refusal to leave more infuriating or comforting. Turning back to the nurse behind the counter, I drew in a deep breath to calm myself before I spoke. The last thing an emergency room nurse needed was *another* shrill voice barking commands at her. I'd developed a pretty good feel for how to speak to hospital staff over the years.

The nurse directed us to bay nineteen, where I found Leslie sitting at my mother's bedside. She smiled warmly at me, then her eyebrows shot up as Daniel trailed in behind me.

"Oh, Krissy. It's so good to see you. Who's this?"

Before I could open my mouth, Daniel reached his hand out to Leslie. "I'm Daniel, Kristin's bodyguard. It's nice to meet you."

Leslie turned to me, her eyes wide with surprise.

I waved off Daniel's comment. "He's not my bodyguard," I said, trying to sound more annoyed than I actually was. "He's a customer who was kind enough to give me a ride."

He turned to me, one eyebrow cocked. "Customer? What exactly am I paying you for?"

I narrowed my eyes at him. "Keep it up and you'll be paying for a one-way ticket back to your car."

My mom exploded into a softly hoarse fit of laughter. "That's my girl," she said, her words thick and rounded from the pain medication.

I stepped forward and placed my hand on her shoulder. "You scared the hell out of me. What happened?"

"It's not her fault, honey," Leslie said. "Some little bastard pulled the fire alarm. I was already outside the building, standing there with the other idiots, when I remembered to check on your mom. Found her laid out on the fourth-floor landing. I'm so sorry, honey. I should've been up there."

I shook my head. "Don't be silly. It's not your fault, Les. I'm the one who should've been there."

My mom clumsily waved off our declarations of guilt. "Oh, please. It's no one's fault but mine and these knotty tree stumps below my waist."

I turned to face Leslie. "Are they going to do another surgery? Why are they holding her here?"

Leslie looked confused. "They didn't tell you? She popped a couple of screws in her knee out of place. She also shattered her elbow." She whispered the last line out of the corner of her mouth, as if my mother wasn't lying three feet away.

My mom laughed again. "I'm crippled, Les, not deaf."

This got a hearty chuckle out of Daniel.

I shot him a scathing look. "It's not funny!"

My mom squinted at Daniel, a lazy smile spreading across her plump cheeks. "Hey, handsome. What did you say your name was again?"

"Daniel," he replied. "Daniel Meyers."

Her eyebrow twitched slightly. "I don't buy this customer thing, Kristin. Do you have a handsome boyfriend you've been hiding from me?" she slurred as she beckoned Daniel to her bedside. "Come here. Let me have a good look at you."

I was mortified. I wanted to protest, but I didn't know what to say. I'd never been in this situation before, introducing a male friend to my mother. Could I even call Daniel a friend? We'd known each other a matter of hours. Yet, he'd already paid my rent and saved me from a sexual assault. And now he was standing at my mother's bedside, when he could be at the cantina tossing back beers or whatever a person in finance did at nine o'clock at night.

Daniel grinned as he approached the other side of the bed. "Actually, ma'am, I'm not her boyfriend"—he looked up at me and winked—"yet."

My mom let out a hoarse cackle. "I like this kid.

He's a keeper."

My cheeks flushed with heat as I gripped the bedrail firmly. "Don't you have a game of real-life monopoly to play or something?" I asked him.

An unreadable expression passed over his chiseled features, then he blinked a few times and the cocky confidence returned. "Actually, I *am* thinking of putting some hotels on Park Place."

Something about his response made me think he was hiding something. "Yeah, whatever," I said, shaking off my confusion as I turned back to Leslie. "So what are we waiting on?"

Leslie tried to go into detail about my mother's injuries, but she found herself fumbling for medical terms she could hardly remember, much less pronounce. In the end, she shrugged and complained that she and my mother had been waiting almost an hour for an orthopedic surgeon to arrive for a surgical consult. As my mother's eyelids fell shut under the heaviness of the pain meds, Leslie urged me to take the opportunity to go home and get my mom at least one change of clothing and some toiletries.

I didn't want to involve Daniel any more, but when I looked up at him the hopeful look in his eyes made me smile. Either he assumed acting as my chauffeur was going to get him laid or he had a major hero complex. I couldn't decide which option was more likely.

I sighed. "Can you give me a ride to my apartment?"

He tilted his gorgeous head to one side and smiled. "I'd love to."

7. Surreal Daydream

"TAKE A RIGHT HERE," I said as we approached Hughes. "There might be some parking in the lot right there on the left."

As he pulled in, I wasn't surprised to find the small lot next to my building was completely full. I silently thanked the universe for this small karmic victory. Daniel would have to drop me off. While he was busy looking for a parking space, I could try to make the apartment look more presentable to someone who was surely accustomed to something a bit more luxurious.

"Just drop me off here," I said, reaching for the passenger door handle. "It's apartment 502. The buzzer at the entrance is broken, so you can just walk right up."

He cocked an eyebrow. "So, anyone can just walk into the building whenever they want? There's no security?"

I rolled my eyes. "In case you hadn't noticed, this is not Fifth Avenue. Not a whole lot of valuables for criminals to pine after."

"Except you," he replied, without a hint of irony.

I opened my mouth to contradict him, but I couldn't think of a single retort. "Um…I'll see you upstairs," I said, grabbing my purse in a hurry as I hopped out of the SUV and power-walked to the front entrance of my building.

My heart raced as I yanked the door with the chipped burgundy paint open and rushed inside. The light in the entryway flickered a bit as the door closed behind me. I glanced at the brass mailboxes on the wall and decided against checking my mail. I needed to get upstairs and tidy the apartment before Daniel made it up there.

My stomach churned with anxiety and hunger. I'd gone too long without food, or this amount of care and attention. I'd be lying if I said I didn't care about making a good impression on Daniel. He was gorgeous and wealthy and, apparently, had a strong desire to help people. Actually, I didn't know if that last quality was true. I knew he wanted to help *me*, but for all I knew, he was a greedy bastard who beat up homeless people in his spare time.

As soon as I entered the apartment, I quickly made up my mom's hospital bed in the living room. I picked up the empty coffee mug and almost completely full glass of water off the side table, and carried the cups to the kitchen. I washed them as fast I could, along with the bowl my mother had apparently used to eat some of her favorite Cheerios. Then, I stashed away the box of cereal she'd left on the counter, because she couldn't stand on her tiptoes anymore to put the box away.

Grabbing a clean rag and a spray bottle of cleaner, I quickly dusted the tops of the tables and TV stand in the living room, which doubled as my mother's bedroom. Exactly twenty-two minutes had passed, and I was just putting away the bottle of cleaner under the kitchen sink when I heard a loud creaking noise behind me.

I thought of what I'd just said to Daniel about criminals wanting nothing from our rundown apartment, and how he'd looked so concerned with our lack of security. But I knew it wouldn't be a criminal walking through my front door this evening. When I turned around, I would find a dangerously handsome man in a suit entering my living room. What would he think of the place I called home?

I spun around in time to see Daniel closing the door behind him. "You found me," I said, running my fingernails softly over my left arm, a comforting mechanism I often resorted to when I was especially anxious.

The door clicked shut and he turned to face me, his expression unreadable. "I'm beginning to doubt that."

"What?" I replied with a nervous chuckle.

He shook his head. "Nothing. Did you pack a bag for your mother?"

I swallowed hard at the realization that he wanted to get out of this apartment as quickly as possible. "Not yet. I just need to grab a few things from the bedroom."

He followed a good distance behind me as I made my way to the bedroom.

I let out a tense sigh as I reached the bedroom door. "Why are you being so nice to me?"

"Am I being nice?"

I glanced back over my shoulder to glare at him, silently communicating that I was not impressed with his habit of answering questions with questions.

He took a few more steps before he stopped not far behind me. "You have a hard time accepting help from people, don't you?"

I gripped the door handle firmly without turning it as his words wriggled their way under my skin. "I guess I'm just used to doing things on my own."

"I see. You're a strong, independent woman who *don't need no man*," he said, snapping his fingers and bobbing his head like a diva.

I turned away and stared at the doorknob to conceal my smile. "Something like that."

"Well, Miss Independent, are you going to open that door, or what? The suspense is killing me," he said, nudging my shoulder.

My entire body tensed. He must have noticed, because he quickly took a step back to give me some space. His question hung in the air like a noxious fume, and I held my breath as I considered it.

...are you going to open that door, or what?

I let go of the knob and turned around to face him. We both opened our mouths to speak at the same time, but I beat him to it. "Would you like to see my sculpture collection?" I asked, my attention focused on his shiny leather Oxfords. When I finally looked up at him, his green eyes were locked on mine.

"I would be *honored* to see your sculpture collection," he replied with the utmost sincerity.

I turned back to the door, gripping the knob even

harder now. "Try not to get too creeped out."

He chuckled. "Why would I get creeped out? Do you sculpt dead bodies or something?"

"You'll see," I replied, unable to muster even a subdued smile in my heightened state of anxiety.

I pushed the door open to reveal my bedroom, which wasn't much wider than a king-sized bed. The small closet in the corner was closed off with a polka-dotted curtain I'd hung on a tension rod. In the other corner, my twin-sized mattress—one of only two pieces of furniture in the room—lay directly on top of the beige carpet, the bed unmade. The rest of the space in the room was taken up by my very large worktable. I had constructed the table out of two-by-fours and plywood scavenged from discarded shipping pallets I'd found on the free items section of Craigslist.

The entire surface of the worktable was completely hidden by the vast collection of sculptures and art supplies: mounds of clays, stacks of mixing bowls and buckets of resin, gleaming sculpting knives, chisels, a bench vice, wire frames, and enough used sketch pads to reach the ceiling when stacked on the floor.

"Holy shit... You're an artist," he whispered, staring in awe at the shelves mounted on each wall of the room, which were teeming with surreal sculptures and heavy books covering all subjects related to art and anatomy.

He didn't say anything about the subjects of my work as he moved closer to the worktable. At least half of my sculptures depicted cubist interpretations of faces and bodies, surreal depictions of hearts melting, hands clawing at the air, and both cubist and surrealist styles of bodies missing various limbs. My heart raced as I watched him staring in awe at my current work in progress: a surreal statue of a decapitated woman in a tattered peasant's dress gently placing her own head in the hands of a skeleton man dressed in a monk's robe.

"These are amazing, you know that?" he glanced over his shoulder long enough for me to see the pure wonderment in his brilliant green eyes, then he leaned forward to get a better look at my work in progress. "How much do you sell these for?"

I shook my head. "I'm not a *real* artist. It's just a hobby."

He stood up straight and looked around at the finished sculptures and monstrous textbooks adorning the shelves. "Just a *hobby*?" he said with a chuckle. "If this is just a *hobby*, I'm frightened to think of how serious you take your career as a waitress."

I grabbed a sculpting knife off the worktable and twirled it between my fingers, the way I did when I worked. "I wouldn't exactly call my job at Joe's a *career*.

I work at the cantina because I can't get enough of Roger, obviously."

"*Obviously*, you majored in sarcasm before you dropped out."

I caught the knife in my hand, wrapping my fingers around the wooden handle. "Actually, I majored in studio art before I dropped out of NYU."

"NYU? You dropped out of *NYU?*"

His mouth hung open in an expression of pure shock. He drew in a breath and opened his mouth a bit wider, as if he were about to admonish me for dropping out of a prestigious university. Or maybe he was going to express outrage that I gave up on something I was perhaps talented in or at least passionate about. Luckily, he stopped himself before he made any such judgments.

As he closed his mouth and turned back to my sculpture, I imagined he had deduced from my earlier admission that I couldn't afford college, and the adjustable hospital bed in the living room of our tiny one-bedroom apartment in the Bronx, that there was a distinct possibility I had dropped out to take care of my mother.

He was silent for a moment, as he seemed to decide what to say in lieu of a lecture about pursuing my dreams. "So…are these sculptures made from the ground bones of baby elephants, or something? Why am I supposed to be creeped out?"

I smiled at his attempt to downplay the darkness reflected in my sculptures. "You don't have to pretend this is normal," I replied. "I know these are a bit...twisted. But..." I paused for a moment, staring at the tattered dress on the subject of my work in progress and realizing I hated the opacity of the fabric. "I guess I feel like...when I turn the painful...*stuff* into something surreal...it makes it less painful."

He held my gaze, but his nostrils flared slightly as his mouth tightened, almost as if he were trying to hold back some sort of strong emotion. Though, I couldn't determine if it was anger or sadness or something else entirely. The muscle in his jaw twitched as he clenched his teeth, then he finally broke eye contact.

"Seems like you've figured out how to deal with things your way," he said, stuffing his hands into the pockets of his expensive slacks. "Good for you."

I felt exposed. I had stupidly shared intimate details of my life with a guy who probably knew nothing about the kind of shit I'd experienced. He couldn't even *look* at me anymore.

What was wrong with me? Why did I feel I could be so honest with a complete stranger?

"Why isn't your buzzer working?" he asked, probably in an attempt to change the subject.

I shook my head as I made my way to the closet to grab my backpack and some clothes for my mom. "I don't know. I think one of my neighbors on the second floor is too lazy to buzz their guests in, so they keep breaking it. Management gave up trying to fix it months ago."

I yanked back the polka-dotted curtain and slipped a couple of my mom's shirts and pants off their hangers. Stuffing them into the backpack, I then pulled a few nightgowns and pairs of underwear out of a plastic rolling cart in the back of the closet. When I turned around, Daniel was once again looking me in the eye.

"I'm going to talk to Jerry about that buzzer," he said, taking a step toward me, and I held my breath as he continued. "And I don't want you to even think about paying back that money I gave them. Jerry's going to fix your rent situation or I'll unleash a legal hell on him that will follow him to his grave."

I slung the backpack over my shoulder. "You don't have to do that."

"Yes, I do," he replied. "You can't do it all alone."

I stared at his breast pocket so I wouldn't have to look him in the eye. "I'm not alone. I have my mom to help me."

But even as I said the words, I knew they were a lie. I had never been more alone in all my life. No boyfriend. No friends. Working two shifts at a place where I was expected to smile and take it when drunk assholes grabbed my legs or described the ways they wanted to fuck me.

"You're a good daughter, you know," he said.

I tore my gaze from his chest and looked up at him, putting on that brave smile I'd perfected. "Yeah, I know," I said dismissively as I set off toward the bathroom to get my mom's toiletries.

I needed to get out of this apartment before this turned into a full-blown counseling session. While I stuffed toiletries into my backpack, I stole glances at Daniel as he stood in the hallway doing something on his phone. When I emerged from the bathroom, he informed me that he'd ordered a town car to take me back to the hospital.

I tried not to let my disappointment show. "Yeah, you probably have to get going. I'm sorry I've kept you this long."

He shook his head. "Please don't apologize. I'm sorry I can't take you myself, but I have an early meeting with some investors."

"Yeah, of course," I said, trying not to roll my eyes

at this obvious lie.

He couldn't get away fast enough.

After he walked me down, we found the town car parked along the sidewalk. I flashed him my brave smile, not wanting to seem upset that he was handing me off to another stranger.

"Can you text me tomorrow…to let me know you and your mom are okay?" he asked, opening the car door for me.

"Yeah, sure. Thanks…for everything," I said, tossing my bag into the backseat of the black sedan.

He held the door open, watching as I clipped my seat belt. "Hey, there's a new art gallery that opened up in midtown a couple months back. Maybe we can check it out sometime," he said. His cool demeanor was back, and he held my gaze as he awaited my response.

I chuckled. "Are you into art?"

He smiled. "I am now."

I pressed my lips together as I tried not to grin like an idiot. He was using his charms on me and I was falling for it hook, line, and sinker, as if he weren't as transparent as glass.

Shaking my head, I looked up at him. "As long as I get to pick the music in your fancy car."

"Deal," he replied, his smile widening.

The butterflies in my belly were having a goddamn field day as I pulled the car door shut. I watched as the front passenger window rolled down and Daniel slipped the driver some cash. He took one more glance at me before he stepped back onto the sidewalk and the car pulled away from the curb.

I could think of nothing but Daniel and that gorgeous smile as I spoke to the doctor at the hospital. As Leslie and I caught an Uber back to the apartment, I used my phone to try to find this new art studio in midtown he wanted to take me to. It wasn't until we arrived at our building that I realized this entire experience with Daniel had not been an elaborate daydream. As Leslie tried unsuccessfully to pull the burgundy door open, I smiled and reached into my purse for the key to the building.

Someone had fixed the buzzer.

8. Step Four

"DON'T FORGET TO SMILE." My mom's voice on the other end of the call sounded urgent as we said our good-byes.

It's sort of hard not *to smile around Daniel*, I thought to myself, then I sighed into the phone. "I know, Mom. I'll see you in the morning," I said, referring to her elbow surgery appointment the following day. "Ask the nurse for something so you can get some sleep. I don't want you up all night worrying about me."

"I'll always worry about you," she said, the urgency in her voice replaced by the usual weariness.

A knot of guilt tightened in my belly as I thought of everything I'd put my mother through in the months after I quit NYU. Inevitably, my mind wandered to Petra.

"I'll be fine," I replied, eager to end the call. "Good night, Mom."

"Good night, sweetheart. I love you."

"Love you, too."

I ended the call with a lump in my throat and shaky hands. Looking into the bathroom mirror, the sheer terror of messing up tonight was plainly evident in my face. I needed to relax before Daniel got here or I was going to pass out at the sound of the doorbell. For the first time in months, my mind conjured a dangerous solution to my anxiety.

My mom kept a bottle of wine hidden in the back of the cupboard above the refrigerator. The bottle was a gift from Leslie for my mom's birthday a few months ago. Leslie didn't know about my past. I was certain my mother kept the bottle because she always had a hard time throwing away gifts.

Since the last time I saw Petra, and the brief stint with binge drinking that followed, I hadn't consumed a single drop of alcohol. Serving cocktails every day at the cantina had never tempted me. According to the therapist who helped me give up booze, I didn't have an addictive personality. My biggest problem was that I lacked coping skills, which she was going to teach me.

I ran down the checklist in my mind.

Step One: Try to sit down in a quiet location and take at least ten deep breaths.

I sat in the recliner next to my mother's hospital bed in the living room. Leaning back, I closed my eyes and drew in a deep breath through my nostrils, letting it out slowly through my pursed lips. I counted off ten inhales and ten exhales before I opened my eyes and cringed as the image of the wine bottle flashed once again in my mind.

Step Two: Remind yourself of the reasons why you gave up your addictions.

Glancing at the bed next to me, I imagined my mother sleeping, her knotted limbs hidden beneath the thin blanket she used during the summer. As hard as I tried, I couldn't stop the image of Petra's bloody face from jumping to the forefront of my thoughts. I squeezed my eyes tightly shut and shook my head in a vain attempt to rid myself of this daymare.

Step Three: Call someone you trust for support.

I had just spoken to my mom. I couldn't call her

right back. She needed her rest. I couldn't call Leslie. It was 7:30 p.m. Leslie and her family would be finishing dinner and getting ready for bed. Besides, she had already gone above and beyond the duty of friendship since my mom had fallen a couple of days ago.

A sharp ache burned inside my chest as I longed to call Petra. I blinked back tears as I realized I would never be able to do that again.

Before I could stop myself, I opened up my phone contacts and dialed the number.

The phone rang twice before a voice answered, "Kristin?"

"Hey, I'm…I'm sorry to call like this. I was just wondering… Did I leave my sunglasses in your car?" I rolled my eyes at this terrible excuse.

Daniel chuckled. "I don't remember you wearing sunglasses when you were in my car. Do you usually wear sunglasses at night?"

"No, I wasn't wearing them," I replied, silently cursing myself. "I just thought maybe they'd fallen out of my purse or something. No big deal. Just trying to track them down."

I shook my head, painfully aware that I sounded like a complete idiot who'd cooked up some lame excuse to call him. He could probably hear the desperation in my voice. Now, he was probably wondering why I couldn't wait a measly thirty minutes—when he was scheduled to arrive at my apartment for our date—to ask him about the sunglasses.

"No, no sunglasses," he said, and I could swear I heard a smile in his voice. "But I'll be there soon. You're welcome to search my car and pat me down, if necessary."

I let out a long sigh of relief as I smiled. "Thanks for the offer. I'll take your word for it."

A brief pause followed, then he spoke again. "Are you okay? You sound… I don't know."

I bit my lip as I realized this man, whom I still considered a bit of a stranger, had just helped me through something difficult, without his knowledge. "I'm fine. See you soon."

I ended the call before he could express any more concern. I didn't want tonight to be a therapy session. I wanted to go on my first date in years without the dark cloud of my past hanging over us. Tonight, I would spend the evening with a gorgeous man in the most beautiful city in the world, and pretend I deserved it.

Step Four: Distract yourself.

The knock at the door startled me out of my TV stupor. I scrambled for the remote and, in my haste, knocked it off the arm of the recliner and onto the floor. Scooping the remote off the floor, I pointed it at the TV to turn it off just as the anchorwoman's face became somber and she said, "We have more details tonight about the deadly crash that left—"

The TV went black and I breathed a sigh of relief that Daniel had arrived at the end of the light and breezy special-interest piece on New Yorkers escaping the hustle and bustle of the city for various seaside vacation hot spots this summer. I didn't usually watch the local news. It was too depressing.

I glanced down at my dress—a black Victoria Beckham shift dress I'd found at the fourth thrift shop I visited yesterday—and the nude slingback heels I'd found at Nordstrom Rack. I'd heard a girl at work once complain about having to spend $600 on a dress for her aunt's third wedding. I'd spent $62 on this outfit and I nearly pissed myself with guilt afterward when I looked at my bank account balance.

I took a few deep breaths as I made my way to the

door in an attempt to settle my nervous stomach. It didn't really work, but it didn't make it worse. I'd have to remind myself to keep finding those silver linings tonight.

I pulled the door open and my jaw dropped at the sight of Daniel.

He looked as if he'd just stepped off the set of a *GQ* magazine cover shoot in his crisp white button-up shirt with no tie and a trim-fit gray suit that showed off his athletic build. But it was the glint of mischief in his eyes that pulled the ensemble together. It was a look that spoke a thousand words—very *naughty* words.

I picked my jaw up off the floor and smiled. "You look…"

"Nowhere near as stunning as you," he said, finishing my sentence, then he nodded toward the stairwell. "Shall we?"

I managed to nod as I fumbled a bit to find my housekey in my purse. Locking the deadbolt, it dawned on me that, with my mom safe in her hospital room, I would be having a night out without having to worry about leaving my mom at home alone. Then, I came to an even more significant realization: This wasn't just my first date since the accident, it was my first night out with *anyone*.

As we walked down the steps, Daniel stole another

glance at my dress. "You really do look amazing, but I sort of regret not planning a date where you could dress more casually."

I smiled. "That's very considerate of you, but I'm really looking forward to checking out a new art studio. I...had a friend in high school who used to go with me to the Met once a month, so I never missed an exhibition. I miss that."

"Sounds like a good friend," he said.

She was a great *friend*, I thought.

His comment silenced me as we descended the stairwells. When we reached his Range Rover, which was parked across the street from my building, he reached past me to open the passenger door. I caught a whiff of his scent and I couldn't help but breathe deeply to inhale more of it. He smelled like a morning stroll through unexplored forest, and money.

The first time I'd smelled the scent of wealth was when my mom and I took our one and only trip to South Dakota to visit her family, when I was nine. We were queued up at the gate, waiting to board our flight, when a man passed us to get in line with the other first-class passengers. My nose was hit with a flurry of air that smelled like a heady mixture of leather, soap, and incredibly good luck. After that, I began to recognize that scent while I rode the subway or stood in line at the café.

I'd never smelled it on the bus.

I sank into the passenger seat as Daniel closed the door, tapping the roof once before he set off around the front of the SUV. As he slid into the driver's seat, I got a strange feeling that something seemed different about him tonight. I couldn't quite put my finger on it, but if I had to guess, I'd say it was the way he walked. No, that wasn't it. It was the way he looked over his shoulder *twice* before he got in the car.

I shook my head, thinking how silly I was. I hardly knew the man. How on earth would I know if this wasn't his typical behavior?

I was reaching. Searching for a reason not to trust him. Desperate for a reason to turn this evening into a disaster before it even began.

"Is something wrong?" he asked, pulling away from the curb.

I looked at him and raised my eyebrows in confusion.

"You're shaking your head," he clarified. "Is something not to your satisfaction?"

I chuckled at this phrasing. "How does someone learn to talk like that?"

He smiled. "Like what?"

"Is something not to your satisfaction?" I said in a

haughty voice.

He nodded as he waited for a pedestrian to cross in front of us. "How would you *like* me to speak? Yo, somethin' wrong, mama?"

I should have laughed, but I couldn't. His impression of the guys in my neighborhood sounded much more realistic than I expected it to.

"You're good at impressions," I replied. "Maybe *you* majored in sarcasm."

He smiled and we drove in silence for a couple minutes, not offering any clarification as to what he majored in or what school he went to. Maybe he could tell I was fishing for information and he wanted to maintain an air of mystery. It wasn't long before the silence became too much for him.

He smiled as he reached for the stereo. Thinking of the deal we'd struck allowing me to choose the music in his car, I immediately reached for his hand to stop him.

He caught my hand in his and laced his fingers through mine. "I didn't realize we had progressed to holding hands, but I'm game," he said, pulling my hand toward him and placing a tender kiss on the backs of my fingers.

I rolled my eyes, ignoring the butterfly parade marching through my belly as I gently extracted my hand from his. "Just following through on our agreement," I replied, focusing my attention on the touchscreen stereo. "I get to pick the music, remember?"

I stared blankly at the screen, which displayed real-time navigation information, then pressed the Home Menu button to the left of the screen. I chose Audio/Video from the selections on the screen. Pressing a few more buttons got me to a decent satellite radio station, which was playing "River" by Bishop Briggs.

He rolled his eyes as he stopped at a red light and relaxed into his seat. "This is the same stuff everyone listens to."

"I'm sorry it's not as cutting edge and hip as your elevator jazz."

He considered his response for a long while. "I don't only listen to jazz," he said.

It was a simple statement, but something in the tone of his voice sounded as if he were divulging a dark secret.

"Okay, what else do you listen to?"

He shrugged. "Do you like underground hip-hop?"

I laughed at the cryptic way he was behaving, as if he was asking if I *too* had a foot fetish. "Not as much as I used to. It's easier to find that stuff when you're in school and still going to parties."

He flicked his head to the right and flashed me a look of utter incredulity. "You don't party anymore?"

I should have felt self-conscious about this question, but I couldn't get over how strange the conversation and his voice sounded. As if the Daniel who picked me up had been left behind, standing on the curb in front of my apartment. This Daniel sounded like someone I'd see at the bodega, chatting up the store clerk while paying for his case of PBR.

He didn't repeat his question. Instead, he moved on to juicier topics. "So…why don't you ask your family to help you take care of your mom and apply for a scholarship so you can go back to school?"

"Geez, why didn't I think of that?" I shook my head as the city lights burned streaks into my retinas. "I don't have family in New York."

His question had made me irrationally angry. I had to chill or this night really *was* going to end in disaster.

"I apologize. That was a stupid question," he said, focusing his attention on the traffic in front of us.

"I'm the one who should be apologizing. That was an inappropriate response. I just… I tried everything I could, but my mom's family lives in South Dakota, and her mom—my grandma, whom I've only met in person once—is also really sick. She's been battling emphysema for almost a decade. My grandpa is dead and my mom's siblings can barely afford the nurse that takes care of my grandma. There's no one who can help me... No one."

My chest ached as the familiar feeling of being utterly alone became overwhelming.

"Hey, you've got Leslie, right?" he said, probably thinking his words were comforting.

I forced a smile. "Right."

A few minutes of awkward silence later, we arrived at The Art Studio in midtown at a few minutes before eight p.m. We parked in an underground parking garage and took the elevator up to the first floor of the nondescript brick building. When we entered Suite 1B, the tension from our conversation in the car vanished in an instant. I couldn't help but laugh out loud. We had just walked into a kid's birthday party.

9. Paintbrush

BEHIND THE CURVED receptionist's desk in front us, a wide white wall displayed a single painting. Off to the right, at a back of a large open gallery space, at least twenty kids and a dozen adults sat on stools behind easels. A mountain landscape projected onto a white wall explained the landscape painted on the canvases in varying degrees of skill. Clusters of pink and purple balloons and a sparkly "Happy Birthday" banner hanging from the ceiling told me we had just walked into the birthday party of a little girl who loved art.

A thin woman with golden-brown shoulder-length hair approached us. "Can I help you?"

Daniel smiled. "I think we may have stumbled into the wrong suite. Is this the art studio that opened in

May?"

"Yes, it is. But as you can see, we're hosting a private event tonight," she replied, looking sincerely apologetic. "I'm Layla, by the way. I'm the studio director."

Daniel appeared undaunted by this bad news. "Nice to meet you, Layla. I'm Daniel. I'm very sorry we interrupted your event."

"Oh, no. I'm the one who should be sorry," the studio director said, herding us back toward the exit. "Sometimes our receptionist forgets to put private events on the website calendar, and I have no idea how to do it myself. I'm very sorry for the confusion. I hope you didn't travel too far to get here."

Daniel answered before I could. "We drove here from Montreal. We're Canadian."

The woman's brow crinkled. "Oh, no. Now, I feel absolutely terrible."

Daniel smiled as he put his hand on her arm. "I'm only kidding. We live down the street. I'm sure you'll see us again soon."

She let out a dramatic sigh as she clutched her chest. "Oh, my goodness. You nearly gave me a heart attack," she said with a weak chuckle.

As Daniel began to apologize, a young girl with bouncy blonde curls walked up to him and yanked on his coat sleeve. "Are you the president?" she asked in a bright voice.

Daniel looked down at her and tilted his head. "No, sweetheart, I'm not the President of the United States. But I am the president of my house. Voted in by a landslide."

She looked skeptical of this answer. "You can't be the president of a *house*," she proclaimed.

Daniel looked appalled by this new information. "Are you telling me my sister lied to me? I'm *not* the president?"

The girl squinted at him in confusion for a moment before she smiled and squealed, "No!"

Daniel feigned sadness. "This changes everything."

The girl tapped her finger on her chin, as if she was pondering something. "You can still paint a picture, even if you're not the president," she said, pointing at the other children and parents, who appeared to be taking a painting class.

In the corner, just beyond the dozen or so easels, a table was piled high with frilly wrapped birthday presents and a three-tier princess-themed birthday cake.

Daniel smiled. "That's very kind of you, but this isn't our party. We're just leaving. You go have fun, sweetheart. I need to go have a stern conversation with my sister."

A rush of warmth flowed through me as I watched this exchange.

Daniel was good with kids.

He was good in business.

Great at tackling belligerent customers.

Even better at repairing broken door buzzers.

He was a natural protector and provider.

He glanced at me as he continued speaking to the girl, and the warmth in his smile made my ovaries explode.

"Kristin?"

"Yes?"

He laughed as he realized I hadn't heard a single word he'd said. "This young lady would like for us to join the party. Care to brush up on your art skills?"

The hopeful expression on the girl's face was too adorable to resist.

"Sure. I could use a refresher course."

The girl bounced up and down with glee. "Yay! This is the best birthday ever!"

The studio director shrugged as we all headed toward the easels. "Rebecca is very exuberant."

"Is this your party, Rebecca?" Daniel asked.

Rebecca nodded forcefully. "I'm six now."

Layla, the studio director, introduced us to the

parents and children, who were busy painting what looked like the same scenic mountain view. When the introductions were over, Layla gave us each an easel, a cup of water, some paintbrushes, and a set of watercolors. The chalky scent of the paints made me nostalgic for the innocence and simplicity of elementary school, where my love of art began.

Layla instructed us to make our best attempt at painting a mountain scene displayed on the wall by a film projector. Oddly enough, I recognized Mount St. Helens from the many photography blogs I followed. It was a common scene due to the sheer beauty of the landscape.

I began my painting by laying out a loose outline of the landscape in a light gray watercolor. When I was done, I tilted my head both ways to make sure the proportions were correct, then I began laying out each part of the scene according to distance and area. I started with the cobalt blue sky and billowy striations of cloud, then I moved on to the snowcapped mountain. This was when I noticed Daniel staring at my canvas. He hadn't so much as touched his own.

"Why aren't you painting?" I asked, dipping my brush into the black paint to darken the gray color I'd already made.

"Because I'm too fascinated by yours," he replied,

his eyes wide with genuine surprise.

I glanced around the room and realized he wasn't the only one staring at my canvas. "It's not even that good," I muttered, barely loud enough to hear myself, but Daniel certainly heard me.

He chuckled. "Are you blind?" he said, rising from his stool so he could stand behind my left shoulder. "You need your own studio."

"I have a studio in my bedroom," I reminded him.

"No, you need a big studio, with huge windows and lots of natural light, where you can spend all day creating your creepy little sculptures."

I rolled my eyes as I added some golden ochre to the gray shadows on the snowy mountain and the grass in the foreground. "Sure. I'll get on that tomorrow, right after I pick up my Ferrari from the shop."

"I'm sorry. That was insensitive of me," he said, sitting down on his stool.

I waved off his apology. "No need to apologize. It's not your fault," I said, suddenly realizing how bitter I must have sounded. "Besides, that came out way more sarcastic than I intended. I shouldn't be complaining. I should be grateful that I finally got a night off work and I'm doing something I love with someone I…think is pretty darn cool."

What the hell was wrong with me? I was babbling

like an idiot.

He smiled as he used his paintbrush to mix some colors on his palette. "So I'm cool?"

"Yeah, of course. You know you are. Don't pretend it's a surprise."

He actually blushed as he mixed together some green and blue, then brushed it onto the canvas in wide swaths. "Can I ask you a question?" he said, trying to sound casual.

"It's a free country."

He was silent for a while, long enough that I thought he'd decided against asking his burning question. Then, he turned to me and looked me in the eye, his expression deadly serious. "What color is this?" he asked, pointing at my painting where I had begun adding the field of flowers in the foreground. "You're so much better at this than I am."

I shook my head. "It's a dark coral. Those are called Indian paintbrush flowers. They're beautiful."

He smiled and went back to his painting. "Do you always apologize for being sarcastic?" he asked casually.

"No. It's just that I dated a guy once who told me sarcasm wasn't sexy. He said it made me sound depressed."

Daniel laughed heartily. "Now that's funny." He

shook his head as he continued brushing more blue paint onto the canvas. "Well, for what it's worth, that guy was a jerk. I find your sarcasm extremely sexy."

"Yeah, okay," I said sarcastically, before I could stop myself.

He laughed even harder. "Never apologize for being yourself," he added.

I tried not to smile, but I couldn't stop myself. He was practically begging me to be myself, but who was I?

I knew who I was with Petra and my mom, the only two people who knew the real me. With them, I was mostly goofy, but often sardonic and borderline fatalistic. But it had been a long time since I'd allowed myself to let go, to be vulnerable, with anyone.

Feeling like my life had been decided for me, and my only purpose was to provide for someone else, had basically made me shut down. It was easy to believe I had nothing more to give, including and especially myself.

I swallowed the anxiety that was threatening to shut me down again. "So... You've seen where I live. How about you? Where do *you* live? Trump Tower?"

He shook his head. "Are you trying to imply that I'm presidential material?"

I turned to look him in the eye. "Answering a

question with a question. Why am I not surprised?"

"Questions. Plural. Miss Nosy Owens."

"How do you know my last name?"

He cocked an eyebrow in confusion. "Jerry said your last name on the day we met."

"I know. I'm just bustin' your balls."

He shook his head and turned back to his painting. "You like bustin' balls, huh? Were you picked on by your siblings or something?"

I shrugged. "I never had any siblings, unless you count my..."

"Your what?"

I focused on my breathing as I pushed the words out of my mouth. "My best friend. My *old* best friend...Petra. She was practically my sister." I choked on the last word as my throat began to swell shut.

He turned back to me. "Where is she now?"

I shrugged, though I knew exactly where Petra was.

We painted in silence for a while. All the while, I was blinking furiously and taking slow, deep breaths to prevent my emotions from spilling over. Daniel was quiet and focused.

"Do you want to know where I live?" he said, his voice solemn.

I sighed with relief at the break in the silence. "Yes."

We half-finished our paintings and, despite Daniel's insistence that I needed to take mine home with me, we left it in the corner with the other discarded attempts. I waited for Daniel near the entrance as he pulled the studio director aside for a private conversation. He handed her something small, possibly money, then made his way toward me.

As soon as we were outside in the corridor, he lightly placed his hand on the small of my back to lead me to the elevator. It was a simple gesture, but it implied I was in some small way his. My inner feminist wanted to push his hand away, but my weary soul felt a kind of relief I'd never felt before.

Why did I feel so relieved? The answer was as simple as the gesture: I wasn't alone.

"What did you give Layla?" I asked as he pressed the call button for the elevator.

He smiled. "Nothing important."

I shook my head. "Your constant refusal to answer questions is infuriating, you know that?"

He was silent for a moment, relishing my frustration as we waited for the elevator. Finally, the doors slid open and we stepped inside. He pressed the button for the second level of the underground parking garage, where he'd parked. As soon as the doors slid shut, he turned to me, his green eyes locking on mine.

"I asked her how much an event like that birthday party would cost. She told me, and I gave her a check for that amount." He tilted his head as he waited for my reply, but he quickly realized I was still confused. "To pay for Rebecca's party."

"You paid for that little girl's party?"

He shrugged. "It was the least I could do. She didn't have to invite us in. She did that out of the kindness of her heart. It ended up being one of the best dates I've ever been on. I thought it would be a nice way to thank her parents for raising a good kid."

I stared at him for a moment, my mouth agape. Before I could stop myself, my hand reached out to touch his chest. "Are you real?" I whispered, clearly feeling the solid warmth of his body beneath his clothes.

He lay his hand over mine, not breaking eye contact as he leaned closer, until his lips brushed against mine, sending a chill cascading over my skin. Each breath he exhaled made my heart race faster. I leaned into him, pressing my lips to his as his hands came up to clasp both sides of my face. A smart move, as I began to feel unsteady on my feet.

Then, as fast as it began, it was over.

Daniel turned away to face the elevator doors, his

hand finding its way to the small of my back again. "Define real," he said as the doors slid open.

10. Dark Truth

DEFINE REAL. It wasn't the answer I was hoping for, but somehow it put me at ease.

He kept his hand on my back, gently leading me through the dimly lit parking garage. I glanced up at him a few times, hoping to meet his gaze for some indication as to what he was thinking, but his eyes were focused everywhere but me. He seemed to be scanning our surroundings, almost as if he were assessing the building for possible threats. Finally, when we were just a few cars away from Daniel's Range Rover, he looked down at me with a look I could only describe as pure conflict.

I didn't know him well, but I considered myself a bit of an expert in human emotion.

In my attempt to become a better artist, I'd read at least a dozen books and completed at least a thousand art studies solely on the subject of facial expressions and body language. If I had to sculpt Daniel's face in this moment, then explain to someone what he was thinking, I would say he was trying to decide between two courses of action: Should he 1) take me home and leave me at my door with a stiff peck on the cheek, or 2) push me up against one of these cars and fuck me right here?

A difficult decision, no doubt.

My mind worried I wasn't being cautious enough with Daniel. My mind voted for option number one. The pulsing ache between my legs and my racing heart meant my body was campaigning very hard for option number two.

As we arrived at the passenger door of the Range Rover, it seemed Daniel's body was going to throw in his vote with mine. He was eye-fucking the shit out of me. He sidled up to the door, effectively blocking me from reaching for the handle.

I looked up at him, my gaze landing on his full lips, then glancing at his hands, and back to his lips, sending him a less-than-subliminal message to slide those strong hands under my skirt.

His eyes were locked on my mouth. As his hand

found my waist, I closed my eyes and held my breath in anticipation. A long, torturous moment passed before, just as I had hoped, the weight of his body leaned into mine. With one hand on my waist, he pressed me up against the side of the SUV as his other hand came up to cradle my face. Then, his mouth found mine, delivering a slow, tender kiss.

His kiss felt downright pornographic. It was straight-up mouth sex, to the point that I could *physically* feel him moving in and out of me despite the fact that we were fully clothed.

As his tongue brushed against mine, my body quaked with desire, all the way down to my bones. Then came the aftershock, rippling through my every muscle as he bit my lip and refused to let go. I whimpered and he responded with a hoarse chuckle that sent chills over my skin.

Holy shit. If he fucked even half as good as he kissed, I was in for the ride of my life.

Suddenly, I was very spatially aware of my body. Without any conscious effort, my right hand had reached behind me, pushing against the glass window. My body was working on its own free will in a carnal attempt to keep Daniel and me pressed together like pages in a book. My left hand clung to the side mirror in a white-knuckled grip.

The breath in my lungs stuttered as I inhaled deeply. His fingers slipped through my hair as he balled up his fist. A brief involuntary gasp escaped my throat as he tugged my hair to pull my head back.

His kiss deepened.

Heat spread over every inch of my skin as his tongue moved in sync with mine.

The blood in my veins burned with hunger as he crushed his hips against mine.

He tugged my head sideways and swept his lips across my jaw, landing on my ear, and the throbbing ache between my legs intensified.

The sound of his breath in my ear sent a shiver of pleasure surging through me.

The heat of his body pressed against mine was reassuring.

The pulsing warmth of his skin was like the soothing hum of a sports car, all revved up and ready to go.

Vroom-vroom.

I lifted my leg to wrap it around him, to relieve the ache between my thighs.

He groaned softly into my ear as he grabbed my leg behind the knee to steady me. He pushed his hips harder into mine, teasing me with his promising bulge. I let out a satisfying moan as he rotated his hips, massaging my spot through the fabric of our clothing. He chuckled softly as he bit my earlobe, then he stopped suddenly and tilted his head back.

I opened my eyes to protest, ready to throw him on the ground and straddle him if necessary. Then, I saw it. An older couple stood behind the sedan that was parked next to us, politely and awkwardly waiting for us to move.

I dropped my leg immediately and smoothed down my skirt as Daniel apologized to the couple and opened my passenger door. I quickly slid into the passenger seat, thankful that Daniel didn't waste any time closing the door behind me. I turned away from the window as the man got into his car. Instead, I watched Daniel slide into the driver's seat with a huge grin on his face.

"That was mortifying," I said, covering my face as I waited for the sedan to pull away.

He laughed as he pressed the button to turn on the SUV. "On the contrary, that was hot," he said, making no attempt to avoid staring at my lips.

I shoved his shoulder to break his trance. "Aren't we supposed to be going somewhere?"

He smiled as he reached up and tucked a lock of hair behind my ear. "Where to, madame?"

I rolled my eyes as I reached for my seat belt.

"Don't act cute. You were going to show me your place."

And just like that, something had shifted.

When I turned back to Daniel, his smile had vanished. He stared straight ahead, lost in thought. Narrowing his eyes, he seemed to be at odds. He was once again the conflicted Daniel I'd seen a moment before he pressed me up against the SUV and thrust his promising package into my life.

He gave a curt nod as he reached for his seat belt. "Right. My place."

He drove along the streets of Manhattan, maneuvering through the Friday night crowds with a deftness I'd only seen in seasoned taxi drivers. A woman in a Prius turned right in front of us, cutting us off as if we didn't exist, and Daniel dodged this near collision with the grace of Neo dodging bullets in *The Matrix*. Nothing would slow him down. He was a man on a mission.

At first, I thought I knew where we were going, but then we seemed to end up on a street we'd already gone down. Were we driving in circles or was he trying to confuse me so I wouldn't remember how to get to his apartment? Or maybe he was one of those paranoid people who always thought they were being followed and he was trying to lose the tail? Or maybe he *was* being followed?

I asked him if we were headed toward the west side, but he told me to be patient, we were almost there. I tried not to get anxious. What if he was driving me to an abandoned warehouse, where he was going to murder me, and no one would ever find me because I didn't know where I was?

I didn't really think he was going to murder me, but I had to at least indulge the possibility, or I would feel even more reckless than I already did. It was reckless to accompany a man back to his place on a first date. I acknowledged that, to myself. But I felt safe with Daniel. That had to count for something.

We pulled in front of what looked like a four-story historic brick townhouse on Prince Street and he turned off the car. "Welcome home, Picasso," he said with a grin.

"Is this where you live?" I was surprised to find that, despite the steady flow of traffic on this street, there was an empty parking space right in front of the townhouse.

"This is a relatively new property. Moved in a few weeks ago, but I still don't have all my stuff here, so it's a little sparse." He followed his last sentence with a long pause and a shrug, as if he was trying to mentally shrug something off. "Anyway, I gave the staff the weekend off."

"The *staff*..." I repeated his words softly, mostly to myself, wondering if he understood that my mother used to be "the staff" before she became disabled.

The front of the townhouse was dark, with no lights on outside or inside. That could be because there was no one home, since he'd given *the staff* the night off. Nevertheless, I began to feel uneasy. What if I was falling into some kind of trap?

"Maybe we should just grab something to eat and call it a night," I blurted out, still staring at the house so I wouldn't have to see his reaction.

"Are you usually this nervous on a first date?"

I turned back to him, shooting him a piercing glare. I wanted to contradict him, but I hadn't been on a real date in so long, I couldn't even remember if I was usually this nervous on a date.

Hookups didn't count as dates. With a hookup, there was no pressure about whether or not you were making a good enough impression, because the last thing you wanted was a follow-up phone call to remind you of your momentary lapse in self-respect. Of course, I also hadn't hooked up with anyone since NYU, so it was possible the rules for hookups had also changed.

I leaned back in my seat. "Yes, actually, I am

usually this…nervous." I stared straight ahead at the pickup truck parked in front of us. "It's been a long time since I've…done anything like this."

"You mean, it's been a while since you've been on a date?"

Though my gaze was still locked on the license plate of the truck, I could hear the smile in his voice. I didn't want to look at him and see the amusement on his face, to see him laughing at my lack of romantic experience.

"Maybe I should just go home," I said, crossing my arms.

"Hey, I'm not smiling because I think it's funny." He turned in his seat so he was facing me, but I kept staring ahead. "I'm smiling because you're full of surprises—the good kind."

I finally turned to him and, as hard as I tried not to, his smile made me smile. "So what kind of surprise do you have waiting for me in there? A dark basement and a pair of handcuffs?"

His eyes widened. "Like I said. Full of surprises. I didn't know you were into that kind of thing."

I shook my head as I threw the car door open and stepped out onto the sidewalk. He quickly appeared at my side with a spring in his step, ready to close the car door for me. Then, he held out his arm and I grasped on to him as if he were a life raft in this sea of uncertainty I'd jumped into. As he led me up the stairs to the front door, I heard a whirring noise followed by a heavy click. The porch lights turned on, as well as all the lights in the two lower levels of the house.

"What was that?" I asked.

He smiled. "That's the smart-home features I added. As soon my cell phone gets within three feet of the front door, I have an app that automatically deactivates the smart lock on the front door and turns the house lights on."

I cocked an eyebrow. "Well, aren't you Mr. Fancypants?"

He shrugged as he opened the front door. "Makes it easier to bring home the unsuspecting young women I abduct and keep in the basement."

"You realize that's not funny," I said, watching as he stepped inside the brightly lit foyer.

"Relax, Kristin," he assured me, holding his hand out for me to take as I entered. "The world is not as scary as you think it is."

I swallowed the angry retort my brain immediately conjured, then I followed him into a living room the size of my entire apartment.

My eyes widened as I took in the beautiful teak floors laid in a sophisticated herringbone pattern. The furnishings were sparse, and a bit modern, but among the gray tweed sofas and stark white walls were soft wine-colored throw pillows, plush ivory throw blankets, and a romantic chandelier hanging in the foyer. The fireplace mantel was honed from what looked like a single piece of gorgeous white marble carved in an ornate pattern.

The space didn't feel very lived in, but it still felt comfortable and inviting.

"Would you like something to drink?" he asked, as I followed him down the stairs to a lower level.

"I don't drink," I replied matter-of-factly, holding back the full, colorful explanation of how I didn't start and quit drinking until *after* I almost got caught driving under the influence.

We only had to take a few steps before I could see he was taking me to the kitchen and dining area, where a wall of windows looked out onto a well-lit, multilevel backyard garden area.

"You don't drink," he said, reaching the bottom floor. "Do you eat? I'm not sure what we have in the fridge, but there might be some berries and cheese."

"What *we* have in the fridge? Do you live here with someone?"

He chuckled as he opened the built-in refrigerator door. "No, I don't. Just a habit, I guess." He grabbed a white bowl of strawberries out of the fridge and placed them on the island between us. "Sometimes, I still wake up thinking I'm going to come downstairs and find my mom and siblings having breakfast."

I took the berry he held out for me, then took a seat on a stool at the island. "Isn't it lonely living in this big house all by yourself?"

He smiled, but only with one side of his mouth. "I keep myself busy with work and social events. I have parties here sometimes. It's…not usually this empty."

I raised my eyebrows as I brought the berry to my lips. "Well, excuse me. I didn't realize I was infringing on your busy social calendar."

He shook his head as he chuckled, and I took the opportunity to eat my strawberry, which, unsurprisingly, was the sweetest, juiciest strawberry I'd ever tasted.

"That's not what I'm implying," he began, plucking another berry out of the bowl and exchanging it for the stem in my hand. "I actually prefer quiet evenings more than the schmoozing and partying. It can get a little stale having to constantly figure out what angle to approach everyone from, as a potential business partner, investor, or a genuine friend. Not to mention the gold diggers and the bloodsucking socialites are just depressing."

I ate the second strawberry and he quickly exchanged the stem for another berry. "So you're not worried that I'm a gold digger?"

He smiled as he watched me bite into my third piece of fruit. "You? Not a chance. You're as real as it gets."

I thought of what he said to me in the elevator: *Define real.*

The lines between fantasy and reality were blurring, and I didn't care. I welcomed this new limbo. Part of me knew it was the old risk-taker in me that was getting high on this experience. But I was certain that if I googled "quotes about taking risks," I would find some famous person who had once said something wise—probably taken completely out of context—that would help me justify my behavior with Daniel. Just knowing this was enough for me.

"That sounds like a compliment," I said, handing him my third stem and refusing a fourth berry.

"Are you always this observant?" he asked, tossing the stems into the sink, then placing the bowl of berries back in the fridge.

"I wish I were more observant."

He turned to face me again, his eyebrows scrunched up in confusion. "How so?"

"I wish I could…" I swallowed hard as I

reconsidered my words. "Nothing. I guess I just have a hard time reading people…sometimes."

"Like me?" He smiled at my raised eyebrows. "I'm not that mysterious," he said, rounding the island until he was next to me. "I want the same things you want." He held his hand out for me to take, then he began leading me toward the glass doors overlooking the patio. "I want comfort and security. I want to feel needed…and I want to need someone."

My heart raced as we stepped out into the brick-paved backyard garden. "It's dangerous to need someone," I replied, breathless as he led me to some stairs leading up to a courtyard on a higher level.

The courtyard was well lit, with pathway lights and spotlights illuminating a few trees, which lined the back wall of the garden. We sat on a concrete bench in the center of the courtyard, a chill racing through me as he laced his fingers through mine.

"We've all been hurt, Kristin," he said, his eyes focused on some distant memory.

"Who hurt you?" I asked, my voice a bit shaky.

He blinked and turned to me to refocus his attention. "Another time," he replied with a smile that barely curled the corners of his mouth. "I promise."

I nodded, gladly accepting this answer because it allowed me to postpone my own dark truth.

He brought my hand to his lips and laid a soft kiss on my knuckles. "I know you work tomorrow and Sunday, but do you think you can get next weekend off?"

I smiled as I continued to feel his lips on my hand, even as he spoke. "I can try. What for?"

He reached up and traced the backs of his fingers over my cheek. "You deserve a relaxing beach weekend."

I chuckled to try to cover up the shiver that coursed through me as he traced his finger down my neck and over my shoulder. "Don't tell me you have a house in the Hamptons."

He smiled as he dragged his gaze away from my shoulder, up my neck, landing on my lips. "Of course I do," he murmured, leaning in until his lips were hovering over mine. "Come with me and I'll tell you everything you want to know about me."

My brain wanted to make a joke about ATM PIN codes, but my body would not allow it.

Every nerve in my body, every drop of my blood wanted...*needed* his lips on mine.

"Okay," I whispered, then I got my wish.

His lips were on mine and his hand was in my hair, holding me firmly in place as his tongue brushed against mine. His kiss was firm and assertive as he held me there, a willing captive. With every breath I took, my body became more liquid than solid. I'd have to be mopped up off the floor if he continued teasing me with his perfect mouth.

I wanted to reach up and wrap my arms around his solid neck, but my arms were like jelly. His lips brushed over my jaw and I sighed as they landed on my neck. He slid the straps of my bra and my tank top aside to plant a lingering kiss on my shoulder. I let out an involuntary whimper in anticipation of what I hoped was about to happen. Then, his lips traced a slow, tender trail up my neck, landing on my mouth again.

He still held my face firmly in his hands, unwilling to break the connection. I wanted to climb in his lap and undo his pants right there in that beautiful courtyard. I opened my mouth to speak this thought aloud, when he pulled away suddenly and planted a kiss on my forehead.

"Sorry, I got a bit carried away," he apologized breathlessly, sweeping my now-messy hair out of my face.

"It's okay. I...should probably get going," I replied, further smoothing down my hair.

He stared into my eyes for a long moment, then he stood up and held out his hand to me. "Come on, princess. We'd better get you back into that pumpkin before the clock strikes midnight."

I smiled as he took me back through the house and out to his car. The drive home was quiet. Daniel didn't attempt to torture me with smooth jazz, and I didn't bother trying to educate him on top-forty music. He held my hand the entire ride home, and walked me all the way up the five flights to my apartment.

He kissed my forehead and the corner of my mouth as he said good-bye. And as I watched him descend the steps to the fourth floor, I tried to convince myself that the physical pain in my belly was not longing. I was just hungry. Right?

11. Happy Birthday, Mom

Four years earlier

PETRA ARRIVED AT OUR APARTMENT at four o'clock sharp. She was usually at least twenty minutes late to parties. When we first became friends, she used to claim she liked to be fashionably late. It didn't take long to realize she wasn't late by any fault of her own.

"I take it your brother wasn't home," I said, following her into my bedroom.

She placed the birthday gift she'd wrapped in bright red paper on my worktable, then collapsed onto my mattress on the floor. "He's probably with his new crackhead girlfriend, Mimi or Minnie, or whatever the fuck her name is. She looks like an anorexic frog."

I laughed at her description, but Petra didn't crack a smile. "What did your advisor say?" I asked, referring to the academic advisor at the community college Petra was considering attending, but she didn't reply. She was probably lost in thoughts of comparing my mom to her parents.

Petra's parents were not model citizens, by any stretch of the imagination. She hated them ninety percent of the time. The two-bedroom apartment they rented on Belmont was paid for with a Section 8 subsidized housing voucher. The money her mom collected through disability due to being legally blind in one eye mostly went to chips, soda, and meth. Her dad only showed up for a few months at a time, or however long her mom needed him until they would inevitably have a blowout fight and he'd leave again. Her older brother wasn't much better.

Nick dropped out of school in the ninth grade, when he began smoking meth. That was also when he began inviting his junkie friends to spend the night in the bedroom he shared with Petra. At twelve years old, Petra was sexually assaulted in her bed by one of Nick's nameless friends, as her brother lay sleeping a few feet away. That was the first time Nick was kicked out of the house. But he always came back.

It was no wonder Petra insisted on always hanging

out at my apartment rather than hers. In the years that had passed since the day we met in the middle school bathroom when we were thirteen, I could count on one hand how many times I'd stepped foot in Petra's apartment.

On the other hand, Petra practically lived here with my mom and me. In fact, she was here today for an impromptu surprise party for my mom's 44th birthday. I'd bet my life that the card attached to the gift she brought was inscribed:

Happy birthday, Mom!
Love,
Your favorite daughter, Petra.

I was even more certain that my mom would read Petra's inscription and agree with every word, reminding me what an awesome mom I truly had.

Petra stared at the ceiling for a while as I sat next to her on the bed, wrapping my gift for my mom. I would hold out my finger and she would dispense the Scotch tape as needed. When I was satisfied with my wrapping job, I placed the gift next to Petra's and collapsed onto the bed next to her.

"You can always move in here while I'm gone," I suggested for the hundredth time.

Petra sighed. "I just need to get a job and move out. Fuck going to college and spending another four years in that nuthouse."

"You'll still be able to go to college if you stay here while I'm at NYU. Don't let them make you give up on your future."

She shook her head. "I love you, Kris, but you know I can't do that to your mom. She's probably dying for you to leave so she can start bringing home some sexy middle-aged men."

"Ew. My mom is not dying for me to leave," I said, flipping over onto my belly so I could see Petra's face. "She'd love to have you here while I'm gone."

My mom and I had discussed the possibility of letting Petra stay here while I stayed in the dorms at NYU, and my mom was completely on board. Though I'd been accepted into NYU on a full scholarship, Petra hadn't been accepted into any of the local four-year colleges she'd applied to because of her SAT and ACT scores. Petra was funny and smart as a whip when it came to social situations, but she froze during tests.

I never said it aloud, but I was afraid that if I went away to stay in the NYU dorms to avoid the forty-five-minute commute, Petra might spiral and take up one or more of her family's traditions.

The even harder truth that simmered beneath the surface of Petra's family issues was her need to know the identity of the guy who unwillingly took her virginity so many years ago.

She liked to pretend she was over it, but on nights that she slept over at our apartment, I would often catch her whimpering in her sleep. She confided in me only once that she still had nightmares about that night.

To say I was afraid to leave Petra alone with her family while I went to NYU was an understatement.

But she'd held her own while living with them for the first eighteen years of her life. I was more afraid of not being there to stop her from doing something stupid if she ever learned the identity of her rapist.

"What time is it?" Petra asked, then answered her own question as she pulled her cell phone out of her jeans pocket. "4:20. Nick's favorite time of day." She sat up and slapped my butt. "Come on. We have forty minutes to whip up one humongous chocolate chip cookie for your mom."

12. MB

THE GLASS OF WATER TREMBLED in my hand as I filled it from the tap. I could feel my mom's eyes on me, watching my every move from where she sat at the kitchen table. She was concerned, looking for signs that I was in over my head.

I was.

And for once, I wasn't the least bit scared.

I guzzled the water down and placed the empty glass in the sink. "Please stop watching me, Mom, you're making me nervous," I said, adjusting my backpack on my shoulder and leaning in to give her a kiss on the cheek. "I'm fine. Everything's going to be fine."

She grabbed my hand and looked me in the eye.

"Promise me you'll call if you need anything," she began. "I know it's two hours away, but Leslie and I will speed over there if you need us."

I shook my head. "Mom, please, stop worrying. I'm twenty-three. It's not like I'm thirteen and this is my first sleepover. Everything's going to be fine. I'll be back before you know it." I planted another kiss on her forehead. "Love you, Mom."

She squeezed my hand one more time before she let it go. "Love you more, baby."

Leslie smiled as she opened the door for me. "Have fun, kiddo," she said with a wink, then she leaned in to kiss my cheek and whisper in my ear, "I'm serious. Your mom is in good hands, so you have fun tonight."

"I don't know what I'd do without you, Les," I said.

She practically pushed me out the door, and I was giddy with laughter as I set off down the stairs. When I arrived outside, I stopped dead in my tracks.

Daniel was leaning against his Range Rover with his head down. He was dressed in blue jeans and a gray T-shirt that hugged his sexy shoulders and arms. But it was the natural, haphazard appearance of his wavy brown hair that nearly stopped my heart. I wanted to leap into his arms and kiss him hard while running my fingers through those luscious locks.

Oh, shit. Maybe I *was* in over my head.

I smiled as I approached Daniel and he finally looked up. His whole beautiful face lit up when he smiled. If I was in over my head, I didn't care. He was worth it.

"You certainly are smiley today," he said, then planted a firm kiss on my forehead as he pulled me into his arms.

I buried my face in the crook of his neck and breathed in his scent. "I've got lots of reasons to smile."

But when I pulled away, Daniel wasn't smiling anymore. I was going to ask if something was wrong, when he blinked a few times and his smile returned, almost as if he were lost in thought for a moment.

"Is everything okay?" I asked, as he slid my backpack off my shoulder and placed it in the trunk.

He returned to the passenger side and opened the door for me. "Never better," he said, wrapping his arms around my waist to pull me close again. "This is going to be the best weekend ever. I just have one request."

I tried to remain calm, but with his lips so close to mine I found it hard to remember to breathe. "What kind of request?"

He brushed his lips over mine, then brought his mouth upward to lay a soft kiss on my cheekbone before whispering in my ear, "You have to let me make you breakfast tomorrow."

I chuckled. "As long as you promise not to poison me, I think I can abide by your request."

"I promise not to poison your breakfast," he said, leaning back so I could see his face. "But I can't promise not to poison your dirty little mind."

He laughed as he let me go so I could get in the car, making certain to give me a light tap on the ass before I sat down. The mischief in his eyes as he closed the passenger door filled me with glee. I knew that no matter what happened at his beach house, I was going to have fun, because I would be with Daniel. And that was all I needed.

The two-hour drive to East Hampton was an opportunity for me to introduce Daniel to some music he could listen to outside an elevator. And he took the opportunity to introduce me to his favorite blues artist, Nina Simone. He started off the introduction with her most famous song, which I had heard of, but had never really listened to: "Feeling Good." But when he played a lesser known song, "Do I Move You," I realized Daniel's taste in music might not be as bad as I had feared.

When we finally made it to East Hampton, I couldn't help but ogle the enormous houses lining the residential streets. Who could possibly need that much space?

Part of me was fascinated, while my more practical side couldn't help but think that all this space and grandeur was such a waste of resources. Still, I couldn't look away.

Most of the houses were hardly visible from the street, as they were hidden by dense rows of trees at the end of long and winding driveways. But the ones I could see were almost all covered in beautifully weathered cedar shingles, with enormous windows and stunning-yet-quaint architectural details.

So much time and thought and care had gone into building and maintaining these behemoths. I hoped the families who went about their day, basking in the sunlight shining through those enormous windows, understood how lucky they were.

When Daniel pulled up to the gate, he punched in a code on a touchpad attached to a pedestal. As the iron gates began to open, I couldn't help but notice a black metal sign on the front of the gate. A golden emblem on the sign read: MB.

"MB?" I asked as he began to pull forward. "Is your real name Mercedes Benz?"

He laughed out loud, perhaps a bit *too* loud. "No, I bought the house recently and haven't had a chance to change the crest on the gate yet. Still a lot of renovations I need to do, actually."

He cast a sideways glance at me and I smiled, though something about his response didn't seem right to me.

It seemed to me that if you were to spend tens of millions of dollars on a house—yes, I had looked up the property values of this neighborhood on the internet—the first thing you would do when you moved in would be to make yourself at home by putting your stamp on it. And Daniel didn't seem like the kind of guy who would want another person's name on something that was *his*.

Maybe I was reading too much into this gate thing.

Then, we reached the end of his driveway and entered a circular drive, where we parked in front of an enormous house that looked like something out of a movie. As soon as the car stopped moving, I threw the door open and stepped out to get a better look at the house. As I admired the lush hydrangeas and the staggering beauty of the wraparound porch, the gate was the furthest thing from my mind.

13. Unsinkable

DANIEL ARRIVED AT MY SIDE with my backpack slung over his shoulder. "Let's go, princess," he said, holding his hand out for me to take.

I grabbed his hand and he led me up the front steps to a set of tall double doors. He entered a code on the deadbolt and the door swung inward. A cool air-conditioned breeze washed over me. The air smelled of lavender and leather and wood polish, probably an assortment of cleaners used by his housekeeper.

"Do you want to hit the beach or the pool first?" he asked, pulling me into the foyer.

The marble floor and wooden banister on the grand staircase gleamed with a mirrored shine.

Through an opening on our left, I could see what looked like a very worldly library or study with rich mahogany shelves lined with thousands of books. The walls in the foyer and the room on our right, which looked like a living room, were covered in fine art pieces. The glass table against the wall in the foyer was topped with a sculpture I recognized.

The clay bust depicted a beautiful child wearing a veil over her sobering expression. Sculpting a realistic bust with the appearance of a wispy veil over the face was not something many sculptors could pull off. This was either a very good replica or it was a genuine Philippe Faraut sculpture entitled "Child Bride." It was a sculpture that had haunted me when I first lay eyes on it in one of my college textbooks.

"Are you okay?" Daniel asked, when he realized I had become immovable.

"You said you weren't into art," I said, trying to swallow the lump of emotion in my throat caused by seeing the sculpture in such an intimate setting. It was even more beautiful and heartrending up close.

I tore my gaze away from the sculpture and Daniel was now staring at it. He was silent for a moment, then he seemed to have a similarly visceral reaction to the piece.

He turned back to me, his expression serious. "I

have to tell you something. This house...it's not technically mine."

My jaw dropped and he held up his hands, a nonverbal gesture I supposed was meant to keep me from jumping to conclusions.

"It's my family's summer home," he continued, setting my backpack down at the bottom of the stairs. "Well, it belongs to me and my siblings now that my mom is gone. It's just easier to say it's mine. They're vacationing in New Zealand this summer."

Now that his mom was gone? I thought his mother died a few years ago and he supposedly just purchased this property, hence the MB sign on the gate. Either he was lying to me or I was making a big deal out of nothing. Or we had a different definition of *a few years*.

I let out a soft chuckle. "You scared me," I said, lightly smacking his arm. "I thought you were going to tell me it was your boss's house, or that you'd broken in or something."

He chuckled, but I could sense tension in his laughter. "Do I look like someone who'd break into a place like this?" he asked. "That's some psycho Norman Bates shit."

I smiled sheepishly. "So...your siblings are into art?" I said, walking very slowly toward the sculpture on the table. "Is this an original Philippe Faraut?"

He followed closely behind me. "To be honest, I wouldn't know an original Philippe Fart from my left hand."

I laughed uncontrollably at his mispronunciation of Philippe's last name. "Philippe Fart?" I repeated, through wheezing laughter.

He smiled as he shook his head. "See? I don't know a fart from my own hand when it comes to art. Can we go to the beach now?"

I quickly composed myself and made my way toward the staircase. "Where can I change?"

"There's a guest bathroom right behind the stairs," he said, pointing to the right of the staircase.

I grabbed my backpack and walked around the staircase toward the door in the corridor behind the stairs, feeling a bit slighted as Daniel ran up the stairs to change. Why didn't he invite me to change in an upstairs bathroom?

The bathroom was deceptively large. I would have expected a bathroom under the stairs to be the size of Harry Potter's bedroom in the Dursleys' house. Of course, the grand staircase was nothing like the Dursleys', and Daniel's beach house was no ordinary house. All surfaces—the walls and the floor—were covered with what appeared to be water-resistant cedar planks. The wall on my left was lined with four modern pedestal sinks and mirrors to match. On my right, a door stood open, which led to a private water closet. Another door to the left of the water closet led to a sauna. The rear wall was lined with hooks, hung with six plush white bathrobes.

Daniel told me he had two sisters and one brother. He also told me his father was in prison, and he was raised by his mother who died a few years ago. I supposed that left two extra bathrobes for guests. I wondered how often Daniel brought female guests here.

I placed my backpack on top of a wooden spa bench next to the sauna, and pulled my bikini out. My heart began to race as I changed into the swimsuit, wondering if maybe I should have brought a one-piece instead.

Would Daniel think I was trying to seduce him? But, *he* was the one who invited *me* to spend the weekend with him. If anyone was trying to seduce anyone, it was Daniel trying to seduce me.

And, boy, was I ready for it.

I bit my lip at this thought, then I zipped up my backpack. I had to stop worrying about who was seducing who and just have fun. I was spending a romantic weekend on one of the most beautiful beaches in the world with the sexiest man I'd ever met.

Like the people who lived in these gorgeous houses, I needed to be less fretful and more grateful.

I felt more than a little self-conscious, coming out of the bathroom in just a bikini, but I was relieved to find Daniel standing right outside in the corridor. He was shirtless, showing off those immense shoulders I'd become so obsessed with. He wore neon green and black board shorts slung low enough for me to notice the well-defined V in his abs, which disappeared below the waist of his shorts.

"Is it okay if I leave my backpack in there?" I asked, noticing the amazingly detailed tattoo of a vintage-style astronaut on his left bicep.

He made no attempt to hide the way his gaze raked over me, from head to toe. "Sweetheart, you can do anything you want here. *Mi casa es tu casa,*" he said in a perfect Spanish accent.

I smiled as he held out his hand to me, and I laced my fingers through his as I got a glimpse of the tattoo on his right bicep, but all I could read were the letters R.I.P. "Can you speak Spanish?" I asked.

"Of course. My mom is Puerto Rican," he replied, leading me through a swinging door into an enormous gourmet kitchen with built-in appliances and two large marble islands. "Do you want some free Spanish lessons?"

I stole sideways glances at his chest, trying to make out the designs of the tattoos, but I couldn't see much from this angle. "Maybe you can start by teaching me how to say, 'Your house is ridiculously gorgeous.'"

He squeezed my hand as he led me through the kitchen and into a casual dining area with a long farmhouse table and galvanized dining chairs. Just beyond the breakfast nook was a sitting area with large, overstuffed gray sofas and more art on the walls and above the fireplace. On our right, a wall lined with four French doors and ceiling-height windows overlooked a gorgeous veranda, which looked out onto a stunning view of the infinity pool. From this vantage point, the sparkling surface of the infinity pool seemed to merge with the glimmering ocean just beyond.

"How about I teach you how to say something else?" he said, opening one of the French doors, and we stepped out onto the breezy veranda that smelled briny like the ocean and sweet like the potted honeysuckle on either side of the doors. "Repeat after me: *No hay nadie.*"

"*No hay nadie,*" I repeated, trying not to laugh at how awful my accent sounded.

"*Mas hermosa.*"

"*Mas hermosa.*"

"*Que yo.*"

"*Que yo.*" I paused for a moment, and when he didn't continue, I asked, "So what does that mean?"

He smiled down at me, but I was unable to hide that flicker of hesitation I was beginning to recognize so well. "I'll tell you later," he said, as his gaze traveled down the length of my body again. "For now, we can pretend it means... You're mine now."

I yelped as he scooped me up in his arms and sped across the veranda, then down the steps to the lower deck. Before I could even register what was happening, or mount a protest, he tossed me into the pool. The surface of the pool smacked my ass before I sank down a few feet into the warm water. Kicking off the bottom, I emerged seconds later just in time to see Daniel cannonball into the pool right next to me. A large splash hit me in the face, filling my open mouth with what tasted like saltwater.

I spat it out and gasped as Daniel resurfaced next to me. "You bastard!" I said, as he grabbed my waist and pulled me close.

"I had to make sure you knew how to swim before we go in the ocean," he said, smiling as I wrapped my arms around his sturdy neck.

I shook my head. "You're a jerk."

"A sexy jerk, right?"

I suppressed a grin. "A mean jerk."

His hands came up to grab my face as he gently brushed the water off my eyelashes. "Thank you for spending the weekend with me," he said, his eyes locked on mine.

"Thank you for inviting me," I replied, wishing he would just hurry up and kiss me so I didn't have to keep staring at his perfect mouth.

Then, my wish came true and his lips were on mine. I tightened my arms around his neck and, before I could stop myself, I wrapped my legs around his hips. He groaned lightly into my mouth, eliciting a soft moan from me in response.

Oh, God. Please let this be it. Let this be the day his promising package is unwrapped.

Almost as soon as this ridiculous thought crossed my mind, Daniel grabbed both sides of my waist and pushed me toward the side of the pool. Before I could protest, he lifted me out of the water and sat me down on the ledge with my feet still dangling on the surface.

"What are you doing?" I asked far too quickly, because my question was soon answered.

He kissed the inside of my thigh and looked up at me with a fierce hunger in his eyes. His lips traced a slow trail of kisses up my wet leg, coming to a stop at the apex. My chest heaved gulps of salty air in anticipation as he reached up and slid the fabric of my bikini bottom aside.

I moaned softly while he kissed my spot as if it were my mouth. His tongue slid into me, discovering my wetness and drawing it upward, where he used it to sweep the tip of his warm tongue over my center in slow circles. I cried out louder this time as I realized there was no reason to temper my passion. We were completely alone.

The way he used his mouth was pure, sweet torment.

It didn't take long before my thighs began to tremble. I leaned back, placing my hands on the pavement to brace myself as my core tightened. But he didn't rush. He drew out the pleasure like a patient conductor leading an orchestra to a slowly building crescendo.

Then, suddenly, like a snake recoiling into a defensive position, all my muscles contracted inward. The wet hair on the top of Daniel's head rubbed against my belly as I curled over him with my thighs locked around his head.

He continued licking ever so softly as the orgasm rocked me, spasms rolling through my legs and abdomen. Just when I thought I could take no more, a blinding, white-hot explosion of atomic proportions sent shock waves through my entire body. Like a spool of ribbon unwinding, my muscles unfurled all at once.

"Oh, God," I sighed as I lay back on the concrete, my body slack, my muscles still twitching as I stared up at the bright blue sky and tried to catch my breath.

"God?" he murmured, and a shiver passed through me as he took his sweet time straightening the crotch of my bikini, his fingers lingering on my swollen flesh. "I know I'm good, but I'm probably not a god...yet." He laid a tender kiss on the inside of my thigh as his thumb rubbed the fabric of my bikini, right over my spot. "But you can be my goddess if it means I get to worship this temple anytime I want."

I let out a high-pitched moan as he kissed my bikini. With a layer of clothing between his mouth and my center, the frustration was unbearable. The longing for his mouth on my skin was so intense that I could think of nothing else but the way his tongue massaged me. The sexual frustration was so infuriatingly hot that I climaxed again within minutes.

I hastily pushed him away, letting out a scream so loud I probably scared the ocean away.

He chuckled as he watched me readjust my bikini and brace my hands on the edge of the pool as I tried once again to catch my breath. "You taste as exquisite as you look," he said, spreading my knees apart so he could stand in front of me and wrap his arms around my waist. "But holy fuck, you scream like a banshee."

I smacked his bicep, right over the astronaut tattoo. "You kind of took me by surprise there."

He planted a warm kiss on my belly and smiled up at me. "Let's go to the beach."

I nodded and he laid another soft kiss on the top of my thigh before he exited the pool. I wobbled a bit as I stood up. My legs were like rubber.

From the poolside, I could see the beach was empty, which probably meant that this was a private stretch of beach belonging to the property. Daniel grabbed a couple of striped beach towels out of a storage building near the other side of the pool, then we set off.

A briny ocean breeze lifted the few dry hairs at my nape, sending chills over my damp skin as we walked down a wooden pathway carved through the shoulder-high seagrass, leading down to the ocean. When we reached the sand, I stopped, wiggling my toes in the warm sand as I closed my eyes and leaned my head back.

Please don't let this be a dream, I begged silently. *But if it is, please don't let me wake up.*

When I opened my eyes, Daniel was still standing next to me smiling as he waited for me to finish having my moment.

"Last one to the water has to make breakfast tomorrow," he said before he took off running.

I sprinted after him, almost stumbling as my feet adjusted to the soft sand. "You said you were making me breakfast!" I shouted.

He reached the water first, his feet splashing through the small waves. I reached him seconds later, gasping as the cold water shocked me out of my playful mind-set and straight into competition mode. I pushed through the frigid water, passing Daniel in a quest to go deeper. He caught up to me quickly, where the water was waist-high, pushing us back a few feet with each successive crashing wave.

"You have to stay within arm's distance," he said, grabbing my hand firmly. "When the tide rolls out, there's no fighting the power of the ocean... I can't lose you."

I turned my back to the water as another wave crashed into us, sending a sheet of water over the back of my head. I turned around, laughing as the stinging saltwater cutting trails over my scalp and face. I licked my lips and couldn't believe how salty the water was. I hadn't been to the beach in so long, I'd forgotten how aggressive the ocean was in its salinity and sheer force.

Tightening my grip on Daniel's hand and digging my feet into the mushy sand, the next wave didn't push us quite as far back. The next wave moved us even less, until eventually we became an immovable force, as much a part of the ocean as the rolling tides.

I didn't know how long this thing with Daniel would last. The beautiful things in my life were never permanent. For now, it didn't matter. For now, I was unsinkable.

We'd been in the water no more than ten minutes, Daniel with his back to the waves, taking the brunt of the force for both of us, when his eyes widened suddenly.

His gaze was focused on something behind me. "Fuck," he muttered under his breath, his voice hardly audible over the gentle roar of the ocean.

I flicked my head around and saw a thin redhead in an off-white ladies' pantsuit stepping off the wooden pathway leading from the house onto the beach. As she walked across the sand, my heart raced. Was this one of Daniel's sisters? Then, I remembered his single-word reaction to spotting this woman. It didn't seem like the kind of reaction one would have to seeing a family member.

Was this woman a girlfriend? Or possibly…his *wife?*

God, please don't let this be true, I prayed to myself. *Please make her disappear.*

"Who's that?" I asked, the high pitch of my voice giving away my sense of uncertainty.

He looked down at me, his arms tightening around my waist as another wave crashed into his back. "A coworker," he said, his eyes locked on mine as he waited for my reaction.

A coworker? A fucking *coworker*? Showing up unannounced at his *beach house*? On the *weekend*?

"Don't you mean, she's an *employee*?" I replied. "Isn't it *your* company?"

He sighed as he grabbed my hand and nodded toward the beach, pulling me toward the shore. "Trust me, Sabrina does *not* like being called an employee."

I didn't know what this meant, but I assumed it meant Sabrina was a bitch. Now I *really* wanted her to disappear.

"Daniel," Sabrina called out in a haughty voice, drawing out the sound of the L.

"Sabrina," he replied, stopping a few yards away from her.

"So sorry to interrupt," she said, glancing at our clasped hands.

I wasn't prepared for what it would feel like when Daniel let go of my hand. That split-second moment of physical pain as an invisible wall emerged out of the sand between us.

"No need to apologize," Daniel replied, his attention focused solely on the pointed features of Sabrina's face.

The corner of her red lips turned up in a smirk. "I wanted to check up on you, see if you need anything. You must be simply *lost* without your house staff."

"We're fine," Daniel said, glancing in my direction.

Sabrina turned toward me, tilting her head as she offered me a phony smile. "My, you're a pretty one," she said, a flicker of something—possibly *jealousy*—flashing in her eyes as she looked me over. "What's your name?"

A pretty *one*? Did that mean I was *one of many*?

Daniel responded before I could. "Kristin and I were just headed inside," he said, grabbing my hand again. He laced his fingers through mine and squeezed so tightly it almost hurt.

He seemed desperate to get away from this woman. Either he hated Sabrina, or he was afraid of what she might say to me. Maybe she would say something incriminating.

I dug my feet into the sand as he attempted to pull me toward the house, then I yanked my hand out of his and offered it to Sabrina. "I'm Kristin. Pleased to meet you," I said, trying on a new haughty accent.

She glanced at Daniel before she took my hand

and gave it a gentle shake. "Very pleased to make your acquaintance, Kristin," she replied, easily out-haughtying me. "You don't really look like Daniel's type. Tell me, how did you two meet?"

Daniel returned to my side, though this time he stood slightly in front of me, as if he were trying to create a physical barrier between Sabrina and me. "It's a long story," he said, answering for me again. "We really should be getting inside."

She pursed her lips. "You should let the girl speak for herself, Daniel," she said, turning her attention back to me. "She looks like she has *so* much to say."

I rolled my eyes, unimpressed with her little rich bitch act. "Actually, I do have something to say."

Daniel looked at me, but I couldn't tell if the intense look in his eyes was pleading with me not to provoke Sabrina or willing me to verbally destroy her. I guess I was about to find out.

I looked Sabrina in the eye and said, "This little *Mean Girls* act may work on other girls, but it doesn't work on me. If you want to make someone feel inferior, you might want to try *not* dressing like Hillary Clinton."

Her mouth dropped open in complete shock. As I marched away toward the house, the sound of Daniel's laughter sounded like music to my ears.

He appeared at my side, planting a loud kiss on my cheek as he grabbed my hand. "That was the most beautiful thing I've ever seen."

My heart raced from the surge of adrenaline. "I'm sorry. That was a really shitty thing for me to say to one of your employees."

He glanced over his shoulder, and I did the same, making sure Sabrina was well out of earshot. "Fuck her. She thinks she needs to haze every new employee."

"I'm not an employee," I said, suddenly feeling sick to my stomach as I imagined that this was how it would play out every time Daniel introduced me to someone in his world of extreme wealth.

"No, you're not," Daniel replied. "But if that were an interview, you'd be hired on the spot. You gave her what she had coming, no more and no less."

I smiled, though my heart was still racing. According to Daniel, I gave Sabrina what she had coming, but did she really deserve that kind of verbal takedown? Or had Sabrina done something else worse to Daniel, something that would make him feel she was getting what she deserved?

14. Too Perfect

AFTER OUR RUN-IN with Sabrina, we decided to forgo another dip in the pool so we could get showered and grab some dinner. Daniel led me upstairs to a guest bedroom with a luxurious en suite bathroom. I didn't bother asking why we weren't sleeping in the master bedroom. If this was a family vacation home, I assumed the master bedroom was probably used by one of his siblings.

I still had questions about why Daniel didn't have a vacation home of his own if he was indeed a successful investor. But I'd always heard that wealthy people were wealthy partly because they earned a lot of money, and equally because they were frugal with the money they earned. Not to mention the fact that Daniel had told me he was only twenty-seven years old. And, as far as I knew, he was unmarried. He probably didn't want to set down roots until he was married or had children of his own.

The rich tumbled stone covering the shower walls and the heavy glass doors were spotless. I felt a little guilty as I remembered the spot of mold I'd seen on the corner of the pink shower curtain at home, which I hadn't cleaned in a few weeks. Daniel did mention that the housekeeping staff had been given the weekend off, but I still wondered how much work they had to do during the summer when the family wasn't around. One thing was certain, I didn't understand the lifestyles of the rich and fabulous, but I also did not begrudge their hospitality.

As I showered, I reveled in the creamy feeling of his fancy body wash, my hand lingering between my legs, recalling the bliss of Daniel's mouth on me. It took a ridiculous amount of self-control not to walk dripping wet out of the bathroom to find him. Instead, I took my time using the expensive shampoo and conditioner, leaning my head back and inhaling deeply as the lather ran down in luxurious ribbons over my skin.

After my shower, I grabbed a clean, folded bathrobe off one of the shelves in a large linen closet. I towel-dried my hair and cursed myself for forgetting my blow-dryer at home. Then, I realized that Daniel surely had a blow-dryer in here somewhere. I pulled open the top drawer of the double vanity and found an assortment of travel-sized toiletries. Opening the next drawer down, I found a very expensive-looking silver blow-dryer and a pink flatiron. Either this room was solely used for guests, or Daniel liked the color pink. Nothing wrong with that.

Using my round brush and Daniel's hair dryer, I was able to dry my hair in less than five minutes, and it had never looked so full and shiny. I noted the brand of the blow-dryer in the event I should ever hit the lottery. Stuffing my belongings into my backpack, I dressed in a beige crepe button-up top tucked into a flouncy nude miniskirt I'd laid out on the edge of the bathtub. The steam from the shower hadn't completely loosened the wrinkles, but I highly doubted anyone would notice in the fading sunlight.

I pulled on my strappy black heels and stepped out of the guest bathroom, where I found Daniel lying on the bed, playing on his phone, and dressed in khaki cargo shorts and a dark-blue polo. He lowered his phone onto his chest so he could look at me, a smile spreading across his face. The first thought that crossed my mind—aside from the fact that his smile never failed to make my insides stir—was that I was overdressed.

"People are going to wonder how I snagged such a looker," Daniel said, getting up and making his way toward me.

"A looker? Next, you'll start calling me your favorite dame."

He smiled as he slid his finger underneath the collar of my shirt. "You're definitely in my top five dames." He laughed at my wide-eyed expression. "Okay, okay, you're in my top two." He laughed even harder and held up his hands to fend off any retaliation. "You have to understand! I'm *really* digging Leslie right now. Without her, you wouldn't be here."

I wanted to roll my eyes so bad, but I couldn't.

He walked around me until he was standing at my back. "My favorite dame is looking very smart this evening," he said, his hand softly clasping my arms as he traced his lips over the back of my ear. "What do you say we blow this joint?"

The throbbing sensation between my legs told me to throw him on the bed and straddle him, but my brain told me I needed to wait, at least until after dinner.

Oh, God. Why did I lose all reason around this man?

Rather than take advantage of the valet parking, Daniel parked his Range Rover on Main Street near the Hedges Inn. We would walk the few blocks to 1770 House. He claimed he wanted to feel the balmy summer breeze on his skin, but I had a strange feeling he was trying to draw out the evening. Maybe he was also nervous about what would happen when we arrived back at the beach house later tonight.

Yeah, right. Daniel did not seem to have a nervous bone in his entire rock-hard body.

The houses on Main Street looked like houses you'd find in a Rockwell painting. Typical white clapboard, two-story houses with black shutters, bright-green perfectly manicured hedges and lawns on large one- to two-acre plots. It was almost too perfect.

I'd only been in the Hamptons a few hours and I already missed the jumbo fried shrimp at City Island and the kids in Little Ireland who sold lemonade on the streets. It was August and I couldn't wait for a golden autumn in Van Cortlandt Park or opening day at Yankee Stadium. Sure, the apartment I shared with my mom was shitty, as was the management of said apartment, but that didn't mean I didn't love the Bronx.

"I'll have to show you around my neighborhood when we get back," I said as we passed yet another perfect house. "I can introduce you to Enrique, the king of dad jokes who owns the bodega across from Tino's Bar."

He looked down at me and flashed me an amused smile. "Sounds like my kind of guy."

He was humoring me. He had no interest in meeting Enrique.

"I'd rather take you and your mom to get a slice," he said, probably trying to recover from his lackluster response. "Your mom seems like a very interesting lady."

We stopped at the corner of Main and Buell to wait for the traffic to pass. "Are you trying to get on my good side? Because I can assure you that it's not necessary. I'm pretty sure I'm incapable of having a bad side right now."

"Sounds like you're in a good mood," he said, letting go of my hand to slide his vibrating phone out of his pocket. "That doesn't have anything to do with our little dip in the pool, does it?"

The last car passed us and I stepped out into the

crosswalk. "You're very proud—"

"Kristin!"

The black car rounding the corner came out of nowhere.

Two years earlier

The darkness was my only friend tonight.

This thought occurred to me as I opened my eyes. My mouth was filled with the warm, metallic gush of fresh blood, and my head throbbed with a deep, persistent ache. A sharp pain in my neck made me cry out as I turned my head to the right. Petra was slumped over and unconscious in the passenger seat.

Did I just kill my best friend?

There was no time to find out. I had to call 9-1-1.

But if I called for an ambulance, they'd surely send a police car, as well. They'd find out what I'd done. What *we'd* done.

In the movies, there were often headlights flashing after a car accident, but there was no light in this dark embankment. Had I even bothered to turn on my headlights when I got in the car? I couldn't remember. I could hardly remember getting in the driver's seat.

I had to get out of there.

No! I had to call an ambulance. I couldn't leave my friend alone, bleeding and unconscious. But how was I going to explain the accident without getting myself arrested when I couldn't even remember what happened?

I would use Petra's phone to dial 9-1-1, then I'd tell the dispatcher where we were.

Where are we?

Oh, God. What have I done?

This was bad. This was very, very bad. This was the kind of bad that ruined lives.

I had to get out of there.

My vision flickered. The broken glass and deflated airbag in my lap transformed into a rainbow of swirling colors. Even in my current state of mind, I knew the problems with my vision meant I had probably suffered a head injury. I thought of the time Petra and I swung as high as we could and jumped off our swings only to land so hard we cracked our heads together and both ended up with concussions. That was only eight years ago, but it already felt like someone else's life.

My hands slashed at the darkness, finding Petra's lifeless body. I felt warm breath on my hand and my body flooded with relief. Sliding my hand into a coat pocket, my fingertips collided with hard plastic. I pulled out her cell phone and dialed 9-1-1.

Hardly able to hear my slurred voice over my booming heartbeat, I attempted to ask for help. The dispatcher wanted to know where we were. I didn't know. It was too dark. She wanted to know who I was. I easily ignored the question. She begged me to stay on the phone, but my consciousness ebbed. The car was a ship, rolling and pitching as I fought to stay afloat. A bitter cocktail of vodka and half-digested orange pill spewed from my mouth onto the center console. I dropped the phone in Petra's lap, leaving the line to the dispatcher open.

After a bit of clumsy fumbling, I found the handle for the driver's side door and heaved it open, tumbling out onto tall, spiny grass. I didn't know where I was or where I would go, but I knew to be grateful for the darkness. It was my only friend tonight. It would shield me from the emergency personnel that would soon arrive.

There would be no hiding from the guilt.

Present day

I was frozen on the spot, a lifeless sculpture, awaiting my turbulent fate. I closed my eyes just as a sudden and violent force slammed into my chest. I flew backward, a bolt of sheer panic lighting up every nerve ending in my body. Unable to make sense of whether or not I'd been hit by the car, I opened my eyes again. Immediately, I landed on my back with a hard bounce, letting out an involuntary grunt as the wind was knocked out of my lungs.

Daniel was on top of me. My fingers searched for the ground, expecting to feel hard asphalt, instead finding warm grass.

Daniel grabbed my face and looked me in the eye, his voice distant as the sound of my panicked heartbeat thrummed in my ears. He looked down at my body, searching for injuries, then he stared me in the eye again. This time I heard him loud and clear.

"Kristin, are you in pain? Can you move your hands and feet, baby?"

A crowd was gathering. An old woman standing behind Daniel looked concerned, and the man next to her was on his cell phone describing something: *Main and Buell... Black. Yes, a black Mercedes... I only saw the first two letters... I think... Yes, definitely New York plates... C-F. Or C-E... I really can't say. Probably CF... Yeah, he's long gone.*

"Sweetheart, you gotta talk to me. Are you in pain?"

I shook my head as I pushed myself up onto my elbows. "No, no pain. Did he hit me?"

"Are you sure you're not in pain?" Daniel asked. "I tackled you pretty hard."

I reached up and scratched my chest. "Just a little out of breath, but I'm fine. Can you help me up?"

Daniel wrapped an arm around my back and helped me to my feet. "He didn't hit you," he said, looking me over from head to toe. "You're sure you're not hurt?"

I nodded slowly as I recalled one of the first questions he asked me. *Can you move your hands and feet?*

The night of the accident was fresh in my mind now. The blinding force, the sheer panic, the way the airbag knocked the air from my lungs, the relief that I was alive. The thousand times I called Petra in the hospital and at the rehab center and at her house. How

I couldn't blame her for ignoring me, but how that didn't make it hurt any less.

Panic rose in my chest and tears filled my eyes as I realized I'd once again narrowly escaped death. But, why? What did I have left to give this world? Why wasn't *I* the one sitting in a wheelchair?

I sank down onto the curb and covered my face. "I want to go home," I whispered, as Daniel sat next to me.

He wrapped his arm around my shoulders and placed a soft kiss on the top of my head as he pulled me into him. "Of course. Anything you want."

The walk back to Daniel's SUV, and the subsequent ride back to the beach house, were filled with a thick, awkward silence. A heavy fog of my memories hung between us. I kept my face averted, pretending to take in the scenery as I wiped away at a steady stream of tears, which never seemed to end. I didn't know what was worse, my brush with death or the embarrassment from the ensuing meltdown.

"I think you'd tell me if you were hurt." Daniel

finally broke the silence as we turned into his driveway. "You would tell me, wouldn't you?"

"I'm not hurt," I replied, unable to disguise the thick emotion strangling my voice. "I'm…" I watched as the giant beach house came into view and thought of how different I'd felt when I first saw it just a few hours ago. Then, I let out a deep sigh. "I don't know *what* I am," I said, my shaky voice sounding utterly defeated. "A monster, probably."

He stopped the car and killed the engine. "Why would you say that? What happened back there?" He was silent for a moment. "Talk to me, Kris."

Something about the way he called me Kris, just the way Petra used to, made me feel exposed. I pulled my feet up onto the seat and hugged my knees to my chest. "Trust me. You don't want to know the things I've done."

More silence. So much fucking silence.

"Hey, I don't know about you," he began, "but I'm fucking starving. How about we go inside and order a pizza?"

The uncertainty in his voice broke my heart. He was trying. He really was. But he didn't know if my mysterious baggage was something he was equipped to deal with. Or maybe he was wondering if I was even worth the effort. At least, he was trying.

I nodded as I unclipped my seat belt. "Okay."

Maybe it was finally time to come clean.

I was glad that Daniel led me into the library instead of the living room, where the walls were covered in beautiful art pieces that reminded me of the future I'd given up. My limbs slack, my expression zombie-like, I propelled myself toward a leather sofa in the middle of the library. Taking a seat on the edge of the cushion, I slid my hands beneath my thighs, so I wouldn't have to figure out what to do with them.

Daniel stood a few feet away, tapping his phone screen, probably ordering food. Though I had no interest in eating, Daniel was a strong guy who probably was not accustomed to skipping meals. He was so strong, in fact, he'd managed to save my life at least once, possibly twice, in less than two weeks. Maybe I did need a bodyguard—to protect me from myself.

I stared at a skull-sized silver world globe, which sat in the center of the mahogany coffee table in front of me. Why would Daniel, or his siblings, decorate this room so formally? If this were my house, I wouldn't weigh it down with dark, heavy wood furniture and leather. I would paint the bookshelves white, then I'd flood the room with light and organize the thousands of books on the shelves by the color of their spines.

Daniel turned off his phone and took a seat next to me. "You know what I do when I need to start working on a huge project, but I don't know where to start?" He didn't flinch at my lack of response, quickly answering his own question. "I start with the worst part, the part I'm dreading the most. It's easy after that."

His attempt to put me at ease was sweet, admirable, even.

"You don't understand," I replied, still staring at the silver globe. "The whole thing is the worst part. From start to finish, there are no good parts."

He was silent for a long time, until I finally turned to look at him. His gaze was intense as he said, "Then, start from the beginning. No matter how bad it gets, I'll be here until the end. I promise you that."

A visceral surge of emotion welled up inside me, stinging my eyes and stealing my breath away. Hiding my face in my hands, I allowed my mind to travel back in time, searching for the beginning of the story I needed to tell. The story that had haunted me every day for two years. The story of the night I became unworthy of the beautiful things in life.

15. Hurricane

Two years earlier

"Do you think they'll hold the scholarship for you to go back?" Petra asked as she applied her mascara.

"Why would they?" I replied, digging through my makeup bag for my eyebrow pencil. "They basically gave me the opportunity of a lifetime and I handed it right back to them. It's NYU. It's not like they have a refund policy or something."

"You should have just asked me. I'd take care of her," she said, stuffing her mascara back into her makeup bag and grabbing some tissue off the toilet paper roll to blow her nose.

I wanted to cry. Not because I had to leave NYU

to come home and take care of my mom. I wanted to cry because ever since Petra arrived at our apartment an hour ago, she'd blown her nose at least half a dozen times. She claimed to have allergies, but Petra had never had allergies in all the years I'd known her.

"I'm worried about you," I said, zipping up my makeup bag as I looked at her reflection in the bathroom mirror.

"Worried about *me*? Why? I'm not the one who had to quit school." She grabbed her bag and pushed past me to get out of the bathroom.

"Talk to me, Petra," I said, following her to my bedroom. "There's something you're not telling me."

She chuckled. "There's a lot of things I haven't told you...for your own good."

I swallowed an angry reply and took a deep breath to calm myself. "I know I've been gone, and I'm probably not the first person you turn to these days. Shit, maybe I'm not even the second or third person. But I'm here now, and I'm not going anywhere." I watched anxiously as she walked slowly along the edge of my worktable, trailing her fingertips over the new sculptures I'd brought back with me from NYU. "Please talk to me."

She stopped in front of a sculpture of a man with his head down, his hand gripping the back of his neck.

"Does this person actually exist?" she asked.

It didn't seem like she was trying to stall, so I answered her question. "Yes. He came in to model in my Figurative Sculpture class."

She smiled and turned back to face me. "I've never been as smart or lucky as you, but I think that's going to change tonight." She took a few steps forward so she was just a couple of feet away from me, her eyes locked on mine. "Nick confirmed that he's going to be at the party tonight."

My heart sank. I knew who she was referring to when she said "he."

I shook my head. "No. I'm not going."

"Kris, don't make me do this on my own," she pleaded. "I just want to find out his last name. That's all I want. I already googled it. There's no statute of limitations on rape in New York. I just need his full name."

"Petra, that's not how it works. You need evidence. Unless you kept your bedsheets or underwear or something else with his DNA on it, then you don't have anything. It's your word against his."

She looked betrayed. "Are you saying I should just let him get away with it?"

"That's not at all what I'm saying," I insisted. "I'm saying that you going there is a bad idea. If all you need is his last name, then send Nick to the party. Tell him to finally step up and be a brother and get that name for you. Then you can report it." I stepped forward and lightly grabbed her face to turn it back toward me. "Don't do this. This is not smart or lucky. This is a bad idea."

Pulling my hands away from her face, she lifted her chin and hardened her expression. "I'm doing this with or without you."

Almost three hours had gone by with Petra downing one whiskey shot after another and still no sign of the loser we were there for. I began to wonder if Petra was even sober enough to recognize him. Four different times, someone had passed around a pill box for anyone to partake. Three times, I'd passed it on to the person seated next to me.

"What's going to happen?" I asked the girl next to me, whose name I thought I must have misheard as Jolie. "Will it relax me?"

My nerves were shot. Every time Petra's gaze lingered on a new guy, I braced myself. Sure, she claimed she was just going to talk to him, to find out his last name so she could press charges, but I didn't know what to believe.

Petra and I had hung out a grand total of seven times in the past eight months. It was September, and tonight was the first time I'd seen her since I came home from NYU in June. I didn't want to believe that Petra had gotten herself mixed up with a bad crowd, or that she was going down the same road as her brother and parents. But I was beginning to think there was no other explanation that made sense for her behavior tonight.

Jolie told me to hold the orange pill under my tongue until it was fully dissolved. In thirty minutes, I'd be fully relaxed, she claimed as she slid an orange pill under her tongue and smiled. I hadn't had anything to drink other than water. I figured I could probably get away with one pill, just to relax me, since everyone else seemed to be downing one pill after another with multiple alcoholic beverages. Besides, I wasn't driving.

I leaned back on the sofa and closed my eyes as I waited for the bitter pill to dissolve. The taste was too bad. I needed something to wash it down.

"What's that?" I asked Jolie.

She smiled. "Vodka soda. Want one?"

"I just need a sip," I said, and she quickly handed

over her teal plastic cup.

I took a large sip and almost spit it out. "This isn't sweet!"

Jolie cackled. "No shit. It's vodka and club soda."

I shoved the drink back into her hand and wiped the excess alcohol off my lips. After a few minutes of waiting for the bitter chemical taste to go away, I finally decided to go to the bathroom and rinse my mouth out. But the moment I stood up, something hit me.

I didn't know if it was the pill or the vodka. Probably the pill, considering I'd only taken a sip of the drink.

My brain felt fuzzy. My mouth and skin became warm and woolen. For some reason, I thought blinking a few times would make the feeling go away, but it didn't. Afraid I would get lost on the way to the bathroom in an apartment I'd only been in for a few hours, I sat my ass back down, thinking I could wait it out.

This feeling can't last forever, right?

Petra would probably know the answer to that question. But when I turned to Petra for reassurance, she was gone.

Fuck.

I sat up straight, teetering on the edge of the sofa

cushion, trying to work up the energy to stand. Using the coffee table to steady myself, I stood up and, with my arms stretched out in front of me like a less-dead version of Frankenstein, I made my way toward the front door, ignoring the curse words spewed at me from people whose toes I'd likely stepped on.

Every step I took felt like it would surely be the last one I'd take before I lost my balance. Somehow, I managed to stay on my feet until I reached the door. Blinking furiously and trying to take deep breaths, I turned the knob and rushed out into the courtyard of the apartment complex.

Smaller groups of people were gathered at various locations in the dimly lit courtyard. *Shit.* I was in no state to walk the entire courtyard looking for Petra, but leaving her on her own was not an option.

I stumbled when the concrete transitioned to grass. Picking myself up, I ignored the sounds of muffled laughter and continued toward an opening at the back of the courtyard, which I assumed led to a street or alleyway. I didn't know why my instincts told me to go that way instead of toward the gated entrance. Maybe it was the way the crowd in that direction appeared more restless, as if someone had just disturbed their space.

"You should stop her. She's fucked up," a female voice said as I passed a couple smoking cigarettes in the yellow glow of a lamp post.

The guy stamped out his cigarette and followed after me, grabbing my hand to keep me from going any farther. "Hey, girl. You're in no condition to leave," he said, as I silently attempted to wrestle my hand from his grip. "Just go lie down in one of the bedrooms until you sober up."

"Let go," I warned him as he began leading me back to the apartment.

"Just chill. It's no big deal. This is my apartment. You can stay in my brother's room. Just make sure you lock the room so no one tries to take advantage of you."

"Fuck you! Leave me alone!" I shouted, pummeling his arm until he finally let me go.

"What the fuck!" he shrieked. "I was just trying to help! Fuck off, then!"

I stumbled toward the rear entrance to the courtyard, ignoring the girl shouting obscenities and the groups of people staring at me. The opening turned out to be an exit, which dumped me out onto a street I didn't recognize.

I didn't see anyone, no Petra or guy she might have followed. *Fuck.* I went the wrong way. I had to go back through the courtyard.

Turning around, I realized I must have been

walking down the street because I couldn't see the entrance to the courtyard. I continued back in the direction I thought I'd come from, when someone yelled my name. *Holy fuck*. I swallowed hard as I realized the pill I took was making me hallucinate.

"Kris!"

The sound was louder this time, and I turned to my left, where I thought it had come from. My muscles went slack with relief as I saw Petra in the driver's seat of a blue sedan I didn't recognize.

"Get in!" she shouted at me.

My limbs felt heavy now as the adrenaline drained from my body. I dragged myself toward the car and stared at the chrome door handle for a moment, trying to figure out how it worked.

"Hurry up!" she yelled, just as a car behind her honked.

Using both hands, I lifted the door handle, but nothing happened. Then, I realized there was a button on the handle. I pressed the button with one hand as the other heaved the door open.

"Hurry, hurry!" Petra urged as I climbed inside and used both hands to pull the door shut.

She slammed her foot on the gas and took off way too fast. "I know where he is, but we have to hurry. Shit! He got away from me."

"Whose car is this?" I mumbled, reaching for the seat belt, but my fingers kept sliding over it. "Where'd you get the car?"

"It's Nick's friend's car. He let me borrow it," she said, taking a wide right turn, narrowly avoiding a car coming toward us in the opposite direction.

"Be careful," I said weakly.

"Geez, you're really fucked up," she commented before slamming on the brakes to avoid a pedestrian. "Fuck!"

"I said be careful!" I cried with a bit more vigor.

"Fuck, fuck, fuck. I'm gonna lose him," Petra whispered under her breath. Then, she took one hand off the wheel to point at something in front of us. "There! You see him? Silver Hyundai. Got him!"

"P, you're scaring me," I slurred, closing my eyes as the blur of the city lights began to make me dizzy. "Let's go home. Please."

"I just need his address, then we can go. I need it."

I don't know how long we were driving around, but the sound of Petra turning the keys in the ignition and the engine going quiet got my attention.

"Stay right here," she said, reaching for the door handle.

I reached out desperately, latching on to her forearm. "Wait! I'll go with you."

"Oh, good point," she said, prying my hand off her arm. "Get in the driver's seat, Kris. In case we have to make a quick getaway."

"What? What are you gonna do? Please don't do this."

"Just get in the driver's seat. I'm not gonna do anything. I'm just gonna talk to him."

And then she was gone.

Fuck.

I climbed over the console and into the driver's seat. Running my hands over my face, I tried to force myself to sober up, but it wasn't working.

My mouth was dry.

I should keep the car running.

Turning the key in the ignition, I proceeded to search the floors and the backseat for a stray bottle of water or soda or something to quench my thirst. Then, I realized I should be watching Petra instead. I looked around the car, my eyes scanning the sidewalks, but she was nowhere.

I had to look for her. I couldn't leave my best friend alone and helpless. But as I reached for the door handle, Petra burst through the passenger door, slamming it behind her as she plunked down into the seat.

"Go! Go! Go! He has a gun!"

Oh, fuck.

My entire body shook as it flooded with adrenaline. I quickly put the car in drive and slammed my foot on the gas, swerving to the left to avoid the car parked in front of us. My heart stopped when I saw a guy in the middle of the street, pointing a gun at our windshield. Before I could second-guess myself, I closed my eyes and ducked my head as I plowed ahead.

The sound of a gunshot was followed by the resounding crack of the windshield shattering into a million pieces. Then, a loud *thunk-thunk-thunk* as we ran into him and he bounced over the hood and the roof of the car.

"Don't stop!" Petra urged me on as the car began to slow.

I couldn't see. I had to duck down to see through the small corner at the bottom left of the windshield that wasn't shattered. My heart raced in time with the RPMs as I tried to listen to Petra's directions, which I assumed were meant to get us as far away as possible.

"We killed him!" I shouted as we finally made our way onto the highway. "We're going to jail."

"It was self-defense," Petra replied. "Just keep going straight."

"We're going to jail for the rest of our lives."

She shook her head. "No way. I know a way out of

this." She was silent for a moment before she continued. "You have to crash the car. Not a bad crash, just enough to cover up the damage from…"

The highway lights burned streaks across my field of vision as my head spun with images of what had just happened. If I didn't pull over soon, I was going to throw up on this steering wheel. The car began to drift to the right.

"Slow down," Petra pleaded. "You're going too fast."

But when I tried to slow down, I realized I still had my foot on the gas pedal. I wasn't slowing down. I was speeding up.

"Slow down!"

The car drifted over the white line onto the shoulder, heading straight for a guardrail. Before I could swerve back to the left, the front right wheel was over the embankment. The rolling was over in seconds. A hurricane of glass breaking, metal twisting, Petra screaming, and then silence.

16. Worthy

Present day

I HAD NEVER FELT so relieved and so frightened in all my life. Judging by the shocked silence that followed my confession, I didn't know if Daniel was going to call the police and turn me in or spit out some sort of platitude about how it wasn't my fault. But I didn't know if I cared anymore. I was ready to face the consequences of what I'd done.

When I finished telling him everything about that night, I told him about the few months I spent trying to binge-drink my guilt away after the accident. How no amount of alcohol could wash away my shame. How I only sobered up because I didn't want to hurt my mom the way I'd hurt Petra.

Daniel sat on the edge of the leather sofa cushion with his elbows on his knees, staring at his hands. "Did he die?"

I smeared my hands over my cheeks to wipe away tears. "No. I don't know if he even reported it because I never got a visit from the cops. Maybe he didn't remember how it happened. I don't know." I swiped the back of my hand across my nose, beyond caring about what a mess I must look like to Daniel. "I tried calling Petra at least fifty times when she was in the hospital. I harassed the fuck out of the staff at the rehab center where she went after that. I didn't want to give up, but she made me. She sent me one text. I still have it."

I slid my phone out of my purse and navigated to my messages app. Just seeing her name on the message made my chest ache. I hadn't looked at this message in months.

Petra:
Stop calling me or I'm gonna call the cops and confess. I'll tell them the truth, that it was all my fault. I'll deny you were ever there.

"She knew me better than anyone. She knew how to get me to leave her alone."

Daniel let out a long sigh. "What did she tell the cops? Who did she say was driving?"

"She probably told the cops she couldn't remember who was driving. I don't think they could prove anything because the owner of the car probably had a solid alibi. All he knew was that he let Petra borrow his car. No one saw me in the car except for Petra and her rapist."

"But the 9-1-1 call. They had your voice."

I shrugged. "I don't know. The call was made from her cell phone. My best guess is they played the 9-1-1 call for her and she either said it was her that made the call or that she couldn't recognize the voice. I was really fucked up and scared when I made the call, and I was crying, so it probably wasn't super coherent. Either way, it would have been an easy lie for her to tell."

He shook his head. "Fuck," he whispered. "This isn't good."

"What...what do you mean?"

He shook his head again. "Sorry. That's not what I meant. I meant to say that..." He reached out and grabbed my hand. "That's one hell of a friend."

I was slightly confused by the difference in his two statements, but I cut him some slack due to the heaviness of what I'd just confessed. "Well, she's not my friend anymore. She made it very clear that she wants nothing to do with me. Besides, what kind of friend leaves their friend unconscious and bleeding in a dark ravine?"

He squeezed my hand. "The kind who doesn't want her friend to go to prison. You both would have gone to prison if you hadn't fled the scene." The muscle in his jaw twitched as he continued with fierce determination in his eyes. "*You're* the one who went with her to the party when you didn't want to. *You're* the one who looked for your best friend even though you could hardly walk. *You're* the one who dodged a bullet to get your friend to safety. *You* dialed 9-1-1. *You* saved her life…twice."

"Yeah, and I'm the one who drove too fast and put my best friend in a wheelchair for the rest of her life."

He sighed as he pulled me into his arms, tucking my head under his chin. "You have to call her again."

"I can't," I whispered into his chest.

"You don't deserve to carry this guilt alone." He leaned back and grabbed my face so he could look me in the eye. "If she won't help you carry it, then I will. But you have to promise me you'll try to call her again.

Promise me, Kris."

I bit my lip as I considered his words. Did he just reach into my dark hole and offer to pull me out? I'd known this beautiful man for less than two weeks, and he suddenly knew more about me than my own mother.

I nodded. "I'll call her."

17. Real

DANIEL KINDLY FORCED ME to eat a bowl of cereal before we headed upstairs to the guest room. I had just enough energy to wash up in the bathroom before changing into my SpongeBob SquarePants nightshirt, which made Daniel smile when I came out of the bathroom.

He was sitting up on a pillow propped against the headboard, beckoning me to his side. "Very sexy pajamas."

I crawled across the foot of the bed and snuggled up next to him, resting my head on his shoulder. "Believe it or not, I left the matching cape at home."

He pulled the covers up to my waist and kissed the top of my head. "I didn't know SpongeBob was a superhero."

"You obviously have never watched SpongeBob when you're feeling sad. Instantly cheers you up."

He wrapped his arm around my shoulders and gave my arm a soft squeeze. "Well, I hope I was able to cheer you up tonight, despite my obvious lack of krabby patty-flipping skills."

I let out a deep breath as I allowed my body to settle into his. "Thanks for listening to me tonight."

"My services don't come free, you know."

I gasped at the insinuation, smacking his chest lightly in protest.

He grabbed my hand. "What a dirty mind you have," he said with a chuckle. "I don't require sexual favors, though I certainly won't reject you if that's the only form of payment you offer." He tightened his grip on my hand so I couldn't inflict any further abuse. "All I ask," he continued, "is that you name your next sculpture Vanessa… That was my mom's name, and I think she'd have really liked you. I think that would make her happy…wherever she is."

I tilted my head back a little so I could see his face, and the sorrow in his eyes broke my heart. "I'm so sorry. I've been so busy talking about myself, I never asked about you."

He shook his head. "You don't have to apologize.

You needed to get that out. I'm honored to be the one you opened up to."

I laid my head on his shoulder again. "Tell me about your mom."

He chuckled. "Oh, man. You're in for a treat. My mom was a total firecracker. Kind of like you," he said, giving my arm a little squeeze. "She used to have all these little sayings that she claimed she learned from my grandpa, but he died when I was eight, so I don't remember him too well. One she liked a lot was '*Mucho ruido y pocas nueces.*' Which literally translates to 'a lot of noise and very little walnuts.'"

I laughed. "Is that supposed to be like all bark and no bite?"

"Exactly. Very quick on the draw, Picasso."

"Nice pun. Tell me more about your mom."

He stroked my hair as he told me stories about his mom. He smiled as he told me how, every Saturday, his mom would turn her favorite Brazilian jazz music on full blast, then she'd dance as she made breakfast. He spoke almost longingly of the hilarious punishments his mom would dole out for bad grades and missed curfews. With every story, my vision of her became more and more clear, until she felt like a physical presence in the room, grand, loud, and beautifully flawed.

"She was only forty-two when she was diagnosed," he said, his tone more solemn. "She was so young, but the first thing she told me when she got back from that doctor's appointment was 'If I die, it's not because you or me or your sisters or your brother deserve that. It's just life, so don't let anyone tell you it's for a reason.'" He paused for a minute. "You see, she knew something important. Bad things happen to good people every day. It's not God or the universe trying to punish you or teach you a harsh, unknowable lesson. It's just life."

I tried to hide the fact that I was crying again by taking slow, deep breaths to calm myself. Though Daniel couldn't see my face, there was no hiding from him. His hand reached up to wipe the tears, which had collected in the corners of my lips. I grabbed his hand to hold it there as I kissed his thumb, tasting the salt of my tears.

He pressed his lips to my forehead and I looked up into his eyes. Even in the dim lamplight, his green eyes were fierce with longing. I let go of his hand and he placed it on my face, holding me still as he leaned in to kiss me. His tongue tasted minty sweet as it slid into my mouth. I moaned as he turned a bit, sliding his leg between my thighs, ever so slowly and cleverly using his knee to spread my legs.

His kiss remained unhurried and steady as his hand moved down to lift up my nightshirt. Daniel tilted his head back to get a good look at me as he pulled the shirt up and over my head. I inhaled sharply as the cool air-conditioned air whispered over my exposed nipples. Daniel looked down at me, taking everything in for a moment. Then, he ran his fingertips softly up my abdomen to the skin between my breasts, raising goose bumps over my entire body.

"You're absolutely stunning," he said as he swept his fingertips lightly over my taut flesh.

The warmth of his skin on mine, and the firmness of the bulge in his boxers, told me he wanted me as much as I wanted him. But the look in his eyes relayed a different story. The conflict I noticed in the parking garage was back, not quite as intensely, but it was definitely there. Either Daniel was cheating on someone with me or there was something, probably even worse, that he wasn't telling me.

Or…he was afraid of hurting me. Not physically. Maybe Daniel was afraid he would lose interest in me after we had sex. Maybe he was afraid of hurting me because he was actually starting to care about me. Of course, that implied that Daniel was the sort of guy to *love 'em and leave 'em.* Somehow, that didn't seem like the Daniel I knew.

The more critical question was, did I know the real Daniel?

I linked my arms around his neck as he cupped my breast in his large hand. "I want you, Daniel," I whispered, hardly able to believe I was saying the words aloud. "I do."

His gaze locked on mine as he lightly stroked the skin over my ribs. He stared into my eyes for so long, I began to feel as if he were reading my soul like an open book. Finally, he looked away, as if something he'd seen had filled him with a sense of defeat or…guilt.

"I don't want to hurt you," he said, looking up to meet my gaze again as his hand slid down my body, coming to rest on my hip. "But I can't promise I won't."

I didn't know if he was talking about hurting me physically, but it had to mean something awful if I was hoping for that to be the case. Awful or not, there was no turning back. If Daniel and I were on a collision course, from this moment forward, I was going to close my eyes and remain blissfully ignorant until the moment of impact.

I pressed my lips together as I looked him in the eye for a long moment, trying to ignore the hormones raging through me, begging me to throttle him.

"I can't promise I won't hurt you, either," I said,

my breath quickening as he slipped his finger under the elastic of my panties and slowly traced the hem down to the inside of my thigh. "But I'll try my hardest not to."

One side of his mouth turned up in a heart-stopping half smile. "You continue to surprise me," he said as he leaned in, his mouth hovering over mine as his hand slid inside my panties. "Let's see if I can surprise you."

As he kissed me deeply, I thought of nothing but his mouth on mine. As he reached for a condom in the nightstand without being asked, my insides warmed at his natural sense of responsibility. As he tugged my panties off and took a moment to admire my body before he settled himself between my legs, I wondered how I could possibly deserve such a gorgeous man.

His weight fell over me like a comforting blanket, then he kissed me for a while before sliding into me. Propping himself up on his elbows, he watched my expression as he moved a little deeper inside with each careful thrust, patiently allowing me as much time as I needed for my body to conform to his. It had been so long since I'd done this, it took a while before I could fully receive him. But when it happened, it was magical.

As he moved inside me, carefully and methodically

fusing every part of our bodies and minds into a single moment of raw cosmic symmetry, I thought maybe, just maybe, Daniel was wrong about the randomness of the universe.

I had never wanted anything more than I wanted to believe I *deserved* to be this happy.

His eyes locked on mine and it was as if the earth had opened up and swallowed every person on the planet except us. We were the only two people who existed in this moment, and the only thing we existed for was this. This avalanche of sensations. This storm of emotion. It was all there in his penetrating gaze, his deliberate rhythm, his fevered kiss.

This was my definition of real.

I slid out of bed quietly, holding my breath until I was safely outside the bedroom. As I made my way out to the veranda, I noted how the house still didn't look lived in despite the fact that Daniel and I had been here for almost a day. I wondered if that was the way it would always look, and something about this thought made me sad.

I quietly prowled across the veranda, past the swimming pool, and down the wooden stairs to the beach. It was still dark out, but a hazy golden promise of sunlight lay just beyond the horizon. Taking a seat in the cool sand a few meters from the reach of the waves, I positioned my feet toward the east, hugged my knees to my chest, and waited. Just as the sun began to crest above the crashing waves, I caught some movement out of the corner of my eye.

"You promised to make me breakfast," I said, as Daniel took a seat next to me.

He wore a pair of gray athletic pants and no shirt, his wavy hair perfectly messy. "I would have never made that promise if I knew you woke up at the butt-crack of dawn," he replied, planting a tender kiss on my shoulder. "Jesus Christ, that's beautiful."

I turned back to the horizon and my breath caught in my chest. The bright, pale-yellow sun rose across a peach horizon, sending brilliant flares of sun rays shining across the sky and dancing on the ocean's surface. Daniel was right; it was absolutely gorgeous.

"You say that as if you've never seen it," I said. "Have you never come out this early to see the sunrise?"

He leaned back on his hands. "You took my Hamptons sunrise virginity. How does it feel?"

"You got a cigarette?"

He shook his head. "You're different today."

"Different? How do you mean?"

He laid a soft kiss on my shoulder and smiled at me. "When we got here yesterday, you were restless. Like a wild animal who escaped its cage."

I chuckled and let out a soft roar. "And today?"

"Your soul is calm. You told your story. Now your heart can rest." He turned his attention back to the sunrise. "Today, you're different. Today, you're you."

A rush of warmth welled up inside me as I realized this man was more tuned into my emotions than I was.

"Have you thought some more about making that call?" he asked.

A pang of guilt beat a steady rhythm in my chest. "Actually, I wanted to ask you about that," I began. "I know you had plans for us today, but I was hoping you could take me back early, like, this morning. So I can make that call today. Is that okay?"

His gaze drifted over my entire face as a smile curled his full lips. "That's one of the best ideas I've ever heard."

I turned back toward the sunrise to hide my grin. "Are you trying to get rid of me?" I teased.

"You really do catch on quickly," he teased back, then he nodded toward the house. "Come on. I think we have time to *relax* in the sauna before we head out."

I shook my head. "Is that your idea of relaxing?"

Sitting up, he reached up to move my hair aside as he leaned in to kiss my neck, then he whispered in my ear. "Trust me, you'll be very relaxed by the time I'm done with you."

By the time Daniel and I had utilized the sauna, showered, and made the two-hour drive back to the Bronx, the clock on my phone read 12:17 p.m. When I entered the apartment, the movie *Turner & Hooch* was playing on the TV as my mom lay in her hospital bed with an ice pack on her knee and her casted arm propped up on a pillow in her lap.

Leslie popped up out of the recliner to greet me. "Hey, kiddo! You're back early. Is everything okay?"

"Did he hurt you?" my mom asked in a harsh growl.

I laughed. "I'm fine. I decided to cut the trip short so I could get some stuff done before I go back to work tomorrow night."

Leslie tilted her head and gave me a pitying look. "Was he bad in bed?"

"Oh, my God!" I exclaimed through nervous laughter. "I am *not* talking about that with you guys."

My mom and Leslie both laughed. "Must have been terrible," my mom said, adjusting the pillow under her arm.

"*Mom!* Can we please not talk about that?"

My mom shook her head. "Rich guys... They get everything handed to them, and they never learn the right way to handle women like us."

"Okay, I'm not having this discussion," I said, my face burning up as I headed for the hallway. "I'm going to my room to unpack."

"I'm heading out, Kris. I'll come by to check on the both of you later," Leslie called to me as I walked away.

I stopped in the hallway and blew her a kiss. "I'll make you some dinner to take back to Jay and the kids."

Leslie smiled. "You're in a very good mood, young lady. I think Daddy Warbucks was better than you're letting on."

I shook my head in dismay as I headed into the bedroom. When I was done unpacking, I sat on the mattress and stared at my phone. I couldn't bring myself to unlock the phone, afraid if I did that I would be obligated to call Petra right away. I wanted to rehearse what I was going to say, but I knew that no amount of preparation would make the call any easier. Not to mention, the conversation would mostly likely not unfold as I imagined.

I had to get it over with, but the butterflies in my stomach were spreading to my entire body. Tiny hairs on every inch of my skin stood on end as I entered my PIN code to unlock the phone.

The first thing I did was go to my phone settings and toggle off the option to show my phone number on caller ID. I still had the same phone number I'd had when Petra was rejecting my calls. But as I touched the button to toggle off this feature, I had a change of heart and turned it back on. I had to give Petra a chance to choose whether or not to take my call, assuming she hadn't already blocked my phone number altogether.

My heart raced as I navigated to the phone app and opened my contact list. Scrolling down to the bottom, I found a contact named Zzz. I had renamed Petra's contact because every time I saw her name as I scrolled through the list, I became sick to my stomach with guilt. Putting her at the bottom of the list meant I would only see it if I scrolled to the very bottom, and I made sure I never did that.

The first thing I did was change her contact name back to Petra. Then, I closed my eyes and took a few deep breaths before I placed the call. Bringing the phone to my ear, my hand began to tremble as my body surged with adrenaline.

"Hello?"

My heart nearly stopped. For some reason, Petra's voice was the last thing I expected to hear. I fully expected to reach her voicemail. I only half-expected her mom or Nick to answer for her so they could instruct me, once again, to leave Petra alone. I never expected her to answer.

"Hello?" she repeated, sounding more annoyed now.

"Petra," I said, sounding out of breath. "I'm sorry, I…I…I didn't expect you to answer."

"Oh, I thought maybe it was your mom," she replied with obvious disappointment.

I should have felt hurt, but all I felt was hope. If she wanted to talk to my mom, and she hadn't hung up on me yet, maybe this phone call wasn't such a bad idea. But with her disappointment being made so clear, I had to make my point quickly.

"Petra, we need to talk," I said, sounding more assertive than I'd expected to sound.

"I really don't think that's a good idea."

"Who's that on the phone?" said a low, muffled voice in the background.

"No one," Petra replied. "Look, I gotta go."

"Wait!" I cried. "Petra, I know I hurt you. I know you're angry. But I'm not asking for anything more than a chat." I swallowed hard as my throat began to swell with emotion. "I'll come to your apartment, or wherever you want. I just want a few minutes to see you, to say what I need to say. Then, you can go on your way and I promise you'll never have to see me again. I just..."

My lips trembled as I considered stopping right there, then I remembered Daniel and how I'd allowed myself to be so vulnerable with him, and I didn't even share with him the kind of history I shared with Petra. I had to be honest. This might be my only chance.

"I miss you." As soon as I said the words, all the fear and uncertainty that had dogged me for the past two years disappeared, and I knew the only thing I could do now was to continue down the path of honesty. "I've missed you so much."

Petra sniffed loudly. "I have to go. I'll text you later," she said, and the call ended.

Letting out a deep sigh, I smiled as tears rolled down my cheeks. I didn't know if Petra was actually going to text me, but I didn't think it really mattered. She answered my call. She didn't tell me to get lost. She may have even cried when I told her I missed her. My heart was full.

I collected myself before heading out into the living room. My mom had fallen asleep with *Turner &*

Hooch still playing on the TV. As I picked up the remote to turn it off, my phone vibrated in my other hand. My heart raced as I raised the phone and turned the screen toward my face.

Petra:
Meet me at Michaelangelo's on Wednesday at 7.

I had to work Wednesday night, but Joe still owed me for the whole Jerry incident. I could probably sweet-talk him into giving me the night off. If not, I could switch shifts with another server. My hands shook as I fired off my response.

Me:
See you then.

PART II: *Daniel*

18. Music Box

A few weeks earlier

TODAY WAS THE FIRST TIME in many years I didn't see the sunrise. It rose at a few minutes past six in the morning, the time I was usually jogging along Orchard Beach, where I took my daily six-mile run. I timed my run so that I always arrived at that beach when the sun was about to rise. Oddly enough, the sunrise reminded me of snow days as a child, sledding down the hill at Crotona Park with my brother and sisters early in the morning before the park got crowded. Simple pleasures taken in simpler times. It was hard to catch the sunrise from inside a morgue.

I made a huge mistake when I began working for

Michael Becker. I allowed myself to start making plans. I should have known better, but I'd never seen a check that huge in all my life. All I had to do was keep this guy safe—which seemed like an easy enough task—and I'd be able to pay off the mortgage my mom left behind and send my siblings to college. I never thought Becker would find a way to get himself killed when I was just one month into the job.

"Mr. Meyers?" The sound of the woman's voice echoed off the walls of the morgue. "This officer would like to speak to you."

I looked up to find yet another boy in blue who wanted to hear the story firsthand. This would be my sixth retelling. I was almost numb to the details now.

Almost.

I told Officer Nowicki the whole story, how I'd been riding in the passenger seat with Michael Becker when some asshole in a silver SUV ran a red light and T-boned our Range Rover. The impact didn't kill Becker instantly. As I frantically dialed 9-1-1, he forced out a few last words from his crushed lungs: *The key…it's in the guesthouse.*

When I relayed these words to the cops, they looked back at me with either confusion or skepticism. But when I called Sabrina Sokolov, Becker's chief advisor, and told her about his last words, I heard a sharp intake of breath on the other end of the line. She knew what Becker meant, and so did I.

As I stepped inside the cavernous foyer of Becker's enormous beach house in the Hamptons, four hours after identifying my boss's body in a New York City morgue, I knew exactly where I would find my *new* boss. Now that Becker was gone, Sabrina would be calling the shots. My fate was now in her birdlike hands.

Sabrina would decide whether I stayed on as a bodyguard with Becker's company or if I received a severance check. Maybe all I'd get for failing to keep Becker safe would be a swift kick in the ass on my way out the twelve-foot-tall front doors.

Becker had never married, and he had no family. As far as anyone knew, he had no heirs to the throne of Becker Holdings, his $400 million empire. But something told me his last words were going to throw a wrench in the smooth transfer of executive power to Sabrina.

Lorena came around the corner from the great room into the foyer, gasping the moment she saw me with a large swath of gauze wrapped around the top of my head. "Daniel! Are you okay?" she cried in her thick Spanish accent as she rushed to greet me.

"Shh! I'm fine," I said, holding a finger to my lips to hush her. "I need you to be quiet. I...I have a little bit of a headache."

She narrowed her eyes at me, probably suspecting this wasn't true, then she nodded. "Yes, of course. Please let me know if I can get you anything," she said, slipping her hands into the pockets of her apron as she crossed the foyer and disappeared through the double doors into the library.

Swiftly and quietly, I made my way up the wooden staircase, past the Picasso in the upstairs hallway, and to the third door on the left. A chill passed over my skin. The house was colder than usual, but it wasn't just the temperature that chilled me to my core. I couldn't get Becker's last words out of my mind. The sight of the door, and the prospect of finding out what lay behind it, had my every nerve on edge.

The door was closed, of course, but I knew if I tried the knob today it would be unlocked for the first time since I'd started working for Becker. Actually, if Becker's other employees were to be believed, it would be unlocked for the first time in at least twenty years. Curling my fingers around the bronze lever, I slowly turned it and pushed the door open.

As I suspected, Sabrina's cherry-red hair immediately caught my eye from where she sat with her back to me. As I had *not* suspected, the room, which had possibly been locked since the day it was built, was not a sex chamber or secret vault full of precious jewels and artwork.

It was a little girl's bedroom.

Sabrina sat at a small white desk, unable to hear me over the sound of her sniffling. Still, I approached quietly. My eyes scanned the bedroom, taking in the details of the space: a fluffy white comforter with ruffled trim, soft lilac paint on the walls, an ornate carousel music box on the white nightstand. It was nothing like my sisters' messy bedrooms. The room felt cold and surreal, like a bedroom you'd find on a movie set. Everything was completely new and untouched. I half-expected a crew of actors and set designers to barge in and begin rehearsing.

As I neared the desk where Sabrina sat hunched over in her grief, I realized she was reading something. On the desk in front of her, a notebook lay open, each page covered in the forward-slanted handwriting I'd come to recognize over the past few weeks.

Was Sabrina reading Michael's journal?

Though the man was gone, it still felt like a gross invasion of his privacy. Of course, if the man was keeping a creepy girl's bedroom locked away in the middle of his sprawling beach estate, maybe he had been keeping the kind of secrets that needed to be brought to light.

Thinking back to the night of the accident, I realized I knew more than I cared to about Michael Becker.

Creeping a bit closer, I held my breath as I peered over Sabrina's shoulder, trying to make sense of the words scrawled on the pages.

Dec. 28, 1999

I saw her playing at the park on 188th today. Sally takes her there a lot. It's a decent park. You wouldn't guess that three blocks west is one of the worst neighborhoods in the Bronx. More than once they've had to leave in a hurry to get away from the hordes of teenagers smoking cigarettes and fighting among themselves. But when they're alone at the park, that's when Kristin shines. My daughter has the brightest laugh I've ever heard.

"*Daughter?*" As Sabrina whipped her head around, I realized I'd said this word aloud.

"What are you doing in here?" she shrieked, wiping hastily at the streaks of mascara running down her smooth cheeks.

"The door was open. I—I was just coming for my last check. I gotta pay rent tomorrow." I nearly stumbled over my words as her gaze bored into me.

Her icy blue eyes flitted back to the open notebook, then she slammed it shut and turned back to me. "What did you see?"

I cocked an eyebrow. Maybe she didn't hear me say the word "daughter." Maybe if I denied seeing anything, I could escape Sabrina's wrath.

"Nothing," I replied. "I saw you, and I saw the room, but that's it. I just want my paycheck and I'll get out of your hair."

She clutched the book tightly against her breast. "He had a daughter." Her eyes were closed as she spoke very matter-of-factly. "Judging by the dates on these entries, I'd guess she's about twenty-two or twenty-three now." She sighed heavily as she opened her eyes and looked up at me. "They've never known each other, and from what I see here, it looks like the mother didn't want her daughter to know Michael." She sniffled and wet her lips as she sat up straight. "He could be a difficult man. I know that. But anyone who could hurt him this way, who didn't want to be a part of his life, doesn't deserve to be a part of his death. Do you agree?"

I closed my mouth as I realized it was hanging open in shock. Did Sabrina really think it was a good idea to keep the news of Michael's death from the only family he had?

Michael had no siblings, and his parents were both dead. If he had any other family—aunts, uncles, cousins—he certainly didn't have any contact with them. Sabrina had told me as much when she informed me that she had been appointed the executor of Michael's estate and the new CEO of Becker Holdings in an emergency meeting with the rest of the management team this morning.

I didn't know much about New York State probate law, but I was pretty certain that a last will and testament could be contested by the deceased's living offspring. Sabrina and Becker Holdings could be held up in probate court for years trying to sort that out.

Sabrina's face softened. "If this gets out, I won't be able to give you your severance."

"Severance?" I repeated the word.

Sabrina had told me to come to the beach house to pick up my last check. She'd mentioned nothing about a severance package.

"I'll have to let all the household staff go," she continued. "Lorena, John Lee, all the security will be laid off until this is settled in court." She paused a moment before laying the notebook on the desk and standing up. "Or...we can do this the right way. We can find out if this girl knows about Michael. If...If she *wants* to know anything about him." Her eyes pleaded with me. "If you do this for me, I'll make sure you receive at least thirty-six months' severance."

My jaw tightened. "Do *what* for you?"

"Four hundred million dollars and more than a hundred employees is a lot of responsibility. And right now, it's all on my shoulders, Daniel," she began, taking a step forward until she was close enough for me to smell the sharp scent of her perfume. "You're a good-looking kid. I want you to get to know the girl. Find out if she's capable of taking on that kind of responsibility."

I attempted to do the math in my head; thirty-six multiplied by my monthly salary was more money than I could calculate in my uneducated brain. I didn't become a bodyguard because I wanted to change the world. I did it because, as the eldest of four children, I'd always been the protector. I might as well get paid for doing something I was good at.

But this assignment Sabrina was offering me didn't involve protecting anyone. Actually, it sounded a heck of a lot easier. All I had to do was find this girl and, what, *befriend* her? It was almost too easy. For all that money?

I thought back to my first day on the job, the day I met Sabrina.

Michael and I stepped off the elevator onto the fourteenth floor of Becker Holdings in midtown. I walked a few steps behind him as he made his way past the receptionist's desk and a vast network of cubicles, where red-faced brokers with their sleeves already rolled up to their elbows at nine a.m. shouted obscenities into their headsets. No one looked at Michael. The ones who did see him quickly turned away. What the fuck did I get myself into?

As we passed an open door in the middle of a corridor, Michael stopped and peered inside. The room was empty except for a few desks. He rolled his eyes and continued down the hallway.

We reached a glass, walled-off conference room, where Michael stopped at the door. "Come inside with me, but stand in the corner. Your strength should be seen, not heard."

I nodded, as it dawned on me how strange it was that this guy needed twenty-four-hour security. He must be in the business of pissing people off.

As we entered the conference room, the frustrated looks on various faces immediately made it clear that Michael was late.

A skinny woman with dark-red hair, wearing a slim-fitting black pantsuit, stood from her chair. "You're late," she barked at him. "We've been waiting over an hour."

Michael pulled off his blazer and tossed it onto the conference table, almost knocking over someone's Starbucks cup. "Yeah, how about you tell me something I don't fucking know. Like where the fuck are the interns I ordered? We need someone to go through the Houseman merger before the audit."

An Asian guy in the middle of the table spoke up. "I called the temp agency, sir, but they said they were informed not to send any more interns."

Michael glared at him. "Why?"

The guy glanced at the redhead, then turned back to Michael. "I don't know, sir. You'll have to ask Sabrina."

Michael shot the redhead a fiery glare. "What is he talking about, Sabrina? Where the fuck are my interns?"

Sabrina rolled her eyes, looking completely unamused by Michael's anger. "You'll get your interns when you learn to keep your hands out of their skirts."

Michael's face turned beet-red. "You, outside." He pushed the words out through gritted teeth, then he waited for Sabrina to begin walking toward the door before he followed after her.

I didn't know if I was supposed to follow them, but I figured if I did, and I wasn't supposed to, Michael would tell me. Better to ask forgiveness than permission.

I followed behind Michael, but he didn't protest. When we were outside the conference room, I took a few steps farther down the corridor to give Michael and Sabrina some privacy, but I could still hear every word they said.

"You're walking on very fucking thin ice, do you understand me?" he whispered.

Sabrina stared at him for a moment, then cocked an eyebrow. "I'm not the one fucking interns and putting this whole company in jeopardy. If you want to make certain the Houseman merger goes smoothly, then you need to learn to keep it in your pants before we're hit with a sexual harassment lawsuit the likes of which you may never recover from. Then it's bye-bye, Houseman merger, and bye-bye, IPO. Do you understand me?"

Michael stared at her for a long time, seething as his face went from red to pink and back to white. "I don't know what I'd do without you," he said, a smile spreading across his face.

Sabrina—aka the Ice Queen—smiled back at him, her cheeks blushing pink through the thick layer of makeup she was wearing. "You'd be broke without me."

Michael got serious again. "Doesn't change the fact that I still need interns to go through the files before the auditors arrive. We need all hands on deck."

"Aye-aye, captain," she replied with a seductive smile.

I had to suppress a laugh. Either these two were fucking, or this woman was begging for Michael's dick. Either way, it was less than an hour into my first day and I'd already learned a very important lesson. If I planned on keeping this job, I sure as fuck did not *want to cross Sabrina.*

The memory of my first day on the job faded away, replaced by the images of my sisters' and brother's faces. If I agreed to do this special project for Sabrina, I'd have enough money to set up Ricky with an apartment near the port, so he wouldn't have to sleep on the sofa anymore. I could set some money aside for Alisha and Geneva's college educations. They wouldn't be stuck living paycheck to paycheck like Ricky and me.

My mother's words echoed in my mind. *"Promise me you'll take care of them, Danny."*

Like Michael's daughter, my father was also a stranger to me. In prison since I was six for robbery and attempted murder, he'd never even met Geneva, his youngest. He was up for parole in a couple of years. I'd always planned on moving Alisha and Geneva out of the Bronx by then, but I couldn't do that on unemployment checks or the average bodyguard's salary. Not to mention that I wouldn't be snagging any high-paying gigs for a while; it would take some time for potential clients to forget Michael had died on my watch.

All I had to do was get to know the girl. I'd be stupid to say no to this.

I nodded before I could change my mind. "I'll do it."

19. Reckless

AS I DROVE AWAY from Kristin's apartment, after our Hamptons getaway, I had to keep reminding myself not to turn around and go back. There was a physical ache in my chest, like the one I got when I dropped Geneva off for her first day of high school. It seemed every time I dropped Kristin off, it was becoming more and more difficult to leave.

I couldn't bear the thought of something happening to her at home or work, or on her way to and from work.

Unlike the wealthy persona I had assumed for this job—a job I was beginning to hate—I had lived in the Bronx all my life. I knew ours was one of the roughest neighborhoods in the country. And after all the lies I'd told, I couldn't help but feel Kristin's safety had officially become my responsibility.

There was no doubt in my mind, I would kill to protect her.

But who would protect her from me?

I didn't know the answer to that question. I didn't know how I could even ponder that question when I didn't want to imagine anyone coming between us. The only thing I knew for certain was where I needed to be right now.

I punched the gas as the streetlight changed from red to green. Today, I had one mission, and one mission only: Find the black Mercedes.

A blanket of darkness had fallen over Manhattan before I was finally able to track down Sabrina at a brasserie on Bleecker Street. I knew the moment the black Mercedes sped away down Buell Lane that the call I received at that moment, from an unknown number, had come from Sabrina or someone working with her.

The first place I looked for Sabrina was back in the

Hamptons. I was not at all surprised to find that the code to enter the six-car garage at the beach house had been changed since I'd left to drop Kristin off at her apartment. The household staff still was not scheduled to return until the next day, so it could only have been Sabrina who changed the code.

It was one thing to conspire to cut Kristin out of her inheritance, but to attempt to run her over was something else entirely.

In fact, the whole idea of Sabrina or someone working for her trying to kill Kristin with a Mercedes was impulsive. It was so impulsive that I was almost certain it had been Sabrina behind the wheel.

Unfortunately, I had no proof to take to the police. I hadn't recorded any of my conversations with Sabrina. And Kristin was so upset last night, after being nearly turned into a pancake and having memories of her best friend dredged up, she didn't want to stick around and file a police report.

Tonight was different. Tonight, I was prepared.

Almost as if she knew I was waiting for her, Sabrina lingered over dinner and drinks for more than three hours. I didn't know what she could possibly have to talk about for that long with Barry and Gene. As far as I knew, she had laid them off weeks ago.

Barry and Gene made up two of the three-man

security detail Michael Becker employed as round-the-clock bodyguards. Barry and I were the newest members, so we had been alternating between day and night shifts. I was the unlucky one who had the night shift on the night Becker died. Gene had worked for Becker almost as long as Sabrina, which made me wonder why she hadn't asked Gene to investigate Kristin.

It didn't take me very long to figure out that Sabrina had probably known about Kristin's existence for years.

This was the only logical explanation for why Sabrina had asked me—not Gene—to get to know Kristin. I was certain she had already looked into Kristin's background and found nothing she could use to justify denying her inheritance. She needed someone Kristin's age who could get close enough to uncover the dark secrets that didn't show up on a background check.

And I fell for it.

How could I not? It all seemed too easy.

It was a piece of cake finding someone to hack the database at Golde Property Management. Making it look like Kristin was past due on her rent was just as simple. Creating a chance encounter was a bit more difficult. It took two eviction notices to bump into

Kristin and *save* her. I cringed at how sleazy it all felt in hindsight.

I gripped the steering wheel as I watched Sabrina from inside the Range Rover she had provided me, to maintain my façade of wealth. The muscles in my forearms tensed into thick tendrils of rage. Rage at Sabrina for being the type of person who could cheat someone like Kristin out of her rightful future. But mostly, rage at myself for taking on this fucked-up assignment in the first place.

I didn't know what I had expected going into it, but I certainly had not expected to find a girl like Kristin, with the weight of the world on her shoulders and very little support to carry the load.

I sure as hell didn't expect to fall so fucking hard for her.

As Stan Getz played a melancholy anthem to my thoughts in "Moonlight in Vermont," I smiled as I recalled Kristin referring to my music as elevator music. The poor girl needed a serious jazz crash course if she thought bossa nova was Muzak. I hoped I would be the one to educate her.

I wanted to take her to Bill's Place on 133rd to show her the true beauty of jazz culture. It always amazed me how many Bronx natives had never been to a historic jazz club like Bill's. In the Bronx, we had so much history and good vibes at our fingertips, and still most of us just wanted to get wasted or stare at our phones on the weekend.

Most of all, I wanted to introduce Kristin to my siblings. As difficult as they could be, especially Alisha and Geneva, I knew they would like her. Kristin was humble and funny and gorgeous in an understated way. But the thing I loved the most about her was that she didn't know she was any of those things.

Did I just admit to myself that I love Kristin?
Fuck.

I shook my head and turned down my music as I watched a server bring Sabrina the bill for their meal. Then, I seethed as I watched her hand over her credit card. If she was covering the entire bill, this had to be a business dinner, paid for with the company credit card.

What kind of business dinner would Sabrina be having with two recently unemployed bodyguards? I was about to find out.

I got out of the car and made my way to the black Mercedes parked about seventy yards down Bleecker Street. Then, I hid nearby as I watched Sabrina get into the car with the license plate CFI-2691. I took a few pictures of her walking toward the car, and a few more of her getting into the driver's seat, with the license plate in frame.

It was one thing to attempt to steal hundreds of millions of dollars from an innocent girl who desperately needed it more than you. It was another thing entirely to attempt to murder that girl for your own selfish reasons.

I was not a professional investigator. Far from it, considering I fell for the subject of my first investigation. But as I watched Sabrina drive away, and I set off a safe distance behind her, I made a sacred vow to myself. Sabrina and her shadowy plans would soon be going down in a perfume-soaked ball of flames.

I couldn't sleep.

I'd nodded off twice and woken up within minutes with my heart racing. Knowing that Sabrina was out there, scheming against Kristin, had me in a state of panic I had never experienced. Before I could talk some sense into myself, I made a phone call I should have made hours ago.

As I ended the call and set the phone back on my nightstand, I let out a deep sigh of relief and fell straight to sleep.

In the morning, I went for my usual run, but when I got to Orchard Beach to see the sunrise, it didn't look as beautiful as it normally did. Not without Kristin.

Once I was showered and dressed in one of the dozen suits Sabrina had me fitted for a few weeks ago, I got in the Range Rover and drove around as I waited for the first text. Eighteen minutes later, text message number one came in from an unknown number.

Unknown:
She's on the move.

Me:
On my way.

Unknown:
False alarm. Looks like a quick run to the corner store.

Me:
Don't lose her.

Unknown:
Not a chance.

I arrived on Hughes Avenue within four minutes, just in time to see Kristin safely entering her apartment building. After parking the Range Rover less than a block away, I fired off a text as my heart rate began to slow.

Me:
I owe you one. See you tonight.

Turning down the radio, I turned on my call recorder app and made my first phone call. As the phone rang, I kept a close eye on Kristin's building from the car, a constant reminder of how my assignment had changed objectives.

Sabrina answered the call after the second ring. "Good morning, Daniel," she said. "Did your romantic beach weekend yield any interesting new leads?"

I took a deep breath to temper my rage. "New leads? Am I investigating a crime?"

Sabrina chuckled, and the sound raised the hairs on my neck. "You tell me. Has Kristin revealed anything dark and untoward during your cuddle sessions?"

I gripped the steering wheel to keep from punching the LCD screen where Sabrina's name displayed on the caller ID. "You nearly blew it when you showed up at the beach."

"*I* nearly blew it?" she replied. "The girl obviously only wants you for your money. Really, Daniel, I didn't take you for such a fool."

"I don't have money," I corrected her.

"Well, *I* know that, but Miss Teeny Weeny Bikini doesn't know that. She thinks she's hit the jackpot."

I took a deep breath to calm myself. "You don't know her. We should meet to discuss this."

"I'm very busy, Daniel. If you have something to say, you'll have to say it over the phone."

Was she recording our conversation?

I shook my head, remembering I'd done nothing wrong. I wasn't the one who had tried to run Kristin over to prevent her from claiming her inheritance.

"Actually," I began, "all I've uncovered is that this girl seems pretty down on her luck. She had to quit school to take care of her mom, who can hardly walk. She's struggling. She could really use a break."

Sabrina scoffed at my assessment. "Is that why you're getting so close to her?"

This woman had a lot of fucking nerve, accusing

me of having ulterior motives, when everything I'd done with Kristin was at her request.

"I got close to Kristin because you asked me to. I asked her to spend the weekend with me because you asked me to. I did my job and I'm giving you my findings. Now I want out."

She was silent for a long moment.

"You don't know her, Sabrina," I continued. "She has a good heart. She deserves her inheritance."

She chuckled. "You slept with her."

"What does that have to do with anything?"

"You're thinking with your dick. Just like…" She paused to collect her thoughts. "Listen here, asshole. You don't get to choose when the assignment ends. You're done when I say you're done."

"That's where you're wrong. I'm not like Michael. I'm not addicted to money. So I don't have to sit here and listen to your bullshit. You can take your severance package and shove it up your twat. I'm done when I say I'm done."

I ended the call as she was beginning to say something.

Either I made a smart decision to cut ties with her over the phone while recording the call, or it was very stupid of me to piss her off, knowing what she was capable of.

I stared at the burgundy door on the front of Kristin's building. I couldn't sit here all day long, watching that door. Keeping Kristin under my watchful eye would prove useless if something happened to her and I wasn't within arm's distance. Sitting in this car, I was basically powerless to help.

Before I did anything, I had one more call I needed to make. This time, the phone rang three times before someone picked up.

"Gruber speaking," said the voice on the other end.

"Peter, it's Daniel. I'm calling in that favor."

After a brief conversation, I ended the call and opened up my text message app to begin typing. I deleted the message and rewrote it at least three times before I finally settled on the correct angle.

Me:
Good morning, beautiful. You still working at six tonight?

Kristin:
Good morning. Yep. Still slinging sandía tonight. Are you gonna drop by for a reunion with Roger?

> **Me:**
> *How about we disappear in the Botanical Gardens for a bit? Grab some brunch. I'll bring you back in time for your shift.*
>
> **Kristin:**
> *Ooh-la-la... So spur of the moment. I like it. What time?*

We hashed out the details and I "arrived" to pick her up thirty minutes later. She stepped out of her apartment wearing a pair of cutoff jean shorts and a loose tank top tucked into her shorts. She took one look at my suit and turned on her heel to go back inside, emerging a few minutes later in the same tank top, black skinny jeans, heels, and a Yankees baseball cap.

"Beautiful," I remarked, taking her hand to lead her down the stairs.

She grinned. "Thank you."

"I was talking about the hat."

She landed a hard shove to my shoulder, but I hardly budged. "You're immovable," she complained.

I brought the back of her hand to my lips and

kissed it. "I have to be," I said, making a vague reference to my job as a bodyguard before I could stop myself.

"Why do you have to be immovable? Afraid you'll blow away?" she asked, cocking an eyebrow at me as we continued descending the stairs.

I searched my mind for a valid response, but continually came up short, so I did the only thing I could do. I changed the subject.

"How's your mom doing?"

Her smile disappeared. "She's okay. Just…I don't know what I'm…"

I gave her a moment to finish her thought, but she never continued. "You can tell me, Kris," I said as we reached the door leading out onto Hughes Avenue.

She stopped in front of the door and tilted her head as she looked up at me with a curious expression. "Have you heard from Jerry about my rent? I haven't heard anything yet, and I'm getting a little worried about coming home to another eviction notice."

Caught off guard for a moment, I finally recovered, placing a kiss on her forehead before I reached for the door. "Don't worry about Jerry. It's taken care of," I said, as we stepped out onto the sidewalk, my eyes scanning every direction. "But I'll give their office a call tomorrow and tell them to send you something official, to ease your mind."

She looked taken aback as I pulled her in front of me with both my hands grabbing her arms, my eyes continually scanning. "What are you doing?"

I led her toward the car, keeping her covered as I opened the door for her. "Nothing. Just saw some shady characters out here earlier. Get in."

She laughed as she sat in the passenger seat. "Yes, sir."

A few minutes later, we arrived at the entrance to the New York Botanical Gardens. Kristin was absolutely euphoric with all the foliage, using her smartphone camera to take dozens of pictures as references for future artwork. I joked about us getting kicked out of the gardens for sexual harassment after Kristin took at least ten pictures of a flower's reproductive organs.

Despite her obvious wonderment, and my ability to interject a joke here and there, she could see something was wrong.

"Why do you keep looking around like that? Are you being followed?" she asked very casually as we ascended the steps toward the entrance of the Enid A. Haupt Conservatory.

"Nope. Isn't there a glass sculpture over by the other entrance?" I said, motioning to the conservatory.

The building was a large glass structure, meant to let in the light for the many plants housed inside. I didn't come to the gardens often, but it was well known that the glass sculpture at the entrance to the conservatory changed periodically. Seeing as there was no sculpture near this set of doors, it had to be near one of the half-dozen or so other entrances. If Kristin suspected me of changing the subject, she didn't let on, as she quickly set off in search of the sculpture.

We were still inside the conservatory, which was quiet for a tourist attraction, when Kristin received a phone call.

"Hello?" she answered. "Why?... What? What kind of violation?... Rodents? Are you *serious*?" She rolled her eyes and let out an exasperated sigh. "Fine. Do I need to come in to clean up, or something? I can still come in if you guys need help cleaning... Okay, all right. Well, thanks for letting me know." She ended the call and stared at her phone for a few seconds, lost in her thoughts.

"What's wrong?" I asked, knowing what the answer would be.

"There was a surprise inspection by the health department today and we were shut down for evidence of a rodent infestation, which is weird because our staff is *super* clean. Helen—one of the other waitresses—said they closed us down for three days until they can come back out and reinspect." She shook her head. "I really needed those tips."

My stomach ached with guilt as I realized I had just literally cost Kristin some of her much-needed income. I needed to find a way to tell her the truth about what Sabrina and I had been up to, but until I figured that out, I had to devise a way to keep her safe. The only way to keep her safe was to keep her by my side. Getting my buddy to call his sister at the health department and close down Cantina Joe's for a few days would buy me some time. But I never considered how it would affect Kristin financially.

With her mom having just spent a few days in the hospital, Kristin probably expected the medical bills to begin rolling into her mailbox soon. I remember when I was driving my mom to her chemo and radiation appointments, I always made sure to check the mail and throw away any medical bills before she saw them. I didn't want her to worry about money on top of contemplating her own mortality.

Right now, Kristin probably felt a desperate need to stockpile her tips and work as many hours as possible to make some extra cash. I may have shut down Cantina Joe's because I was willing to do anything to protect Kristin, but her safety wasn't the only part of her that needed protection. If I didn't sack up and fess up to her soon, I was going to lose her in more ways than I cared to imagine.

"Hey," I said, lifting her chin so I could look her in the eye. "I don't want you to worry about whether or not you make enough tips or work enough hours. If you come up short, I'll take care of it." I grabbed her face to hold her head still as she tried to shake her head. "That's not an offer, it's a fact. I'm going to take care of you."

She smiled as I reached up and turned her Yankees cap backward. "You only like me because of my taste in sports teams," she teased.

I leaned forward and placed a soft kiss on her warm lips. "That's just a bonus. I like you because you're *my* Picasso," I said, looking her in the eye. "You're priceless."

Kristin smiled as her cheeks flushed pink and I pulled her into my arms so she couldn't see the uncertainty in my eyes. I didn't know how long I could keep her safe, but I knew I would stop at nothing to try. I had no fucking choice. I was recklessly in love with her.

20. Rich Asshole

I HAD NEVER BEEN so startled by a knock at the door in all my life.

As I made my way across the living room, I replayed in my mind the post-accident statement I'd given to the police less than a month ago. No matter how hard I tried, I couldn't remember what I'd said to the officers on the scene.

Maybe the gaps in my memory were due to the mild concussion, or a severe case of shock. I could only imagine I was about as coherent as a drunken toddler when I gave that statement. However, I did remember the events leading up to the accident. Unfortunately, I remembered that very well.

I hated being a clock watcher. It wasn't as if I wasn't accustomed to sitting in cars waiting for people. Sitting around and waiting was ninety percent of my job. The reunion reception was supposed to end at ten p.m. But as the parking lot began to empty, and the clock crawled past midnight, I began to worry.

Exiting the BMW i8, I made sure to press the button on the key fob to activate the alarm, even though I knew the alarm was automatically activated as I walked away. It was not every day that I drove my boss around in his new $160,000 sports car. And, because I couldn't resist, I glanced back at the car to make certain it was still in the parking space where I'd left it—and to admire it—before I entered the Vanderbilt Hall reception area.

A group of men in expensive suits had gathered in the far corner. They all laughed and gestured raucously, most of them still holding empty cocktail glasses in their hands. A bartender was cleaning up behind the bar as janitorial staff picked up trash off the floors and empty wine glasses off tables.

A gentleman who looked like a waiter in a starched white shirt and black slacks approached me. "Excuse me, sir, but you'll have to leave. We're locking up soon."

I nodded at him. "I'm just here to pick up my boss, Michael Becker."

His eyes widened a bit at the mention of Michael's name, then he nodded. "Of course, sir. Can you please tell him that we were supposed to clear the building and lock up by midnight?"

"Will do," I said, continuing toward the corner.

Michael Becker stood at the center of the group of men, telling a story or joke that had the other men enthralled with laughter. I walked slowly toward the group, giving Becker time to finish his tale before I interrupted. When I was within a few yards, he noticed me and insisted a few of the men make way as I approached.

"Good evening, sir," I said, nodding at Becker as I glanced around the group, taking in everyone's face. *"I've been informed by the university that they will be closing the doors to Vanderbilt Hall very soon. We should get going, sir."*

"Gentlemen, this is my bodyguard, Daniel...Daniel...? What's your last name again, Daniel?" Becker said, draping his arm across my shoulders.

"Meyers, sir."

He smiled as he tightened his arm around my neck and pointed at me with his other hand, which was still precariously holding a half-empty cocktail glass. "Good-looking kid. If...and I mean if *I had a daughter, Daniel would get my blessing. Everyone knows it's aesthetics that matter above all else. Right, Meyers?"*

I politely wriggled out of his grasp. "Of course. We should get going, sir."

Becker cocked an eyebrow as he stared into his glass. "Yes, aesthetics matter, but so does power. Did any of you see my i8 in the lot?" he asked, looking around at the other men. "That beauty is power personified—357 horsepower, to be exact. Wanna have a look?"

The men, who seemed to be in some sort of drunken trance, all voiced their agreement with slurred variations of "Fuck, yeah."

I trailed closely behind the group, nodding at the cleaning staff in a modest gesture of apology and reassurance that we would soon be out of their way. After a bit of redirecting, I herded the men toward the exit leading to the parking lot on the 3rd Street side of the building.

The balmy July heat had melted into the earth, leaving behind a sizzling promise of trouble that hung in the air. I hoped the rest of these men were taking taxis or calling for a ride, because none of them seemed sober enough to drive, except Michael.

I had worked for Becker for less than a month, but I'd already seen him plastered on at least two occasions. When he was drunk, he had a very obvious tell. It was my job to notice these things. When Michael was drunk, he forgot people's first names.

It made sense, considering he probably knew a thousand Bobs, Tims, Richards, Johns, and Daniels. Last names were often more distinct. Either Michael wasn't aware of his own shortcomings when he was tipsy or, more likely, he was signaling to me that he wasn't really drunk. He was putting on a show for the guys.

Or he was using reverse psychology on me, trying to make me believe he wasn't drunk when he was actually wasted. Fuck. *This job was becoming more complicated by the minute.*

It was a beautiful summer night in New York. A few of the men closed their eyes and tilted their heads back to savor the fresh air on their faces. I shook my head as I led the way to Becker's new BMW i8. The few with their eyes open either whistled or let out various curious words at the sight of the crystal-white electric sports car with the blue accent stripe.

They discussed the virtues of the i8 over the Tesla for a few minutes as I kept a vigilant watch over the various entrances to the parking lot. A group of drunk, unarmed, presumably rich assholes was a robbery waiting to happen. Finally, the men said their good-byes and wandered off into various directions, muttering about their intentions to catch cabs and Ubers. Obviously, these men were not as well off as I had assumed.

Michael held his hand out to me palm up. "Key fob."

I cocked an eyebrow. "I'm sorry, sir. Are you telling me you want to drive?"

"Don't play dumb with me, Meyers. You know I'm not drunk. This is my *car. Now, give me the key fob or tomorrow you can look for a job elsewhere."*

I looked him in the eye, waiting for him to tell me he was kidding, but he clearly wasn't. "Sir, I really don't think that's a good idea. You may not be drunk, but you've—"

"If you don't give me that key, so help me I will call the

police and charge you with theft."

I chuckled. "I'm sorry, sir, but I'm pretty sure the police will understand why I'm not letting you get in that driver's seat."

He shrugged. "Maybe. Or maybe they'll believe the rich asshole over the poor schmuck. You want to take that chance, Meyers?"

I gritted my teeth as I realized he really wasn't drunk, but that didn't mean he was sober enough to drive. I was fucked either way.

"When was the last time you drove this thing?" I asked, slipping my hand into the pocket of my slacks to retrieve the key fob.

"I drove it last week!" he replied impatiently, glancing in the direction of the sidewalk, where one of his former law school cronies was watching our exchange.

I handed over the key fob and he snatched it out of my hand. "Just try not to kill us," I muttered under my breath as I walked around the back of the car toward the passenger side.

"What did you say?" he asked as he slid into the driver's seat.

"Nothing, sir," I said, getting into the passenger seat and shutting the door. "Please feel free to pull over if you get tired or just don't feel like driving anymore."

"Jesus Christ. Give it a rest, already. I'm fine!"

I buckled my seat belt and watched as he tossed the key fob into the cup holder and pressed the START button on the *dashboard. The car didn't start, and he shook his head as he seemed to remember he needed to press down on the brake as he pushed the START button.*

Once the car was idling, I gently reminded him to put his seat belt on, but he waved off my suggestion as he lowered his window to let in some fresh air. I tried to think of what, if anything, I could do to prevent a car accident from where I was seated. I didn't know how the BMW i8 worked, but it was possible I could hit the START button to kill the engine if it became clear Michael wasn't driving safely. But that wouldn't help much if we were barreling over a guardrail or into a brick wall.

I could kill the engine at the first sign that he wasn't fit to be driving tonight. Then, I could grab the steering wheel and guide the car to safety. My other hand would grab the key fob and toss it out the window, away from the vehicle, so Michael wouldn't be able to restart the car.

Fuck. *This job was getting way too fucking complicated.*

His driving was a bit choppy as he made his way out of the parking lot onto 3rd Street. But as soon as he was on the road, he smoothed out, and I allowed myself to relax a little. Big mistake.

"See, this is not so bad, right?" Becker said, taking a smooth left turn. "It's not so bad to let your boss remember what it was like before he became a rich asshole and had everything done for him like a fucking invalid. Right?"

"Right," I said, unable to decide if I felt more angry with

him or sorry for him.

We were six blocks from Becker's townhouse, and the traffic light had just turned green, when he pulled forward and BOOM! We were T-boned in the middle of the intersection, by a woman who was distracted by her phone.

I stared at the doorknob, willing myself to turn it so I could finally face the person I knew was standing on the other side of the door.

"Who is it?" Geneva shouted from the bedroom she shared with Alisha.

"It's not for you!" I shouted back as I reached for the doorknob.

Taking a deep breath before I opened the door, I was not at all surprised to find a man in a freshly starched white shirt and slacks, a badge hanging from a chain that dangled around his thick neck.

"Detective Jones?" I said, opening the door wide to invite him inside.

"Mr. Meyers. May I come in?" he replied in a deep, authoritative voice.

"Please," I said, stepping aside and motioning to the sofa my little brother slept on every night. "Have a seat."

He pulled a notepad and pen out of his back pocket before he took a seat on the sofa.

"Would you like something to drink?" I offered. "All I have is water and OJ."

"I'm fine, thanks," he replied, writing something on his notepad. "I'd prefer to just get right to it, if you don't mind."

"Not at all," I said, swallowing hard as I took a seat in the armchair to the right of the sofa. "Ask away."

Jones cleared his throat. "You said in your report—"

"I actually don't remember what I said in that rep—"

He held up a hand to stop me. "Let me finish, please. Then, you can speak."

I nodded and pressed my lips together tightly to keep from calling the guy a prick.

"Okay, as I was saying. You said in your report that you didn't know Mr. Becker had been drinking that night. If you're his bodyguard, weren't you supposed to be watching him all night long?"

I paused a moment to collect my thoughts. "Mike—I mean, Mr. Becker asked me to stay in the car. It was some kind of college or fraternity reunion. I can't remember. Anyway, he said he didn't want people to think he was an asshole—his words—for bringing a bodyguard."

Jones pursed his lips as he stared at me for a

moment, lost in thought. "So...you didn't assume that Mr. Becker would be drinking at a fraternity reunion?"

I sighed as I leaned forward, resting my elbows on my knees. "Look, I never personally saw him drink anything. And he was my employer. If he said he wasn't drunk, I wasn't going to call him a liar."

"But your job was to protect Mr. Becker from all possible threats, even himself. Was it not?"

I shrugged. "I didn't want to lose my job."

"So you risked losing your life by allowing a possibly intoxicated man to drive a car while you were in the passenger seat."

"He threatened me. He said he would fire me or call the cops and say I was trying to steal his car." I closed my eyes and gritted my teeth as I tried to block out the images of Michael's head, lopsided from the impact. "He said he just wanted to remember what his life was like before he became a rich asshole."

I opened my eyes and Jones was looking at me through narrowed brown eyes, one eyebrow cocked skeptically as he sized me up. As he opened his mouth to speak, the phone attached to his belt buzzed loudly. He slipped it out of the clip, glanced at the screen, then answered the call.

"Jones." His eyebrows scrunched together as he listened to the person on the other end. "I told Reyes to interview the mother. She's the alibi witness... How am I supposed to fucking know where he is? Am I his fucking wife?... Well, someone has to do it before the 72-hour hold is up or that little fucker's gonna run... No, I'm in the middle of an interview... The Becker accident..." He shook his head and let out an angry sigh. "Just get me the *fucking* address. I'll do it."

I looked Jones in the eye as he ended the call. "Look, Becker threatened to make up a story that I was trying to steal his car if I didn't give him the keys. I had no choice."

He shook his head. "I can see you're upset. We'll continue this conversation later. I'll give you a call."

"I'm fine," I insisted, eager to get this interview over with.

He stood from the sofa. "I have somewhere else I need to be. We'll resume this interview later."

He followed me to the door.

"Should I have a lawyer present?" I asked, placing my hand on the doorknob without turning it.

He raised his eyebrows. "I don't know. Do you think you need one?"

I sighed as I opened the door. "I guess we'll talk later."

Closing the door behind Jones, I turned and leaned my back against the cool wood slab, still gripping the knob as I shook my head. This was like a game to him, but to me it was my life, and I wasn't playing it right.

I had to get a lawyer before I spoke to Jones again. The last thing my family needed was another father figure in prison.

Maybe I should have told Jones about Sabrina, and her plan to defraud Kristin out of her inheritance. Then, I ran my hand roughly down my face in frustration. If I told Jones about that, I'd have to tell him about my involvement in Sabrina's scheme. I was officially fucked.

21. Hush-Hush

I TOLD OLLIE AND ZANE to meet me at Tino's Bar to get a drink and pick up some girls, because if I'd said we were just going to get a drink they would have suggested we get a case of PBR and drink at Ollie's apartment instead. But I really didn't feel like being around Ollie's mom and sister, Betty, right now.

Betty had had a crush on me since elementary school, and his mom was constantly trying to force greasy food down my throat. I couldn't maintain my alluring physique on a diet of macaroni and cheese and fried pickles. Alisha would throw her phone at my head if she heard me say that out loud.

The truth was, I just wanted to get out of the

house to a friendly—and relatively noisy—bar, where I could have a chat with my two best friends without being overheard by any of our family members.

Ollie and I had been friends since I kicked his ass in first grade. Zane joined our little brotherhood in middle school, when he moved to the Bronx from Cleveland. We were all knuckleheads back then. Well, Zane was still kind of a knucklehead, but at least he had moved out of his mom's house, even if it was to live with Yasmin, who hated Ollie and me with the fire of a thousand suns.

"Why the fuck are we at Tino's?" Ollie complained. "There hasn't been a decent girl in this shit-hole in at least thirty years."

"Hey, watch your mouth, Dumbo," Patty the barmaid barked at Ollie.

Zane and I laughed as Ollie subconsciously ran his finger along the back of his ear and said, "Come on, Patty. You know my mom couldn't afford to get my ears pinned."

Patty looked much too small and old to be working behind a bar in the Bronx. Her father had opened the place in the '60s, when Patty was a teenager. Now in her early sixties, with her father having passed away almost a decade ago, Patty knew every single person who walked through the doors. And by *knew*, I meant she knew almost everything about them, from their family history to their relationship woes. Patty was everyone's grandmother, mother, aunt, sister, friend, whatever you needed her to be.

Patty pursed her thin lips, then leaned forward and pinched Ollie's cheek. "I know, sweetie. I'm just teasing you, you handsome little devil."

Ollie blushed. "Aw, man, Patty. You're embarrassing me."

I shook my head and ordered a couple pitchers of beer, then carried them to a table in the corner of the dimly lit bar. Bobby Nunzio and his cousin, whose name I couldn't remember, were playing darts about ten feet away, just out of earshot.

I barely participated in the conversation, nodding my head when Ollie asked if he could borrow some of my tools so he could work on his thirteen-year-old Altima, and shaking my head when Ollie asked if he could bring a girl to my house while my sisters were at school. Then, Zane started reminiscing about the time we snuck a bottle of Bacardi 151 into school, and got so blasted from a couple of sips that we spent the entire next period in the wrong classroom. This memory, and the way he laughed so hard as he recalled it, made me think of what Kristin had confessed to me.

I didn't think of myself as the type of guy who

sought out women who needed to be saved. Kristin might argue otherwise. But the girls I'd dated before were nothing like Kristin. Unsurprisingly, they were more like my mom: loud, opinionated, and fiercely independent.

Kristin had the Miss Independent act down pat, but that wasn't who she was. She was strong on the outside, with a fragile heart, which had not been handled with care up to this point.

I downed another beer as I realized that, very soon, I would be just another person in a long line of people who had queued up to break Kristin's heart. When I was four and a half beers down, and my courage meter had leveled up, I decided it was time.

"I think I met a girl," I said, staring at the sweat collecting on my fifth glass of PBR.

"You *think* you met a girl?" Zane replied in his unnaturally deep voice. "Is this the girl you have me stalking while you're asleep?"

I ignored Ollie's high-pitched laughter as I continued, "Dude, you have no idea what I've gotten myself into. I met a girl, and I like her."

Zane cocked an eyebrow. "You *like* her? What are you in, fucking second grade? You *like* her?" He glared at me incredulously. "Why the fuck am I watching this girl's apartment for you? Is she one of your rich clients? 'Cause that's a shitty place to live if you're rich enough for a bodyguard."

I shook my head. "She's not a client. Well...not really."

Ollie tilted his head. "Seems like a pretty straightforward question to me: Is she or isn't she a fucking client? Why are you being all spooky about it?"

I stared at the bubbles on the surface of the beer in my mug for a while, trying to figure out how to word my answer without giving away Kristin's identity. "She's...She's someone I met recently."

"Why the fuck do you look like you've just seen a ghost?" Zane asked, clearly confused by my cryptic answer. "Is the pussy that good? Can I get in on that?"

I shook my head as Zane and Ollie bumped fists. "Nah, man, she's not like Yasmin. She actually has standards."

Ollie laughed even louder. "Third-degree burn!" he said, pointing at Zane.

Zane pushed Ollie's finger out of his face and turned back to me. "Why the fuck do you have me watching this girl's apartment in the middle of the fucking night?"

I sighed as I wrapped both hands around my glass and tried not to think about how I was leaving Kristin's apartment unattended while we were sitting here. "Because it was her dad…"

Ollie's laughter sputtered to a stop. "What the fuck are you talking about?"

I tore my gaze away from the glass and looked back and forth between Zane and Ollie. "My boss…the one who died in the accident… He was her father."

Ollie scrunched his eyebrows together in confusion. "Did you meet her at the funeral or something?" he asked, then he smiled as he shook his head. "That's sick, man. You've got sick moves with the ladies, bro."

I rolled my eyes. "I didn't meet her at the funeral."

"Then how the fuck did you come at her?" Zane asked, a note of anger in his voice.

As much as Zane liked to talk about cheating on Yasmin and pretending like girls were just objects to be toyed with, he actually had a very low tolerance for men who disrespected women. Having grown up in a household of females, and dealing with the aftermath of his cousin's rape in high school, Zane did not fuck around when it came to men who took advantage of women.

"Ah, fuck," I whispered, as I realized I'd probably already said too much. I couldn't let Zane and Ollie in on the arrangement I'd had with Sabrina, but I also couldn't lie to my best friends. "I'm supposed to be...interviewing her or something."

"Or something?" Ollie said. "Or what...fucking her? Is that what you mean? Why the fuck are you being all hush-hush about this? Spit it out, motherfucker."

I drew in a deep breath and tried to ignore the feeling that everyone in the bar was staring at me. "It's just...I told you my boss was rich, and...so now that he's dead, all that money has to go somewhere, but...my new boss asked me to do a little...reconnaissance."

"Reconnaissance?" Zane interrupted. "Is that what you were hired to do? 'Cause I seem to remember you telling me you got a job as a bodyguard, not a fucking Secret Service agent. What the fuck?"

Shit. If Zane could already see where this was going, and he was this annoyed, that meant the situation was even more of a clusterfuck than I thought it was.

I shook my head, then downed the rest of my beer. "Forget it, man. I know what I have to do. I'm gonna take care of this. Trust me."

Zane and Ollie looked at each other, then Ollie said something I'd be repeating in my mind as I lay in bed later that night. "I don't know what the fuck you're into, Danny, but you've got your sisters and bro to think about. Don't fuck that up."

22. Come Clean Again

I WOKE ON WEDNESDAY morning with a sense of dread weighing on me so heavily, I could hardly drag myself out of bed. Today was the last day of the three-day shutdown I had orchestrated at Cantina Joe's. Kristin would return to work tomorrow. As much as I dreaded this conversation, I had to tell Kristin the truth about me and, most importantly, the truth about her father today.

Once Kristin knew the truth, there would be no reason for Sabrina to try to remove her from the equation. And Zane could go back to using his late nights and early mornings to play video games, the way he normally did after he worked the late shift.

Once I was showered and dressed, I disabled the

anti-theft tracking service in the Range Rover. If anyone tried to look up its last location, it would ping from my apartment building. Then, I shot off a text to Zane. He responded to my message from his burner phone with a seven-word reminder of last night's conversation at Tino's.

Me:

I'll take it from here. Thanks for helping me out. I owe you at least two pitchers for this.

Unknown:

Fuck the pitchers. Think of your family.

Harsh words, but he was right. I had been thinking of my siblings' long-term futures when I made the deal with Sabrina, but I hadn't been thinking of their immediate futures. I should have considered the possibility that, other than being completely immoral, the deal I made with Sabrina might actually be illegal.

Blinded by the possibility of a huge payout, of not having to stress about money anymore, I allowed my greed to overrule my reason. Plain and simple, I was blind and stupid. Maybe I was more like my convict father than I thought.

I pulled onto Hughes Avenue just in time to see Zane's car turning the corner to leave. It was still dark out. I hated to wake Kristin this early, but I was selfish. I wanted one last quiet moment with her. I figured it would be safer to meet her early in the morning, before the morning shift change, where Gene would normally come in for work at eight a.m.

Gene and Barry were obviously still working for Sabrina, despite her claims she had laid them off. I didn't know what kind of work they were doing for her, but I had to assume the worst. I also couldn't allow them to keep Kristin and me locked away in our apartments like prisoners.

The phone rang twice before Kristin answered. "Daniel? It's so early," she said, her voice groggy and rough.

"I know. I'm sorry to wake you. I just wanted to show you something. Can you take a ride with me?"

She cleared her throat before she responded. "I'll be down in a few."

Of course, I couldn't allow her to come down by herself. Luckily, it seemed Kristin's neighbor had broken the buzzer again. I raced up to the fifth floor and waited in the corridor outside apartment 502. My heart raced at the thought that I was being reckless by asking Kristin to go out in public with me. But I had managed to keep her safe since we came back from the Hamptons. I needed to share this one thing with her before I made her hate me.

She came out of her apartment with her brown hair in a messy bun, wearing a pair of pink sweatpants and a faded black tank top, but I'd never seen her look more beautiful.

"You're stunning," I said, planting a kiss on her forehead.

"Yeah, real fucking gorgeous," she said, closing the door behind her.

"Did you lock the door?"

She looked at me like I was crazy. "Uh, yes, Dad."

I smiled at her joke, though inside I cringed at the irony that she had jokingly called me Dad right before I was about to tell her the truth about her real dad. Despite my efforts to remain inconspicuous, I was beginning to realize that Kristin was quite observant. As we walked to the Range Rover, she shot me another crazy look as I used my body to block her when a stake-bed truck drove past us.

"You should think of applying for the Secret Service," she said with a chuckle as she slid into the passenger seat.

"Very funny," I replied before I closed the passenger door and took a quick glance up and down the street.

As I got into the driver's seat, I could feel her staring at me.

"You've been pretty jumpy lately. Mind telling me what the fuck is going on?"

I smiled as I pulled away from the curb. "I'll tell you everything very soon. I just need you to see something first."

She shrugged and slumped down in the seat, not bothering to change the jazz radio station as she made herself comfortable. Good. The lower she sat in the seat, the safer she would be if we were ambushed. The more relaxed she was, the less likely she was to be seriously injured in a car accident.

I was completely aware that my thoughts sounded like the thoughts of a paranoid crazy person. I had accepted that my behavior would seem overprotective and possibly extremely strange to Kristin. It was a small price to pay to keep her safe.

We arrived at Orchard Beach about fifteen minutes later, having encountered very little traffic on Pelham Parkway at this early hour. Switching off the car, I sat for a moment, savoring the quiet companionship of this amazing woman. Then, I reached out and grabbed her hand and brought it to my lips.

"I'm going to show you something you've

probably never seen, but you have to promise me that you won't forget who showed it to you."

She laughed. "This better not be a trick. I don't want to go out there just so you can show me a tent where the bums go to jerk off."

I couldn't help but laugh. "You think I'd do that to you?" I said, shaking my head. "Get your mind out of the gutter and follow me."

I made sure to glance around as we exited the SUV, letting out a sigh of relief as I saw no other cars in the dark parking lot. Grabbing her hand, I led her down the beach access road. We passed the empty Pelican Bay Playground on our right, before the narrow road deposited us onto the promenade.

"Have you ever been here this early?" I asked as we approached the waist-high railing that separated the paved promenade from the sandy beach.

She grabbed the railing as she looked sideways at me. "No, I'm not crazy. I don't wake up at the crack of dawn like you do."

"Only when you're in the Hamptons, right?"

She smiled at my reference to how she woke up early after we spent the night together. "That's different. I don't get to wake up in the Hamptons every day."

"Well, you're in for a treat, young lady. This is by

far the best place to watch the sunrise in the Bronx."

She turned toward me now, tilting her head. "And how do you know the best place to watch the sunrise in the Bronx?"

"Look over there," I said, pointing across the water toward Oyster Bay, where a hint of golden glow began to creep up the horizon. "This is where I come every morning—well, haven't had a chance to run for the past three days—but this is where I come most mornings to run."

Her gaze was still focused on the horizon, where I'd directed her to look. "Wow..." she whispered as the sky burst into an array of golden light shooting out of an apricot sun. "What's the name of that feeling you get when you see something too beautiful for words?"

I stood in awe of her as she stood in awe of the sunrise, unable to tear my gaze away from her. "Kristin."

She smiled as she flicked her head around to look at me. "It's not called Kristin," she said, then she landed a weak shove to my shoulder. "Why do you come to the Bronx to run? Aren't there better places to do that in the Village?"

I shook my head. "Kristin, I don't live in the Village."

Her smile quickly faded. "What do you mean?"

I stole a glance at the glorious sunrise I'd seen a thousand times before, then I looked her in the eye and steeled myself for her reaction as I said, "I live in the Bronx, not too far from you, actually. I don't drive a Range Rover, and I don't have a beach house in the Hamptons. I've been pretending to be someone I'm not, someone with a lot of money, so I could get close to you… for my boss."

She cocked her left eyebrow and chuckled nervously. "What? Is this some kind of joke?"

I shook my head. "I fucking wish. I began working for your father, Michael Beck—"

"My *father*?" she interrupted. "What are you talking about, Daniel? You'd better not be fucking with me."

I held up my hand. "Please just breathe. I know this is a lot to take in, but I need to tell you everything."

She drew in a deep breath and let it out slowly.

I nodded. "Okay," I began. "I started working for your dad, Michael Becker, a couple of months ago. But we were in an accident about a month ago and… he died." I gave her a moment to absorb this information before I continued. "Michael was worth hundreds of millions of dollars. When I went to collect my last paycheck, my new boss, Sabrina—whom you already met—was reading some kind of journal your dad had left behind. There was a lot of stuff in there about you and your mom."

Her eyebrows scrunched together in a pained expression that ripped me apart. "My mom? My mom knows about this?"

I shook my head adamantly. "No, your mom knew nothing about this." I braced myself as I prepared to tell her the worst. "Sabrina must have thought I was going to tell someone about you and that was probably going to affect how much money and control she got over your father's company. So she offered me a ridiculous amount of money...if I got to know you and reported to her what I found out."

Her lips began to tremble as tears collected in her eyes. "You were paid to be with me?"

"I wasn't paid anything," I assured her. "Sabrina expected me to find out something about you that would make you unworthy of your inheritance, but I told her you deserved every penny of it." I reached for her face and she smacked my hand away.

"Don't touch me," she said as she began walking down the promenade. "You mean, you didn't tell her how I nearly killed my best friend? How *noble* of you."

"Please don't go in that direction," I said, catching up to her. "There's more you need to know, and it's better if we stay still."

"Was it all a lie?" she said, not looking at me as she continued to walk. "Oh, God... Is your mom even dead?"

"It's not safe for us to walk out here. Please stop, Kris."

She stopped in the middle of the boardwalk and glared at me. "Don't call me that! You have no right to call me that!"

"You're right," I agreed. "I have no right to even be near you after what I've done. I fucked up. I hurt you, probably more than anyone has ever hurt you. I know that. And I'll never stop regretting it. But I need you to listen to what I have to say because, as fucked up as this whole situation is, I'm in *love* with you...and what I'm about to say could save your life."

She covered her mouth as she looked up at me with pure heartbreak in her eyes. "How could you do this? What did I do to deserve this?"

I pulled her hand away from her mouth and wrapped my arms around her, surprised when she allowed me to pull her close as she sobbed into my chest. "You need to go home and tell your mom everything I just told you. Tell your mom and everyone you know. It's the only thing that will keep Sabrina from hurting you. Promise me you'll do that."

She pushed me away roughly. "My mom wouldn't

keep this kind of thing from me. You're lying!"

I followed as she continued down the promenade, glancing around to make sure we were still alone. "Kristin, you have to believe me. You're in real danger," I said, trying to grab her arm to stop her, but she smacked my hand away again. "Kristin, please, I'm a professional bodyguard. I assess security risk for a living, and your risk is sky-high right now, unless you get home and tell your mom you know about your real dad. You need to go now."

She shook her head as she continued walking. "You're a bodyguard? That explains the thing with Roger and all the paranoia. God, I'm so stupid."

We passed the swimming facility on our right and I tried to look into the dark shadows created by the building, but the sun hadn't fully risen yet. Kristin and I were a couple of sitting ducks out here on this open promenade. I needed to get her back to the parking lot, to the safety of the SUV, so I could take her home.

"You're not stupid," I insisted, "but you need to come back to the car with me before something bad happens."

"Are you threatening me?" she shrieked as she wiped away tears.

"No!" I yelled, letting my frustration get the best of me. "I told you, it's Sabrina that wants to hurt you.

She's the one who tried to run you down in the Hamptons."

She finally stopped walking, and that was when I saw it, a black Mercedes coming slowly down the access road near the swimming facility with its headlights off. Unfortunately, whoever was driving saw me see them, and they gunned the engine, coming straight toward us.

"We have to run!" I shouted, grabbing Kristin's arm and racing down the boardwalk toward the grassy park area ahead of us on the right.

The Mercedes skidded right onto the promenade, about a hundred yards behind us, as we began to cut across the park. The car would only have minor difficulty getting over the concrete curb into the park area, but it might be enough for us to lose them in the small wooded area along the parkway. Then, we could come out the other side of the road and flag down a passing vehicle on Park Drive.

"Are they coming after *us*?" Kristin shouted as we continued running across the grass toward the tree line.

"They're after *you*!" I replied. "Don't look back! Just keep running until I tell you to stop!"

A loud clunking noise startled us, and we both looked over our shoulders to see the Mercedes barreling over the concrete curb and bouncing onto the grass. As we made it to the tree line, the squeal of the Mercedes' wheels sliding over the dewy grass became softer. They would need to slow down to drive around the trees, which, unfortunately, weren't close enough together to completely prevent them from following in the car.

Kristin screamed as she tripped on a fallen branch. The adrenaline coursing through my veins gave me the strength to slide my hands under her arms and lift her off the ground as if she weighed nothing. We continued toward the highway, with no choice but to slow down as we attempted not to get tripped up on the brush and branches again. The sound of the Mercedes' engine continued to get closer as it cut a careful path through the trees.

Kristin glanced behind her and screamed again.

"Don't look back! Just keep running!" I shouted.

"They're getting closer!"

I could see the headlights of the passing vehicles on Park Drive. "Keep running!"

As soon as the road came into view, we burst out of the woods, racing across the narrow parkway, putting more obstacles between us and the Mercedes. But the moment we slowed down to attempt to flag down a vehicle, the first shot rang out. My first instinct was to push Kristin to the ground and throw myself on top of her.

The second shot hit me in the shoulder, feeling more like a powerful punch than a piercing sensation. I braced myself for more gunshots, as the sound of the blast echoed inside my skull. Was it an echo, or were they still shooting?

I kept Kristin's body covered with mine. I was about to raise my head, when the loud screech of tires encouraged me to keep my head down. The screeching came to an abrupt stop. For a few seconds, everything was quiet. Then, the sound of Kristin's sobs cut through the silence.

PART III: The Heiress

KRISTIN

23. Batman

BEFORE WE WERE CHASED through the woods and across the highway, Daniel asked me to tell everyone I could about the things he'd told me. And, as I waited to be updated on his condition, I did just that.

The first person I told about my real father, Michael Becker, was the woman who nearly ran over our attacker.

The attacker had exited the black Mercedes to chase Daniel and me across the parkway. Luckily, nearly being spread across the highway like butter on toast had scared him off, and he didn't attempt to pursue us or attack the woman who nearly killed him.

He fled the scene, but not before he had let off two gunshots, one of which ripped through Daniel's flesh and bone.

The second person I told was Officer Henley, who was the first to arrive at the scene.

Then, I told the medics who worked to stabilize Daniel as they slid him into the back of the ambulance.

When I arrived at Bronx-Lebanon hospital in the back of Officer Henley's cruiser, I rushed inside and told the triage nurse, who had been told they were bringing me in to be treated for possible shock.

I wasn't in shock. I was determined not to let Daniel down.

I wanted to be angry at Daniel for deceiving me. I wanted to rage at the injustice of discovering most of my life as the disadvantaged daughter of a single mother was a sham. I wanted to curse my mother for keeping something so important as the identity of my wealthy father from me. But all I felt was a hurt so deep and so profound that it actually felt empowering.

I would probably never again in my life be as painfully betrayed as I was today. There was nowhere to go from here except up and out of the dark hole I'd dug for myself two years ago. Today, the downward descent was over. And I was hysterical with relief.

As I sat on the hospital bed, waiting for the

emergency room doctor to examine me for signs of shock, I repeated the lines in my head so I would be ready to tell him or her my story.

My father's name is Michael Becker. He died last month. One of his associates named Sabrina has been trying to keep me from my inheritance. Today, she tried to kill me.

As the curtain surrounding my hospital bed began to stir with movement, I prepared myself to see a man or woman in a white coat. When the curtain was pulled aside, Leslie's concerned face looked back at me. In a wheelchair at her side, my mom stared up at me with pure fear behind the tears in her eyes. Whoever had called her, possibly Officer Henley, had probably repeated the story I'd told so many times this morning.

"You knew this whole time," I said, my voice hardly louder than a whisper.

"He was a bad person, Kristin," she said, wheeling herself to my bedside so close that my dangling feet touched the side of her wheel. "A very mean man who would have abandoned us the first chance he got."

"You didn't even give him a *chance* to abandon us?"

She shook her head. "You don't understand. It's...a very long story. Yes, I should have told you, but you were always too young to understand. And then, when you got older, I thought it had been so long that it wouldn't matter anymore."

"It wouldn't matter?" I replied, the relief I'd felt earlier disintegrating into grief. "You thought it wouldn't matter that my father was *alive*, not killed in some bogus car accident when I was a baby?"

"Kristin, please—"

"I'll never get to know my father because now he really *is* dead! And I had to find that out from his former bodyguard, who also happens to be the man who was pretending to be interested in me for what I am instead of *who* I am."

That was when I broke. As the epiphany rolled over me, I realized this was what would hurt the most, never knowing if Daniel had been interested in me because of the kind of person I was. Or if he only got close to me because of my inheritance. Would I ever be able to trust anyone again?

I didn't want to consider the possibility that, if Daniel made it out of that surgery room alive, I would never see him again. But I didn't know what other option I had, knowing he had so thoroughly fooled me. If he was such a good actor that I was convinced he was extremely wealthy, how did I know he wasn't acting when he said he was in love with me?

"What happened to Daniel?" Leslie chimed in, probably trying to ease some of the tension.

I shook my head. "He was shot," I said, my voice

cracking on the last syllable. "He was pretending to be rich to impress me, or something. He was my dad's bodyguard before he died." I looked into my mom's eyes as I delivered the next line. "It's a long story."

My mother's expression hardened. "You have every right to be angry with me. You have every right to lash out at me. But you have no right to judge me. I made a decision, a decision I thought was the best for *you*. Everything I've done, I did for you." Her features softened again. "You're the most precious thing in my world. Please believe me when I say I never meant to hurt you. I was trying to protect you."

I wiped at the tears running down my cheeks as I slid off the hospital bed. "I can't sit here doing nothing. Tell the doctor I left because I was feeling fine. I have some calls to make."

My mom grabbed my hand as I began to walk away. "I love you so much, sweetheart. I am *so* sorry that I hurt you."

I let out a deep sigh, then I kissed the top of my mom's head before I set off out of the emergency room, up one elevator, and down a few corridors, until I determined that I was sufficiently lost. Finding a relatively quiet waiting room in the radiology department, I took a seat on an uncomfortable metal bench and began typing a message.

Me:

I'm so sorry, but I'm probably not going to make it to Michaelangelo's tonight. I'm at the hospital. I'm waiting for a

I couldn't even finish typing the sentence "I'm waiting for a friend to get out of surgery." Daniel wasn't a friend. Was he? What kind of terrible person would I be if I canceled my meeting with Petra, the friend I'd betrayed so badly, so I could be a good friend to the man who'd betrayed me? I deleted the last line and continued typing.

Me:

I'm so sorry, but I'm probably not going to make it to Michaelangelo's tonight. I'm at the hospital. I was shot at today. I'm fine, but I'm waiting to see if the guy who was with me makes it through surgery.

The guy who was with me? That made it sound like I was hanging out with a random guy and we were involved in a random shooting. It wasn't random. I needed to tell Petra the truth or I would doom our possible reconciliation from the outset. Shaking my head, I deleted the entire message and started again.

Me:

I'm at the hospital. Someone tried to kill me today. I'm fine, but I'm waiting to see if my friend who was with me makes it out of surgery. It's a long story I really hope to share with you, but I may not make it to Michaelangelo's tonight. I'm so sorry.

God, my life must seem like a total shit-show to her right now.

I waited impatiently for her response, trying to busy myself by browsing through my Facebook and Instagram feeds. The happy pictures of people I hadn't spoken to since I quit NYU were too much to bear. I switched off my phone's screen and tried to slide it into my pocket, shaking my head in dismay as I realized I had no pockets because I was still wearing my pink sweatpants.

What kind of person leaves the house in sweats and gets shot at while running across a highway?

Someone whose life is a total shit-show.

My phone vibrated and I nearly jumped off the bench. Turning the screen to my face, I unlocked the phone and smiled as I read the message.

Petra:

Are you at Bronx-Lebanon? I'm actually pretty fond of hospital food. ;) Wanna have lunch in the café?

My hands trembled so visibly, I hid them under the lacquered wood tabletop so as not to attract the attention of the people seated at nearby tables in the Grand Café. Clasping my hands together, I tried taking deep breaths to calm my nerves, but nothing worked. Despite her cheery text message, I was terrified of what Petra would say when she saw me, walking around and probably taking careless risks with my life while she was confined to a wheelchair.

Leslie and my mom watched me from the countertop of the cafeteria. After my mom's sixth voicemail, I finally told her where she could find me, but she had to promise to remain in the background until Petra was ready. Based on Petra's initial reaction when I called her a few days ago, I was almost certain she would be more excited to see my mom than me.

I watched my mom and Leslie from across the café, too nervous to watch the entrance. The moment my mom's eyes widened and she covered her mouth, I knew Petra had arrived.

I turned to look over my shoulder at the cafeteria entrance and my muscles went weak.

Petra sat in a wheelchair, wearing blue skinny jeans and a chunky ivory cardigan—despite the summer heat, she was still trying to keep covered up the way she used to with her oversized T-shirts. She had lost a bit of weight, and my chest ached as I realized her legs seemed almost too thin for the rest of her body. Her ginger hair was pulled up in a perfect ponytail, and her makeup looked as if it had been perfected through countless YouTube makeup tutorials.

Happy tears stung the corners of my eyes. She was still as beautiful and vibrant as ever.

My limbs felt almost too weak to support me, but I pushed myself to slide out of the dining booth. I took the first three or four steps slowly and deliberately, before the urge to get to Petra became too strong and I broke into a jog. Spurred on by the smile on her face, I dodged an old man with a walker who was moving at a snail's pace. When I finally arrived at the café entrance, I was surprised and grateful to see tears collecting in her eyes.

"You look like you've had a shitty day," she said, holding her arms out.

I chuckled through tears as I gently embraced her. She returned my hug vigorously, the way she used to.

"It's getting better," I replied.

She laughed as she released me and wiped fresh tears from her rosy cheeks. "Great. Now *I'm* crying."

I looked up at the tall, handsome man standing behind her wheelchair. He nodded to my right, and I nearly jumped when I looked behind me and found the old man with a walker standing so close to me I was surprised I hadn't felt his breath on my neck.

"Oh, I'm sorry," I said, moving out of his way so he could pass.

"Dumb kids. You're blocking the entrance," he complained as he shuffled past us and out into the corridor.

As soon as he was out of earshot, I looked at Petra and we burst into laughter. We collected ourselves as we made our way to an empty table, where Petra finally introduced her male companion.

"Kris, this is my fiancé, Trey," she said with a proud smile.

I glanced at the modest ring on her finger and the equally modest smile on his face, and my heart soared. "It's an honor to meet you," I said, holding out my hand.

Petra waved off my suggestion of a handshake. "Get out of here with your honor and give the guy a hug."

Trey chuckled as we hugged briefly and set off to find an empty booth with room for Petra's chair. "It's good to finally meet you," he said, positioning Petra next to the table in the corner. "Petra never stops blabbing about you."

She smacked his forearm as he slid into the tan vinyl bench seat. "No one likes a tattletale," she chided him with a smile.

As I slid into the booth, I looked away to try to hide the pang of jealousy I felt as I admired their dynamic. It reminded me of what I thought I'd shared with Daniel.

"Whoa. You just got serious," Petra said, cocking an eyebrow at me as I tried to recover from my moment of envy. "You wanna tell me how the hell you almost got killed today?"

I swallowed hard and looked her in the eye. "I will,

but first I have to say how sorry I am for what happened in that car two years ago."

Petra's smile disappeared, but she didn't speak.

"I don't know if I can ever be forgiven for leaving you in that car," I continued, "but I want you to know that not a single day goes by where I don't regret the choices I made that night. I even became a pretty crazy alcoholic for a few months afterward, but my mom nipped that bad habit in the bud pretty quickly."

Petra smiled again, her eyes brimming with pure admiration. "I'll bet she did."

I chuckled as I tried to hide my fear that Petra had agreed to meet me just so she could get back in touch with my mom. "But I still…I can't stop thinking of how badly I betrayed you," I said, staring at the table. "I was a bad friend."

Petra was silent, allowing my words to hang in the space between us, then she let out a soft chuckle. "It's been two years, Kris," she said as I looked up to meet her gaze. "If you're still beating yourself up over the mistakes you made two years ago, you don't need my forgiveness. You need therapy."

I smiled uncomfortably. "I guess I should have seen that coming."

Petra sighed. "What did you expect me to say? I forgive you, Kris. Let's be BFFs again!" Her gaze didn't falter as she spoke. "You're not the only one who made mistakes that night. I should be apologizing to you for getting you into that situation in the first place. You didn't deserve that any more than I did." She drew in a shaky breath and continued. "Yes, we fucked up. We fucked up like we were getting paid to fuck up. But I didn't need your forgiveness to move on with my life. And neither do you. What you need is to forgive yourself."

I glanced at Trey, but he was staring at the tabletop, doing a very good job of staying out of this exchange. "You're right," I said, letting out a sigh as I sank into the vinyl seat. "I don't know what I expected out of this meeting... You're also right that I have some serious issues that need serious therapy. Issues that have nothing to do with whether or not you can forgive me."

She looked at Trey for a moment, lost in thought, then she turned back to me. "I spent a long time being angry, Kris. Hell, I'm still a crazy bitch to Trey most of the time," she said, and he chuckled. "I get frustrated with my...*limitations.*" She cringed as she said the word, then continued undaunted. "I've raged at you for leaving me, for driving too fast, for not convincing me to stay home. I've raged at myself for all those things and more, but mostly for ruining our friendship." She held up her hand to stop me from interrupting. "I know you want to take all the blame because that's just who you are. You take on the responsibility for everyone in your life, and you never let anyone make their own fucking mistakes... You should have told me to go to that party alone, but you couldn't, because that's not who you are. You *need* to take care of everyone. And I love that about you, Kris, I really do. But you need to let others take care of you, too."

I couldn't bring myself to look her in the eye, staring at the tabletop as I replied. "I did. I let Daniel take care of me and it nearly got me killed."

She shook her head and wagged her finger. "Nuh-uh. You can't stop there. Tell me what the hell happened today."

I let out a deep sigh. "I wish I knew more, but what I do know is that I was happy. Really, truly happy for the first time since... Then, it all went up in flames. I was suckered into a lie. God, I was a complete fool." I raised my head to look her in the eyes again. "My father's name is Michael Becker. He died last month before I ever met him. But, apparently, he was really rich and one of his employees... Well, a few of his employees didn't want me to get my inheritance, so they cooked up this...scheme, where one of them, Daniel, was supposed to get close to me and, I guess, find dirt on me."

"That's disgusting!" Petra snarled.

"I know," I replied. "The worst part is that it worked. Daniel got close to me, so close I told him about what happened to us two years ago and…and I fell in love with him."

Petra sucked air in through her teeth as she shook her head. "Is he good looking?"

I laughed. "Ridiculously."

"Ooh, that's tough," she said with a smile, clearly pleased that she had made me laugh. "Listen, there's obviously a lot more to this story than what you've told me, but I do actually have some advice for you, believe it or not."

I smiled. "Very hard to believe."

"I know," she said, nodding. "But here's the hard truth: Love is messy as fuck. It looks nothing like the shit you see in Disney movies and rom-coms. Real love is *fugly*. It's holding your hair back when you vomit and wiping your snot when you cry, and that's just two of the many bodily fluids involved."

I snorted with laughter. "Jesus, Petra. I was almost killed today. I'm not supposed to be laughing right now."

She waved off my words. "Bullshit. This is exactly when you should be laughing."

I shook my head. "I've missed you so fucking much."

"I've missed you too, babe. But right now, you have to finish telling me about this Daniel guy. Start at the beginning, and don't leave anything out."

As Trey left to get us some hospital food at the counter, I told Petra everything.

I told her how I met Daniel at the property manager's office, and how his smile could light up the night sky. I told her how he saved me from creepy Roger, and our amazing first date at the art studio. I told her about my brush with death in the Hamptons, and how Daniel could always be counted on to protect me.

I couldn't so much as look at the food Trey brought us as I took my time telling Petra how incredible it felt to finally tell someone what had happened two years ago. How I had brushed off all the little signs that something was off about Daniel. How desperate I was for something to go right, for someone to take care of me.

How I wished I had known Daniel and I were from the same neighborhood, so we could bond over our shared misery and nostalgia. How I wondered if I would have fallen so hard for Daniel if I'd known he wasn't wealthy.

That was when I stopped. I had been so worried that Daniel only fell for me because he knew about my inheritance. I never considered that he probably wondered if I had fallen for him because of his pretend wealth. If I was being honest, his wealth was one of the many qualities in Daniel I found so fascinating.

Petra smiled. "You look like you're having some kind of epiphany."

I sat up straight. "I am," I said, staring at nothing in particular for a moment before I snapped my focus back to Petra. "There are no do-overs."

"Damn fucking straight," she replied.

I smiled. "Yes, you and I failed. Daniel and I failed. But there's no path around failure, only through it. There are no do-overs. I just have to keep doing."

Petra wiggled her eyebrows. "Ooh, are you gonna *do* him in his hospital bed?"

"Petra!" my mom's voice startled me.

Petra laughed as Leslie pushed my mom next to her and they hugged vigorously. "Mom!" Petra bellowed as she squeezed harder, unconcerned with the dirty looks she was getting from our fellow diners.

I scooted out of the booth so Leslie could have my seat, and excused myself to allow my mom to catch up with Petra. "I have to check if Daniel's out of surgery," I said, kissing my mom's forehead. "Don't have too much fun without me."

As I walked away, I took one more glance over my shoulder. I never thought I'd be this happy to discover Petra had found someone to love her and take care of her. She was right. I had to move past the mistakes and make things right with Daniel, not just for me, but for Petra and my mom. They deserved to feel as happy as I felt right now.

I deserved it, too.

The elevator doors opened, and I stepped out into the corridor to make my way to the intensive care unit. My stomach curdled with the familiar sensation of guilt as I realized the last time I was here was to see my mom, and I was with Daniel. It seemed the people I loved were dropping like flies around me.

I wasn't the praying type, but I said a silent prayer for Daniel that he would be okay. I didn't think I could bear it if Daniel was permanently disfigured—or worse, *died*—while trying to protect me.

After a brief inquiry, a harried ICU nurse informed me that Daniel was in room 422. She didn't even ask me for identification. I wanted to question this lack of security, but I figured I probably should keep my mouth shut if I wanted to see him.

"Kristin! Kristin! Over here!"

I whipped my head around at the sound of my name being called, only to find a reporter with a microphone and a cameraman trailing behind her. "What the fuck?" I whispered.

"Kristin," the woman called out to me again as she approached with her microphone. "How does it feel to know you're the sole heiress to a $400 million fortune?"

"Ma'am, you can't be here," the ICU nurse said, rising from her swivel chair and coming around the desk toward us. "Media is not allowed in the hospital. You have to wait outside in the parking lot."

The reporter yanked her arm out of the nurse's grasp. "I'm just asking a few questions."

The nurse gave her a scathing look. "Well, you can go ask your questions in the parking lot. Now go!"

The reporter rolled her eyes at the nurse, then looked me in the eye. "I'll be right outside. We can *pay* you for an interview!" she yelled in haste as the nurse herded her and the cameraman back into the elevator.

As the nurse pressed the button to take them down to the ground floor, I shook my head. This woman was offering to pay me for an interview *right after* informing me that I was the sole heiress to a $400 million fortune. She was either a liar or an idiot, and I had no desire to find out which it was. I was beginning to understand why people hated reporters.

The nurse waited until the elevator doors had fully closed before she turned around and returned to her desk, shaking her head. "Sorry about that, honey. They're sharks. Go into a damn feeding frenzy at the first sign of blood," she said, taking a seat in front of her computer. "Who did you say you were here for again?"

I swallowed hard as I realized she was going to probably ask for identification now. "Actually, you already gave me the room number," I replied with a smile. "Thanks for taking care of that. I've never actually been approached by reporters before. That was kind of weird."

She looked up at me with her lips pursed. "Honey, you'd better get used to it with that kind of money."

My smile faded as I spun around, setting off down the corridor before turning the corner. A large group of people were gathered at the end of the hallway, talking animatedly among themselves. As I read the ever-increasing room numbers on the doors, I realized they were likely standing outside Daniel's room. They were probably his family.

I wanted to turn around and leave. I had no right to be here. Not only was I not family, but I was the reason Daniel was in that room, possibly clinging to life.

Before I made up my mind, a guy who appeared to be about the same age as Daniel noticed me standing motionless in the middle of the corridor. He broke away from the group and began walking toward me. My heart raced as I realized there was rage in his dark eyes. This could be one of Daniel's siblings or cousins coming to hit me, or worse. I closed my eyes and braced myself for whatever was about to happen.

After a brief moment of silence, he finally spoke. "Danny's gonna be so happy to see you."

I opened my eyes, realizing that what I had mistaken for anger in this man's eyes was actually grief. His eyes were slightly puffy, as if he had recently been crying.

"He was scared shitless of something bad happening to you," he continued, blinking furiously, probably to hold back more tears. "You don't know me, but I've been helping Danny keep an eye on you this week. I'm Zane."

He held his hand out for me to shake, but I hugged him instead.

"Thank you," I whispered.

He chuckled as he gently pushed me away. "Yeah, no big deal," he said, looking over his shoulder at the group of people.

"No, I mean, thank you for not being mad at me," I clarified.

His thick eyebrows scrunched together in confusion. "Why would I be mad at you? Unless you're the one who shot him?"

I smiled and shook my head. "Definitely not. I just thought you guys might be mad at me because he got shot protecting me."

He waved off this suggestion as a skinny guy with big ears came over to join us. "Girl, you should know by now. Nobody can stop Danny from trying to be the hero. It's just in his nature. That motherfucker thinks he's Batman."

"For reals," the skinny guy replied, shaking his head as he turned to me. "Who's your friend, Zane?"

"Remember that chick Danny was trying to tell us about the other night at Tino's?" Zane replied, then he addressed me. "This is Ollie," he said, indicating the skinny guy. "Actually, I don't think we properly introduced ourselves. Danny never told us your name."

"Oh, I'm sorry. I'm Kristin."

Ollie smiled as he looked me up and down. "Pleased to make your acquaintance. You here to see my boy?"

I glanced at the group gathered outside Daniel's room. There were two young girls who looked to be in their teens, one older woman who looked about Daniel's age, and another guy who looked a lot like Daniel, only younger.

"I don't know," I replied hesitantly. "Looks like there's already a lot of people here to see him. I don't want to get in anyone's way."

Zane and Ollie looked at each other, a silent exchange happening between them before Ollie spoke. "You think Danny wants to see his brother and sisters when he wakes up? He sees those little fuckers every damn day of his life."

I tried not to laugh at this, but it was difficult. "Do you know if Daniel's...okay?"

It felt strange calling him Daniel when they clearly all called him Danny. It made me feel even more like a stranger who didn't belong there.

Zane smiled. "Don't tell him I said this, but that fool could probably take a dozen bullets and be okay."

Ollie laughed. "Thank you for that blackmail material."

"Fuck you," Zane replied, rolling his eyes, though

he was clearly uncomfortable.

I glanced at the group of people outside Daniel's room again, then I turned to Zane, my new ally. "Can you introduce me to his family first?"

A huge smile spread across his sharp features. "It would be my pleasure."

DANIEL

24. Pretend

MY FIRST THOUGHT, as my eyelids fluttered open, was that I'd never felt this thirsty in all my life. Then, my vision began to focus and I had to speak my next thought aloud.

"You're still in your pj's," I croaked, my voice hoarse with thirst.

Kristin bolted up out of the chair she had been slumped in just a second ago. "Are you thirsty?" she asked urgently. "The nurse said you might be thirsty."

I nodded, watching in amazement as she made the simple act of pouring water from a plastic pitcher look beautiful. "Are you okay?" I asked, hardly able to muster more than a whisper.

I wasn't just thirsty. I was drowsy, but not the kind

of drowsy that came when you took too much cold medicine. I felt as if I'd been out partying until five a.m., then I got run over by a train and injected with a horse-sized dose of morphine. I was fucked up.

Kristin laughed as she held the cup with the straw up to my mouth for me to sip. "You're asking *me* if I'm okay?"

I could only manage a couple of sips before the liquid in my belly began to curdle. "I hurt you," I said, my voice clearer now that my throat was wet. "You're not okay."

Her smile disappeared as she pulled the chair closer and took a seat. "Yes, you hurt me. But we can talk about that later. You have to get your strength up first."

"So you can punch me?"

She laughed. "No, I don't want to punch you. Well, maybe just a little."

I flashed her a lazy grin. "You're so beautiful."

She looked down, as if she was trying to hide her face. "Yeah, well, you're really high on pain meds right now."

"I'm sorry I lied to you," I said, reaching out to grab her hand with my good hand. "I thought I was doing what was best for my family. But it all got so complicated when I started to imagine you as part of my family."

She looked up again with tears in her eyes. "I just met your family and friends outside. They love you so much." She paused for a moment, then she smiled. "Zane said you think you're Batman."

I tried to shake my head, but a sharp pain in my clavicle stopped me. "Zane is a liar. Don't believe anything he says."

"He also said that you're so strong you could probably take a dozen bullets and still be okay."

I smiled. "I take that back. Zane always tells the truth."

She squeezed my hand. "Thanks for saving my life, Danny."

I chuckled at her use of my nickname. "I never got paid for that, you know."

She let out a short burst of laughter, which was followed by a heavy silence.

"I didn't expect to fall in love with you. That changed everything," I said, squeezing her hand. "I got into this for the money, but no amount of money is worth losing you. You know…" I took a moment to compose myself, swallowing hard as my throat began to ache. "After my mom died, I had to start pretending to be happy around my siblings. I wanted to be their rock. But…I never had to pretend to be happy with you. I hope you can forgive me for pretending to be someone I'm not."

She wiped tears from her cheeks, which were looking a bit hollow. "I can forgive you, if you can accept my thanks for saving my life, even if you don't get paid for it."

"You don't have to thank me for that. I had no choice."

She tilted her head. "Why?"

I smiled. "Because you're not like the high-value targets I normally protect. You're not high-value at all. You're priceless."

KRISTIN

25. Never Again

As I helped my mom up the stairs to our fifth-floor apartment, it struck me that this might be the last time we would ever have to do this painful dance. Then, I thought of the many times Leslie and I had helped my mother up these stairs. I thought of the many times I'd come home from work and stood under a shower of scalding hot water in a vain attempt to wash away the dirty feeling I got from putting up with men like Roger *for the tips*. And all the times I sat at my mother's bedside in the hospital, worried sick about her, and the eventual medical bills, as she recovered from yet another surgery.

Angry tears stung my eyes as I opened the door to our apartment and helped her into her bed in the living room.

"You're mad at me," my mom said as she adjusted the pillow behind her back. "And you have every right to be."

I wanted to shout at her, "*Admitting you've hurt someone doesn't make the hurt go away!*" But as soon as the words entered my mind, I thought of my conversation with Daniel, which had occurred less than two hours ago.

"*I hurt you… You're not okay.*"

"*Yes, you hurt me. But we can talk about that later.*"

If I could show Daniel mercy after how thoroughly he'd deceived me, I had to do better for my mom.

I yanked the hair tie out of the loose bun on top of my head, letting the brown, tangled mess fall over my shoulders as I sank into the recliner. "Mom, even if you tell me your 'long story,' the truth is that I'll probably never understand why you kept me from knowing him," I began, pulling my legs up onto the chair to sit cross-legged. "But there's no sense in letting it get between us now. You're my only mom. I have to trust that you did it for the right reasons, because I can't lose you and my father at the same time."

My mom was silent for a long while as she wiped tears from her pale cheeks. She had hardly seen the sun for two years straight, spending most of her time in this apartment or in hospital rooms. She had also suffered. Nothing would make me happier than to take her to that beach house and see her basking in the sun on that beautiful stretch of sand.

"Not a day went by where I didn't question whether I was doing the right thing," she said, her voice thick with regret. "I used to work for your father. We had a brief fling that ended when I told him I was pregnant. I was young and stupid. I thought he really cared about me. I didn't care that he didn't take me on dates or introduce me to his non-existent family. I didn't care that most of our time together was spent in the bedroom. I was charmed by his charisma and, very stupidly, enchanted by his riches."

I cringed as I realized I had been just as foolishly captivated by Daniel's pretend riches. Like mother, like daughter. It seemed the only thing I could be angry about was that she didn't share this story with me in time for me to learn from her mistakes.

Her voice took on a hard edge as she continued. "When I told him I was pregnant, he fired me on the spot. He told me I'd better get a lawyer if I ever expected to get a dime out of him. Then, he laughed, because he knew I couldn't afford a lawyer." She looked up at me with shame in her eyes. "You were about four months old. I was feeling particularly overwhelmed and lonely one day, and I called him to ask if we could meet. He told me he was in the Hamptons, and invited me there to hash out the visitation details over brunch.

"So I buckled you into your car seat and I drove all the way to his beach house to offer him another chance to be a part of your life. But when I got there...I found him having sex with not one, but *two* women in his hot tub. He invited me there to humiliate me." The shame in my mother's eyes turned to steel. "And I decided right then and there that I wouldn't allow it. Never again." Her gaze locked on me as her eyes pleaded with me to understand. "He proved to me that day that I didn't know him at all. You might as well have been conceived in a one-night stand with a random stranger. The thought of allowing a stranger to have unsupervised visits with you terrified me. In my mind, my only choice was to forget him."

I gritted my teeth, still attempting to temper my anger. "But you didn't know if he would have been a good father. You never gave him a chance to try," I said, feeling sick with myself for defending this man who was obviously an emotional sadist.

My mom stared into the distance, thinking carefully before she spoke again. "You're right. Maybe he would have done a complete 360 and turned into the Father of the Year." She shrugged as if this was a vague possibility. "I honestly believed it was much more likely that he would have toyed with our emotions and our livelihoods. I'm almost certain he would have reeled us in and tossed us back out over and over again for his own personal enjoyment. Then, his lawyers would have terrorized us until I agreed to some kind of settlement that would only devalue your true worth. You didn't deserve that."

I glanced around the apartment, very obviously taking in the value of our furnishings and the decrepit apartment they were housed in. "This is what I deserved instead?"

She beckoned me to her side, patting the mattress for me to sit next to her. "Come here, sweetheart."

I felt like a dejected child who had just been given a very reasonable explanation for why they were too young to attend a sleepover. I didn't want to believe my mom had a good reason for keeping me from my father. But the more she spoke, the more I realized that I probably would have done the same thing in her position.

When I sat on the edge of her bed, she swiftly pulled me into her arms and held me so tightly it actually hurt. But I didn't pull away. I couldn't, because it was exactly what I needed.

I wept into her shoulder-length graying hair that smelled distinctly like coconut, which managed to make me smile as I cried. "I'm sorry if I sounded ungrateful, Mom," I said, releasing her and still wiping away tears as I looked her in the eye. "You worked your ass off to take care of me on your own. You resisted the temptation of money to make sure I would always feel loved. I hope I can be half as badass as you when I get my inheritance."

She smiled from ear to ear as she reached up and grabbed my face. "With or without that money, you were always destined to be more badass than me."

We laughed as she took me into her arms again, where I settled in for a long while.

Daniel

26. Priceless

RICKY HELPED ME PACK UP the get-well cards and gifts—mostly sports gear and gift cards—in my hospital room as the nurse helped me sign my discharge papers. I didn't know how I was going to pay the hospital bill for this twenty-day stay. I didn't know if Sabrina had taken the time to officially fire me and cancel my health benefits. I supposed I would find out soon enough. In the meantime, I tried not to worry about it, or the fact that I might never regain full use of my left shoulder.

I had to focus on the positive things in my life. Like the fact that Ricky's boss, when he found out I'd been fired and nearly killed by the same person in a span of two weeks, gave Ricky the promotion and raise he'd been pining after for almost a year. Or the fact that seeing me in the hospital, and hearing the story of how Kristin had to quit college to take care of her mom, made Geneva and Alisha swear to me that nothing would stop them from going to college and getting a degree.

Of course, the most amazingly positive thing in my life was still Kristin.

I knew she was strong when I found out she was taking care of her mother on her own. But I could not have foreseen how gracefully she would handle this whole experience—the deceit from me and her mother, the reconciliation with her best friend, the death of her absent father, and her new position as de facto CEO of Becker Holdings, as specified in her father's will. I had no doubt she would answer the call of duty for Michael's empire the way she had when her mother needed her.

The nurse gave me the copies of the signed discharge papers and disappeared into the corridor. I sank into the visitor's chair as Ricky finished collecting more cards and gifts from the small closet in the corner of the room. I closed my eyes and tried to think of people I could contact for leads on a job. Manhattan was chock-full of rich people. There had to be a rich woman out there looking for a devastatingly handsome crippled bodyguard.

"Yo, Danny. You got a visitor," Ricky said.

I opened my eyes and the hairs on my neck prickled. Detective Jones stood in the doorway wearing a look so deadly serious, I was certain he was going to deliver some very bad news.

Bracing myself for whatever it was, I stood gingerly and walked over to him, holding out my good hand to shake. "Detective."

He shook my hand and broke into a toothy grin as he eyed my left arm in its sling. "Looks like you could use some good news."

I turned to Ricky and nodded toward the corridor. He easily took the hint to leave us alone. Once Ricky was gone, I motioned for Jones to have a seat in one of the two visitors' chairs. I grabbed the other one and pulled it a little farther away before I took a seat.

"Shoot."

Jones laughed. "Interesting choice of words," he said, glancing at my shoulder. "Well, I won't beat around the bush. I'm here to tell you that, based on the department investigation and the coroner's findings, Michael Becker's death has officially been ruled an accident. The investigation into his death is now closed."

I let out a huge sigh of relief. "Thank God. And

thank *you* for coming to tell me personally," I said, shaking my head. "That's a huge weight off my shoulders."

He glanced at my injured arm again. "Doesn't look like you'll be doing much heavy lifting with that shoulder anytime soon," he said, with a grin that told me he was enjoying my injury a little too much.

"Ah, this is nothing," I said, pretending to brush some dirt off my shoulder. "It's just what happens when you're out there putting your life on the line every day."

He laughed. "Really," he said, nodding his head. "So how does that work? Does getting shot make you a good bodyguard or a bad bodyguard?"

I laughed as I shook my head. "Probably a stupid bodyguard."

We both stood up at the same time, but he spoke first. "You're a good guy, Meyers. Keep up that bravery and you might become a great one someday."

"Thanks," I replied. "So…before you leave, you mind updating me on Sabrina Sokolov? Should I be looking over my shoulder as soon as I walk out that door?"

This new line of questioning tempered his smile a bit. "They're working on gathering evidence for the indictment right now. The photos and voice recordings you provided will help with that.... Hearing is in two days. But, from what I hear, they left a paper trail a mile long. So my advice to you is... Get a lawyer, because when the shit hits the fan, they're gonna start pointing fingers at the first mention of a plea deal." He nodded once before he headed for the door. "But you didn't hear that from me. Take care, Meyers."

I smiled as he stepped into the corridor and the sound of his footsteps faded away. "Take care, chief."

Ricky backed his pickup truck into a parking space a couple blocks from our building. "Oh, shit! I almost forgot!" he said, reaching into the backseat and coming up with a large sealed manila envelope. "A messenger dropped this off for you this morning. I haven't opened it."

I took the envelope and turned it over in my lap a couple of times, looking at both sides. There was no return address, and only my first name was written on the outside in nondescript black marker.

"Did the messenger say who it's from?" I asked, hesitant to open it.

Ricky shrugged. "He didn't say shit. But he also left a big-ass package at the apartment."

I looked at Ricky to see if maybe he was trying to trick me. "Am I gonna open this up and find pics of myself high on morphine getting my bedpan changed or something?"

He laughed. "How the fuck do I know? I swear, I had nothing to do with that. For all I know, that envelope contains anthrax."

I glared at him. "Thanks for easing my mind," I said, shaking my head as I broke the seal on the envelope and reached inside.

I pulled out a packet of what looked like a dozen or so pages stapled together, with a check paper-clipped to the front of the packet. The top of the check indicated it was a severance check. The bottom portion of the check was made out to me from Becker Holdings in the amount of $1.00. It had to be a bad joke orchestrated by Sabrina to rub my nose in my unemployment.

I ripped the check out of the paper clip and began to crumple it up when I noticed the packet of paper behind the check. It looked like some type of letter. Then, I read the name typed beneath the signature at the bottom of the page: Kristin Owens, CEO.

My eyes scanned the letter, and I nearly vomited

with relief when I realized it was an offer of employment. Attached to the back of the letter was a nondisclosure agreement and an employment agreement to work as Kristin's bodyguard earning double what Michael had paid me.

"Fucking hell," I said, shaking my head. "I thought this was going to be from Sabrina and we were going to have to evacuate the whole fucking building."

"So…is this a good thing?" Ricky asked, looking confused.

I nodded as I reached for the door handle. "It's a very fucking good thing, bro. Now, come show me this package."

Ricky helped open the wooden box that looked like it contained a flat-screen TV. But I highly doubted Kristin would send me a television. If she did, I would question her judgment. I didn't need to be wasting away on the couch. I had to get back into the gym as soon as possible so I could be in top shape to protect her.

Inside the wooden box was a cardboard box. Inside the cardboard box were Styrofoam corners, encasing something that was wrapped in thick white canvas fabric. On every container, the words DO NOT USE SHARP INSTRUMENTS TO OPEN were printed very large and clear. I helped Ricky remove the foam corners and unwrap the fabric to reveal something completely unexpected and totally outrageous.

It was the Picasso that had hung in the upstairs corridor of Michael's beach house.

"Is this..." Ricky said, tilting his head. "Is this a fucking Picasso?"

I shook my head in utter disbelief. "If it is, we have to keep our voices down," I said, suddenly feeling as if the walls separating our apartment from the one next door were way too thin.

Ricky tilted his head some more to get a better look at the back side of the painting. "There's something on the back."

I walked carefully around to the other side and found a Post-it note affixed to the back of the canvas, which I took as proof that this was a real fucking Picasso. In black marker, written in neat cursive, were the words: Because you're priceless.

KRISTIN

27. Catching Rays

MY MOM OPENED AND CLOSED one kitchen drawer after another in obvious frustration. "How many sets of silverware does a person need? Jesus criminy, where are the chopping knives?"

I smiled as I opened the drawer below the chopping block next to the range and pulled a Japanese chef's knife out of the built-in knife block in the drawer. "Here," I said, passing it to her.

"This house has been renovated a lot since the last time I was here," she said, looking around the enormous kitchen at the beach house. "It's going to take some getting used to."

Today was the first day my mom would spend the night in the beach house. Leslie had stayed in the apartment with her for the past eleven days, while Petra, Trey, and I scoured the house for anything we would not be keeping. But before I even stepped foot in the house again, Petra and Trey removed everything from the bedroom my father had created for me.

I didn't want to see any of it. I didn't want to see the frilly fabrics and princess decor. I didn't want to be reminded of the kind of daughter he had wanted. Most of all, I didn't want to be poisoned by the belief that somewhere deep down, he loved me.

Petra insisted that whether I wanted her to or not, she would take lots of video and plenty of pictures of the room. And everything they removed would be saved, in case I had a change of heart later on.

We brought surprisingly few boxes of my belongings from my apartment. I moved my things into the guest room, where I'd slept with Daniel almost two months ago. I put my mom's things in the guest bedroom downstairs. Neither of us were keen on sleeping in the master bedroom.

"Where's the mint?" Petra asked, peering into the enormous refrigerator.

"It's in a glass of water by the sink," I replied.

We had been preparing tonight's dinner for almost two hours and I still felt as if we were forgetting something. Despite the fact that Daniel and I had reversed our roles, I couldn't help but think of him as a sophisticated gentleman I needed to impress. After all, he was the one who got lessons in how to be a fancy rich guy from Sabrina.

Daniel was the number-one reason I was certain money couldn't buy class, because he was the essence of class from the moment we met, and every day since.

I finished cubing the watermelon and tossing it with the feta and mint leaves Petra had retrieved for me. The doorbell rang as I placed the salad on the large twelve-seat dining table that overlooked the veranda and the ocean.

Petra wiggled her eyebrows. "Is that Kevin Costner?" she said, calling Daniel by her new nickname for him, which referred to Kevin Costner's role in the movie *The Bodyguard*. "And Iiiiiiiiiiii-ee-Iiiiiiiiii will always love youuuuuu..." she sang as I left the room to answer the door.

As I walked through the kitchen and down the corridor toward the foyer, I couldn't help but recognize how strange it felt to walk such a long distance just to answer the door. In our old apartment, when the doorbell rang, my mom would sometimes stretch her arm out to open the door from her hospital bed. It almost made me feel guilty.

Arriving at the front door, I pulled it open and was

not prepared for how happy I would be to see Daniel, or how devilishly handsome he would look, after not seeing him for almost two weeks. Unable to control myself, I threw my arms around his neck. He grunted from the force of my hug, and I quickly remembered his shoulder injury.

"Oh, my God. I'm so sorry," I apologized as I let him go, and immediately reached for his left shoulder, stopping just short of touching him.

He laughed. "I'm fine. It's been more than a month," he said, reaching up to grasp my hand and place it on his shoulder. "I've been working with the physical therapist, and she thinks I should be able to start lifting again in a couple weeks. And with the titanium plate in there, I may end up even stronger than before." He flexed his muscles for me to feel.

I rolled my eyes. "Did she say when you'd be ready to graduate from Superhero Academy?"

He smiled. "God, I fucking love you. Come here," he said, pulling me into a bear hug.

I buried my face in his smooth neck, breathing in the clean scent of his skin and wishing we could just spend the rest of the day right here in this position. Unable to control myself, I licked his neck, savoring the sound of his laughter.

"Settle down, Picasso," he said, releasing me and

turning around to grab a silver gift bag off the front step. "This is for your mom."

I smiled as I took the bag and tried to peek inside.

"Watch it, young lady. That's not yours," he said, grabbing my free hand and leading me across the foyer toward the corridor.

"Is it weird that you probably know this house better than I do?" I asked, as he led us through the swinging door into the kitchen.

"Everything is weird to you," he said, as I allowed him to lead me through the kitchen and into the dining area.

Petra gasped when she saw him. "Holy shit!"

Daniel looked back and forth between Petra and me, clearly confused. "What? What's going on?"

I shook my head, then whispered in his ear, "Be prepared for Petra to say something very inappropriate about how handsome you are."

Daniel chuckled as he turned back toward the table. "You must be the famous Petra."

Petra glanced at Trey, who was sitting next to her at the dining table. "You must be...very, very, ridiculously good looking."

Daniel smiled, unable to hide the slight blush in his cheeks. "Uh...thanks?"

Daniel helped me serve dinner, after which my

mother wanted to open her gift from Daniel, but he insisted she open it in private. When he said this, he and Petra exchanged a look that made me wonder if she knew what was in the silver bag.

My mom was all too eager to have a secret she could keep from me. She gladly hid the gift under the table and out of my reach.

After Daniel and I cleared the table, Trey and Petra insisted on doing the dishes, while I took Daniel upstairs to show him something.

"No funny business while you two are up there," my mom said as Daniel and I began to leave. "No one wants to hear that. We just ate."

Petra and Trey laughed as they loaded the dishwasher. "You tell her, Mom," Petra agreed, pumping her fist in the air.

I shook my head as I dragged Daniel out of the kitchen to avoid any more embarrassment. "You'd think they've known you all their lives the way they act," I said, leading him up the stairs.

"They're real. I love that."

We entered the guest room and suddenly the atmosphere changed. It was as if someone had flipped a switch and all the memories of the things we'd done in this bedroom were projected onto every surface. When I looked at Daniel to see if he felt the same shift in the mood, the hungry look in his eyes made me feel naked.

As if there were a magnet in his hand, he automatically placed his hand on the small of my back as he looked down at me. "Maybe we should give them a little concert," he said, flashing me a seductive smile.

I smiled as I reached up and placed my hand on the scruff of his jaw. "First, I have something you need to see."

He lay his hand over mine, then he turned his head slowly and placed a tender kiss on the palm of my hand. "The stage is yours."

"Before I show you, I want you to know that I spoke to my old academic advisor at NYU."

His eyes widened with excitement. "Go on..."

"He said I could probably still return on my scholarship if I returned by next fall. But I told him I don't need the scholarship. I just need to know I can come back. So, once I get all this probate stuff worked out, I'm going back to school."

He clenched his jaw as he seemed to be having some type of emotional reaction I couldn't read, then he shook his head and planted a hard kiss on my forehead. "You make me proud to know you."

I chuckled uncomfortably. "Well, I hope I don't let you down."

"You could never," he replied, with complete conviction. "But, before you show me whatever it is you brought me here for, I forgot I also have a gift for you."

I feigned surprise. "Oh, you mean this is a gift I can actually open?"

He smiled. "Actually, Miss Smartypants, this gift isn't even wrapped." He pulled a silver USB drive out of his jeans pocket and handed it to me. "This is a collection of my favorite elevator music," he began, ignoring my laughter. "You can see the gift I gave your mom once you've memorized every song on this USB drive."

I shook my head. "You're like an evil mastermind of torture. This is sadistic."

He shrugged unapologetically. "You'd better break out those earbuds, baby, 'cause you've got work to do."

I sighed as I tossed the USB drive onto my unmade bed, half-hoping that it would somehow get lost before I had to listen to it. "My turn," I said, grabbing his hand and leading him to the windows overlooking the swimming pool and the ocean, which was when I saw Leslie wheeling my mom over the wooden pathway leading to the beach. "Look at that…" I said, my voice trailing off as I watched them.

"Is that what you wanted to show me?" Daniel said, but almost as soon as the words were out of his mouth, he saw what I had brought him upstairs to see.

Standing on top of a round table a few feet away, in front of the center window overlooking the ocean, was my latest sculpture. I'd spent most of my nights over the past two weeks obsessing over this piece.

Realism was not my strong suit, especially since I began my foray into surreal and cubist styles so many years ago. But I wanted this piece to convey emotion that Daniel could easily interpret.

The woman wore a flowing dress, the skirt of which she gripped in her slender hands as she danced to what I imagined was a lush, romantic rhythm. Her eyes were closed and her lips slightly parted as she felt the music deep inside her.

"I put her here so she can dance in the sunrise," I said, feeling even more exposed and vulnerable than I had when we stepped into the room.

Daniel stood in complete silence as he stared at the sculpture. Maybe he didn't mean it literally when he asked me to name my next sculpture after his mom. Every moment that passed as I waited for him to break the silence made me more certain I had messed up.

Then, he turned to me and gently grabbed the back of my neck, pulling me close so he could look me straight in the eye. "Are you real?"

I sighed with relief as I smiled up at him. "Define real."

His mouth fell over mine, stealing my breath as he parted my lips with his tongue. He held my face firmly as my arms fell slack at my sides, as if his kiss was siphoning the energy from my entire body. My knees were about to buckle when he pulled away, resting his forehead against mine.

"I have another surprise for you in my car," he said, his voice a hoarse whisper heavy with longing. "I'll be right back. Stay here."

As he let go of my face, I had to stop myself from reaching for him. He reached the bedroom door and my stomach fluttered as he glanced back at me and smiled before disappearing into the corridor. As I waited for him, I wandered toward the bed, thinking I would search for the USB drive. But when I reached the foot of the bed, I thought of what Daniel had said when he'd handed me the memory stick. *"You can see the gift I gave your mom once you've memorized every song on this USB drive."*

The first image that popped into my mind was a diamond ring. I shook my head at the silliness. Daniel and I had known each other less than two months. His gift to my mother would be something more immediately meaningful. But, then, why wasn't I allowed to see it yet?

I let out a frustrated sigh as I began digging through my messy bedsheets for the USB drive. "Aha!" I said, holding up the memory stick and staring at it, wondering if perhaps, hidden in one of the songs, was the reason Daniel had kept my mom's gift a secret.

Walking around to the side of the bed, I shook my head in dismay as I surrendered to the harsh reality that I would have to listen to every song on this drive. I placed the stick on the nightstand. When I turned around, I found Daniel standing in the doorway, watching me with a gorgeous smile.

"Stay there," he said, then he stepped out of the doorframe for a moment, disappearing into the hallway.

He reappeared with a cardboard box in his good hand. The box looked to be about the same size as the box I'd sent him, which had contained a very expensive original Picasso. He gently set the box down on the floor, propping it up against the wall, then he disappeared into the corridor again. He returned with another cardboard box, smaller than the first, which he propped up against the wall next to the other one.

"What are those?" I asked.

He grabbed my hand and pulled me toward the

packages. "This is actually not a gift for you. It's a gift from you to me," he replied, smiling at my obvious confusion. "It's the only gift I want from you. Well, other than your sexy body."

I rolled my eyes as he let go of my hand and began lifting the top flap of the box. "This is turning out to be a very interesting gift-giving session," I muttered.

He looked up at me as he reached his hand inside. "Oh, it's going to get even more interesting later," he said with a wink. His hand emerged from the box, lifting out a canvas artwork I recognized as the mountain scene I'd painted on our first date. "This is the only gift I want from you," he said, gently resting the canvas against the box it came out of. "I have no doubt that one day this will be just as priceless as that one," he said, pointing at the other box, which was obviously the Picasso.

I cocked an eyebrow. "How the hell did you get that?"

"I know people," he replied, then laughed at my unamused expression. "I called Layla, the director of the studio, and she told me Rebecca, the birthday girl, took your painting home that night. Layla was kind enough to give me the parents' phone number, and they were very understanding when I told them why I wanted it."

"You took it away from Rebecca?"

He shook his head. "No, no. It wasn't like that," he said, walking toward me. "Rebecca's mom said that once they got it home, Rebecca didn't want the painting in her bedroom. So it's been sitting in their garage for the past month and a half."

I breathed a sigh of relief. "Oh, good."

He reached forward and my heart raced as he grabbed my waist to pull me flush against him. "Rebecca's mom said she would give me the painting in exchange for sex."

"In exchange for *what*?" I shrieked.

He leaned in and kissed the corner of my mouth, lingering long enough for me to feel his smile curving against my lips. "God damn. You're sexy when you're jealous."

I made a very weak attempt at pushing him away. "So that first box is my gift to you... Then, why is that other box here?"

He grabbed both my hands as he looked me in the eye. "I know you wanted me to have that Picasso, but I can't accept that kind of gift from you. That's just not the way my mother raised me." He pressed a finger over my lips as I opened my mouth to protest. "No, you won't change my mind. My mom raised me to take care of her and my siblings. I've always been the one who protected them. The one who cared for their every need. If I take that painting, it won't be me taking care of them anymore. And, before you say it, *no*, this does not make me a sexist little shit."

I laughed. "Oh, really? Because it sure sounds like a giant load of sexist bullshit."

He shook his head and pointed to the painting of the mountain scene. "Remember what I said to you in that art studio while you painted that beautiful piece: Never be afraid to be yourself. Well, I take that to heart. Especially after pretending to be someone else for so long, I don't *ever* want to pretend with you again." He grabbed both my hands again, giving them a gentle squeeze to emphasize his point. "Baby, this is just me being me. If this is going to work between us, you have to let me take care of you."

"But you *will* be taking care of me, as my bodyguard," I said, mentally cursing myself as I realized I was pouting like a teenager.

He smiled as his hand cupped the side of my face. "And I'll kill for you, as your bodyguard or not." He softly swept his thumb over my cheekbone as he gazed into my eyes. "There are a lot of good things that came out of this deception, and the best thing is you. But the crash course Sabrina gave me in rich guy manners and 'How to Sound Like a Warren Buffett Wannabe' actually lit a fire in me... I'm going back to school, too, to get a degree in finance."

An enormous grin spread across my face as tears welled up in my eyes. "We can be study partners?"

He chuckled as he reached up and wiped a tear from my cheek. "Hell fucking yes."

I wrapped my arms around his waist as I buried my face in the warmth of his solid chest. "I'll take back the Picasso if you agree to acknowledge that I did nothing to earn that Picasso or any of this other crap I inherited."

He kissed the top of my head. "I guess."

"So technically," I continued, "the only reason this wealth is mine and not yours is because my parents boned then my dad died, which is a pretty stupid way to earn something." I tilted my head back to look up at him, seeing the look of recognition in his eyes. He knew what I was going to say. "Which means that I have about as much of a right to this money as you do."

His face was serious as he looked me straight in the eye and said, "I don't want any of it."

I swallowed hard as I stared right back into his brilliant green eyes. "I don't either, but I'm stuck with it. And you're stuck with me. And just like you, I was also raised to take care of the people I love."

His serious expression softened as he seemed to surrender to these words. "That's not fair."

"What's not fair?"

He smiled as he tucked a lock of hair behind my ear. "That it will be at least four more years before I'll be able to outsmart you in these kinds of arguments."

I shook my head as I smiled up at him. "Never gonna happen."

PART IV: Epilogue

Seven years later

THE SUN ROSE at 6:53 a.m.

All along the edges of the bedroom curtains, the sunlight changed from indigo, to green, to gold, then to peach and back to gold. With every change in hue, I was rapt with attention, watching as the shadow on the duvet created by the small protrusion of Kristin's belly became more and more defined by the growing light.

She slept peacefully, trusting I would not wake her until it was absolutely necessary. She loved sleeping on her back, but I knew from experience that she would not be able to indulge in her favorite sleeping position much longer. At four and a half months pregnant, she had no more than a month before the weight of the baby would force her to start sleeping on her side—with that damn pregnancy pillow—the way she had when she was pregnant with Amelia.

I let her sleep for another hour and a half, while I stared at my phone, responding to emails and checking on the markets. Kristin hated when I checked the markets before getting out of bed on a day off. She said it affected my mood for the rest of the day. That wasn't entirely true. It was just that, obviously, when the markets were down, I tended to get more doomsday messages from clients than I did when the markets were up.

The Dow was up today. I turned my phone off and tossed it into the top drawer of my nightstand. I wouldn't be needing it anymore today. Today, Kristin would have my undivided attention.

The clunk of the phone hitting the bottom of the drawer made her stir.

I slid my hand under the comforter, finding her swollen belly. "Happy anniversary, baby," I murmured, as I leaned in and kissed the soft skin on her neck.

She groaned as her eyelids slowly flickered open. "Happy anniversary," she whispered.

"How are you feeling?" I asked.

My mind was clearly set on one thing, and one

thing only: anniversary sex. But she'd been having some morning sickness lately, so I had to at least check in with her first.

A lazy smile spread across her face, as her brain woke up and registered what I was *really* asking. She nodded. "Yes," she replied, answering my implied question rather than the one I'd actually asked.

I chuckled as I slid my hand inside her panties. "Can't hide anything from you, can I?"

Her mouth fell open and she let out a small gasp as I found her spot. "Five years of marriage has a funny way of turning a person into an open book."

"Are you calling me transparent?" I said, my hand frozen in place.

She grabbed my hand and I laughed as she began using my finger to touch herself. "Stop talking and just fuck me."

I pulled my hand free of her grasp. "As you wish."

Knowing how she liked it best, I grabbed her hip and rotated her body away from me, so she was facing the window. She giggled as I slid my hand over her baby bump, continuing down between her legs again. Closing her eyes, she let out a blissful sigh as I found her spot.

I slid my leg between hers, spreading her knees apart like butterfly wings. Then, I draped her leg over mine, giving my hand easy access to her center. She whimpered as my finger whispered over her sensitive skin, being as gentle as possible. When the volume of her cries increased, I slid a finger inside her.

She was primed and ready.

"Oh, God," she breathed as I pushed into her from behind.

I paused for a moment, my mouth pressed against the back of her ear as I savored how perfectly I fit inside her. Keeping one hand between her legs, I slid my arm underneath her and caught her breast in my other hand. I thrust into her slowly at first, reveling in the soft warmth of her body against mine. But it didn't take long for both of us to lose ourselves in the moment.

"Harder," she begged.

And harder I went.

I yelped as Daniel pulled out of me and scooped me up onto all fours in one impossibly swift yet careful motion. He grabbed my hips and I laughed as he yanked me backward, so he could stand on the floor behind me. His hand slid down my backside and between my legs again, instantly finding my spot. Sometimes, I was certain he knew my body better than I did.

I looked back at him over my shoulder and his eyes locked on mine as he massaged my center. His other hand reached forward, grasping my shoulder to hold me steady as my legs began to quiver. I hung my head, breathing heavily as the orgasm rippled through me. Before I could collapse, he slung his arm around my waist and plunged into me.

His body curved over mine, his mouth landing on my shoulder as he sank in and out of me. He was slow and deliberate at first, his teeth scraping gently over the back of my neck as he took his time to draw out the pleasure. But as he traced the tip of his tongue over the back of my ear, I heard the moment his breathing quickened and I curled my fists around the comforter to brace myself.

My eyes widened and I gasped as he stood up straight, grabbing onto my hips as he pounded me from behind. His skin smacked against mine and I laughed heartily as I realized I was going to come again. My increased sensitivity and seemingly endless sex drive was my favorite perk to being pregnant.

"That is one sexy fucking laugh," he said, his body

quivering against mine as he slowed his thrusts until he had finished inside me.

We were both silent as he pulled me up onto my knees, his body pressed against mine as he took my breast in one hand, his other hand landing on my belly. I turned my head and his mouth curved against mine as he twitched inside me.

As he began to soften, he pulled his head back and looked me in the eye. "I have a surprise for you."

I smiled. "I know."

His eyebrows scrunched together and his green eyes looked stricken. "You know what it is?"

I laughed and shook my head. "No, but I know you have a surprise. I mean, I figured you'd have one since you've surprised me on every other anniversary."

He rolled his eyes and laid a gentle smack on my ass before he pulled out of me. "You scared the fuck out of me," he said, holding out his hand to help me off the bed. "Come on, dirty girl. It's shower time."

As we lathered each other up in the shower, I thought of all the surprises Daniel had sprung on me before this one, trying to work out what this one might be.

The first time he surprised me was on the one-year anniversary of the day we met at the offices of Golde Property Management. He dressed up like a cop and handed me a fake eviction notice, then he pretended to arrest me and take advantage of me in my jail cell. Definitely one of my favorite surprises.

Another memorable surprise was our third anniversary, which was traditionally supposed to be a leather gift, but had more recently been replaced by crystal or glass. Daniel surprised me by taking me to the art studio of Arturo Uribe, Manhattan's most sought-after glass sculptor. Arturo spent all day teaching me everything I'd ever wanted to learn about glassblowing and sculpting.

I knew that this year's surprise would probably be found in my new art studio. I had been using the master bedroom at the beach house as my art studio for the past seven years. It had the best view of the ocean; therefore, it had the best lighting. It was also the biggest room on the second floor. Unfortunately, this meant my studio didn't exactly meet all my needs.

I still had to trudge downstairs and into the laundry-slash-utility room to wash clay and paint off my hands. I'd learned that lesson the hard way when I backed up the plumbing system with bits of hardened clay. The utility sink downstairs was equipped with a special constant-flow sink trap and filtration system to prevent any paint or sculpting material from hardening in the pipes.

It took a few years before I finalized the architectural design for my art studio, and we began construction six months ago. The new two-story building sat on the east lawn, just to the right of the pool if you stood facing the ocean. The building was completed last month, and I'd spent most of the past three weeks working with an interior designer to make the inside my perfect combination of beautiful, practical, and inspirational.

"Do I need to get dressed up for this surprise?" I asked, looking at Daniel's reflection as I towel-dried my hair in front of the double sink.

He disappeared through the doorway that led into the walk-in closet. "You know your surprise is in the studio," he said, confirming what I already knew. "You can walk across the lawn naked, for all I care. Not like you haven't done it before."

I pulled on a pair of cargo shorts and a T-shirt in the closet. When I emerged, Kristin shot me a nasty glare from across the bathroom. She knew I would never let her live down the time she went alone for a swim, and her bikini top snapped, floating away into the depths of the ocean. Then, as she ran topless from the beach into the house, she bumped into the gardener.

As hilarious as it was, I felt a little bad that I had to fire the gardener. Poor kid always turned away every time he saw us coming, but he couldn't hide the fact that he kept getting a stiffie whenever he saw Kristin. I gave him good references.

I came up behind her and placed my hand over her abdomen. "Have you thought more about what you want to name him?" I murmured into her ear.

She tossed her towel onto the vanity and lay her hand over mine. "What was that gardener's name again? Roberto?"

I glared at her reflection in the mirror. "All right, you got me back."

She grinned as I rested my chin on her shoulder. "How about Daniel?"

I shook my head. "Come on, baby. For a professional artist, that's not very creative."

She elbowed me in the ribs and I backed away to escape her wrath. "Well, what do *you* want to name him?"

I stepped forward again, wrapping my arms around her waist. "Something manly, like Brutus."

She cringed. "Brutus? That's gross."

"Gross?" I laughed.

"Yes. Brutus sounds like bruise. Might as well just name him Bruiser."

My eyes widened. "Bruiser is good. Bruiser is a kid no one fucks with."

"Bruiser is a dog's name! And not even a *cute* dog's name," she said, shaking her head. Then, she stared at the reflection of my hands on her belly for a while, before she looked up at me. "How about...Theodore?"

I smiled as I rubbed her belly. "Little Teddy Bear."

She beamed at the sound of this. "*My* Teddy Bear."

"Hey, kid. Don't forget who your first teddy bear was," I said, turning her around and planting a soft kiss on her forehead as I pulled her into my arms.

She coiled her arms around my waist and pressed her cheek into my shoulder. "I love when you call me kid. It almost makes me forget I'm turning thirty next month."

We stood there for longer than we probably should have, but it was okay. Amelia could sleep in a little longer while I indulged in some alone time with Mommy.

As I held Kristin, I didn't know how I was managing to keep my cool on the outside. Because inside, I was a mess. This was the first anniversary where there was a distinct possibility that my surprise might genuinely upset Kristin.

I kept thinking back to the first time I shared a family dinner with Kristin, her mom, and Petra in this house. I brought a gift for Sally that day, and I told Kristin she couldn't see her mom's gift until she'd memorized all the songs on a USB drive. Of course, she found out soon after that, that this was just a joke. The gift I gave Sally contained a note stating that she could share her gift with Kristin whenever she was ready. I figured, it was the least I could do for the woman who had raised the girl I'd fallen in love with.

To Sally's credit, she didn't shy away from sharing her gift with her daughter. The journal Michael Becker had kept became a gateway to understanding for Kristin. Still, she insisted Sally keep it. And when I asked her if she wanted to keep the pictures Petra had removed from the bedroom her father built for her, she insisted we should get rid of them.

I had been keeping this year's anniversary gift a secret from Kristin for seven years. If this surprise didn't work out the way I hoped it did, I just prayed it didn't end in divorce.

I stepped into Amelia's bedroom, shaking my head when I saw she had kicked off her covers again. She was splayed out across the mattress with her mouth hanging open, waves of golden-brown hair falling across her angelic face. Her pajama shirt with the bunny rabbit print was scrunched up, exposing her soft belly. It took everything in me not to wake her with a loud raspberry on her stomach.

I slowly sat on the edge of her bed, and her eyelids clicked open. The golden flecks in her green eyes shined in the morning sunlight.

"Good morning, sweetheart," I said, placing a gentle kiss on her forehead.

She reached up to brush her hair out of her face as her eyes widened with pure wonder. "Mommy, I dreamed—I dreamed—I dreamed I could fly."

I smiled as I helped her get the rest of her hair out of her face. "Really? Where were you flying?"

She blinked furiously as she sat up, her face full of utter amazement as she stuck her arms out as if she were flying. "I flew over—over the pool. And you—and you and Daddy were watching me. And Daddy—

Daddy couldn't catch me!" she said, covering her mouth as she giggled.

"That doesn't sound right." Daniel's voice startled us as we turned to watch him approach the bed. He took a seat on the other side of the mattress and pulled Amelia into his lap. "Daddy would never let you get away," he said, kissing her forehead and squeezing her tightly.

There was nothing in the world that made me happier than the expression of pure love and adoration on Amelia's face whenever her Daddy held her. It didn't even matter to me that she might never adore me as much as Daniel. Her love for him was too beautiful and unadulterated to ever begrudge.

"Good morning, baby," he said, loosening his hold on her.

"Good morning, Daddy," she replied, making no attempt to leave his lap.

I reached for her chubby toes and she giggled as I rolled them between my fingers, like plump peas. "Can we all see the surprise together?" I asked Daniel, loving the way Amelia's face lit up at the mention of the word "surprise."

"I want a surprise! Pleeeeeeee-ase!" she howled.

Daniel shot me a very unimpressed look, then he smiled down at Amelia. "Of course, baby. I'll take you swimming today, then I'll read you a book. A *surprise* book."

Amelia clapped her hands together. "A surprise book about magic?"

"It wouldn't be a surprise if I told you what the book is about."

Her wispy eyebrows scrunched together, pleading with him. "Please, Daddy. I want a magic book."

It never failed to amaze me how Amelia never stuttered when she spoke to Daniel. It was almost as if she drew strength from him, the same way everyone else did. Like when Daniel's sister Alisha almost gave up on college so she could move in with her loser boyfriend after graduating high school.

Daniel never scolded her. Instead, he took Alisha and her boyfriend out to lunch with us, treating the guy as if he were already part of our family. Throughout the meal, I could see Alisha's body language changing, leaning away from her boyfriend as she slowly began to realize he didn't have strength of character. The next day, Alisha announced she had decided to continue her education.

It was an interesting symbiosis. Daniel gave us strength by taking care of us. By being Amelia's rock, she never felt frightened or uncertain around him. This made her stronger and more confident whenever

Daddy was around. It was a beautiful thing to see.

As we walked along the brick-paved path toward the new art studio, I focused on chatting with Amelia to distract myself from speculating on how Kristin would react to her surprise.

"You want to visit Grandma today?" I asked her, but she didn't reply, too busy contorting her hands and fingers into circles and squares and triangles. "Huh, baby? Wanna go see Grandma?"

Her eyebrows shot up and she nodded her head vigorously. "Can I take my Buddy?"

I smiled at the way she always remembered to ask permission. "Of course, baby."

Amelia had been begging us for a dog since the moment she could speak. She was in love with Grandma Sally's golden retriever, Bobo. We got Amelia a stuffed golden retriever, and it didn't surprise me one bit when she named the toy dog Buddy. I planned on getting her a real Buddy for her fourth birthday in a couple of months.

We arrived at the door to the two-story studio, a

stunning building with a pitched roof, floor-to-ceiling windows, and golden cedar shingles, which would soon turn a dusty gray from the salty breeze. The curtains inside had been drawn shut for days as I prepared this surprise. I hoped she liked it.

We stopped at the arched red door and I turned to Kristin. "If you don't like the surprise, just say the word and I'll get rid of it."

She rolled her eyes. "You have impeccable instincts when it comes to surprising me. I'm sure whatever it is you're hiding in there will be exactly what I need, even if it's not exactly what I want."

I smiled at her diplomatic way of preparing me for the possibility that she may not like the gift. "I guess we're about to find out if that's true."

I entered the code on the deadbolt, and the lock clicked. Pressing down the latch, I pushed open the door and the smell of fresh paint slammed into us. As planned, my surprise gift was the first thing you saw as you entered the studio. It would be the first thing she saw when she arrived in the morning, and the last thing she saw as she closed the door when leaving the studio for the day.

She stared at it for a very long time, my stomach doing cartwheels as I waited for her say anything. But all I could think was *I fucked up*.

I stared in complete shock at the framed black-and-white pictures on the wall, which surrounded a large porthole-like circular window that overlooked the ocean. My throat swelled shut as I was overwhelmed with emotion. From the instant I saw them, I knew the pictures were taken by my favorite photographer, Mikki Slayer. But Daniel must have hired her to take candids without my knowledge, because other than the few email messages we'd exchanged, I'd never met her in my life.

"How did you do this?" I whispered, though I already knew the answer. It was the same answer as always.

No one could resist Daniel. Not even the reclusive sculptor, Arturo Uribe, who Daniel was able to convince to give me private glass sculpting lessons. Apparently, Mikki Slayer could also not resist him.

The wall was covered in candid photos of Daniel, my mom, and me. In some photos, we were alone, and in others, we were with Amelia. The pictures were stunning. No one could capture an honest moment the way Mikki could. But it was the pictures that were obviously *not* taken by her that surprised me most.

Photos of my father, and photos of me that were obviously taken by my father, told a story of a man I'd never known. A man I thought I'd never wanted to know. A man who it seemed, at some point in his cold, wretched life, may have actually loved me.

I pulled the neck of my tank top up to wipe the tears from my face, then I took a few more steps forward.

"Is it what you needed or what you wanted?" Daniel asked tentatively.

I turned to him and the uncertainty in his eyes made me love him even more. "It's both," I whispered, shaking my head as I held my arms out so he could hand over my baby girl. "I don't know how you do it, how you continue to surprise me."

He passed Amelia to me, then stood behind me, placing a heavy hand on my shoulder as we both gazed at the wall of memories. "It's easy," he said, placing a soft kiss on my ear. "You know all the times I complained about not being able to read your mind? Well, that was a lie. I can actually read your mind."

I smiled as Amelia wiped some moisture from my chin. "Oh, really? What am I thinking now?"

He wrapped his arms around me, his hands

cradling my abdomen. "You're thinking... Hmmm, I really like the name Brutus."

I shook my head and planted a loud kiss on Amelia's cheek. "What do you think, baby? Do you want to name your new dog, Brutus?"

Amelia's eyes widened. "I get a dog? Where's my dog?"

"Let's go to the shelter and get you a puppy," I said.

Amelia threw her arms into the air, her face lighting up with sheer glee as she cheered. "Thank you, Mommy!"

Daniel leaned forward and whispered in my ear. "Very clever, offering my son's name to a dog."

I smiled triumphantly as I turned to face him. "You should have seen that coming, mind reader."

He shook his head, clutching his chest dramatically. "How could you Brutus to me?"

I looked up at him, my heart full with admiration. "Because I know you can take the heat. After all, you are my superhero."

The End

Her Guardian Playlist

1. Taken Care Of
"Half The World Away"
Aurora

2. Karma
"Karma Police"
Radiohead

3. Blood Sisters
"Heartlines - Acoustic"
Broods

4. Hero
"A Real Hero"
High-Highs

5. Smooth Jazz
"River"
Leon Bridges

6. A Keeper
"New York"
Milk & Bone

7. Surreal Daydream
"Bird"
Billie Marten

8. Step Four
"Recovery"
Broods

"River"
Bishop Briggs

9. Paintbrush
"Paper Thin - Live From Studio"
Astrid S

10. Dark Truth
"Issues - Acoustic"
Julia Michaels

11. Happy Birthday, Mom
"We Had Everything"
Broods

12. MB
"Boardwalks / Remastered"
Little May

13. Unsinkable
"Wait"
M83

14. Too Perfect
"Dark Side"
Bishop Briggs

15. Hurricane
"Way Down We Go"
Kaleo

16. Worthy
"Save Me"
Nicki Minaj

17. Real
"Slow It Down"
The Lumineers

18. Music Box
"I Want It All"
Natalie Taylor

19. Reckless
"Fire-scene - Alt. Version"
S. Carey

20. Rich Asshole
"Nobody's Fault But Mine"
Nina Simone

21. Hush-Hush
"Pray (Empty Gun)"
Bishop Briggs

22. Come Clean
"Grand Piano"
Nicki Minaj

23. Batman
"Hello"
Adele

24. Pretend
"Better - Piano and Voice"
Regina Spektor

25. Never Again
"Mother and Father"
Broods

26. Priceless
"Close To You"
Rihanna

27. Catching Rays
"the Whale - End Credits Song"
Olly Alexander

Epilogue - Daniel
"Bridge"
High-Highs

Epilogue - Kristin
"Wings - Acoustic"
Birdy

Listen to the playlist on Amazon
bit.ly/heiressplaylist

Listen to the playlist on Spotify.
bit.ly/heiressplaylists

ACKNOWLEDGMENTS

When I began writing this book in 2016, I set out to write a story that would speak to those of us who have often struggled with self-worth. We've all made mistakes, but some of us carry the guilt from those mistakes like a boulder chained to our ankle. We often over-identify with our mistakes, feeling like our worst moments define us. As Adam Parker from the *Shattered Hearts Series* once said, "It's not our mistakes that define us. It's the lessons we learn that show our true character."

Huge thank you to my beta readers: Paula Jackman, Cathy Archer, Kristin Shaw, Sarah Arndt, Erin Fisher, and Beverly Cindy. This book has a conventional Cinderella storyline, told through the point of view of unconventional characters with modern problems, and these girls never failed to keep me in check. They saw me through the most difficult period of my writing career and I will be forever grateful.

Thank you to Tamara Paulin for being there with positive words and the occasional reality check when needed.

Big thanks to my editor, Jessica Anderegg of Red Adept Publishing. Thank you for those extra eight days! And, as always, thank you for not being afraid to call me out on the issues I'd prefer to ignore.

Huge thanks to my copy editor, Marianne Tatom.

Thank you to all the bloggers who shared the release! And a big thank you to Alyssa Garcia of Inkslinger PR for making this launch utterly painless. And to all the bloggers and readers who took the time to read the book, post your reviews, and still take the time to cheer me on and pimp the shit out of my books. You are what makes this indie book community thrive. Keep supporting the indie authors you love and we'll keep writing the romance books you love to read.

To the readers who have messaged me and

shared your excitement for the release of this book and your frustration with my extended break, thank you for your kindness and for the occasional kick in the ass. Depression sucks, and it's even harder to deal with when you lose someone close to you. It took a while for me to come out of my fog, but words cannot express how much your messages meant. Thank you for taking time out of your day to think of me and reach out to me. Your enthusiasm lit my path during a very dark time.

To Arielle, for helping me develop the idea for this book and for being the backbone of my support system.

OTHER BOOKS BY CASSIA LEO

CONTEMPORARY ROMANCE

Stand-alones

Black Box

Shattered Hearts Series

Forever Ours (Book #1)

Relentless (Book #2)

Pieces of You (Book #3)

Bring Me Home (Book #4)

Abandon (Book #5)

Chasing Abby (Book #6)

Ripped (Book #7)

EROTIC ROMANCE

LUKE Series
CHASE Series
Edible: The Sex Tape (A Short Story)

EROTIC SUSPENSE

UNMASKED Series
KNOX Series

ROMANTIC COMEDY

Anti-Romance Duet
Anti-Romance (Book #1)
Pro-Love (Book #2)

PARANORMAL ROMANCE

Carrier Spirits Duet
Parallel Spirits (Book #1)
Kindred Spirits (Book #2)

More books at cassialeo.com/books

ABOUT THE AUTHOR

New York Times bestselling author Cassia Leo loves her coffee, chocolate, and margaritas with salt. When she's not writing, she spends way too much time re-watching *Game of Thrones*. When she's not binge watching, she's usually enjoying the Oregon rain with a cup of coffee and a book.

CPSIA information can be obtained
at www.ICGtesting.com
Printed in the USA
LVHW090712221218
601308LV00032B/360/P

9 781721 766611